LIES

Have No Memory

YVONNE DEAN ANDERSON

LIES HAVE NO MEMORY
Yvonne Dean-Anderson

ISBN: 978-1-7347430-8-1
ISBN: 978-1-7347430-9-8
Library of Congress Control Number: 2020918434

Front cover and book design by Jenette Antonio Sityar.

Printed in the United States of America.
First printing edition 2020

Pecan Tree Publishing
Hollywood, FL 33020
www.pecantreebooks.com

Pecan Tree Publishing

www.pecantreebooks.com

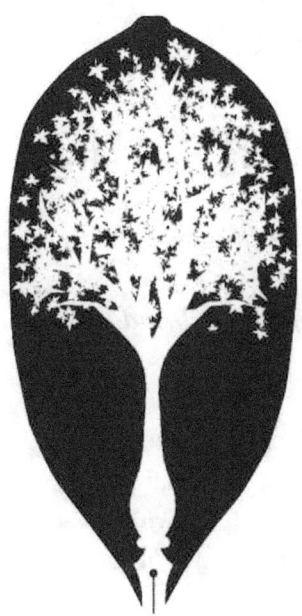

New Voices | New Styles | New Vision
Creating a New Legacy of Dynamic Authors and Titles
Hollywood, FL

DEDICATION

My truth is, I would not be the who I am if you all were not who you are.

The 11 best teachers of my good, bad, and indifference; my children:
Tosca,
Nakei,
Alphonso,
Cherise,
Nakinja,
Michelle,
Arthur,
Bertette,
Beejay,
Montiera
Jah-Mere

TABLE OF CONTENTS

CHAPTER ONE

The Broken Vessels

*A*s the machines beep at a steady pace, acknowledging the fact you are still alive; I stare. I stare at nothing; trying to remember what you smelled like before the smell of another woman's perfume replaced mine. I try to remember the admiration in your eyes when you were looking at me; before your playful glances turned into stares of discontent. I try hard to remember the sound of your voice that comforted me before everything you said became lies. I try to remember what it was like being loved by you before your touch felt empty and cold. Above all, I try to remember not to hate you, not to despise you, not to want you dead. However, to all these things I try to remember; I can remember yesterday morning; when I turned over and saw your side of the bed empty yet again. As I turn to reach for your arms, and they don't reach back. All I can remember is the pain I feel once again thinking you were where you wanted to be, without me.

After ten years of marriage, and two beautiful children, I thought nothing could destroy the heaven I was allowed entry to. The pearly gates that allured me in with inviting music of harps playing ever so delicately in the background. The voice; your voice that beckoned me to enter in, the shining streets of gold that hypnotized me, blinding me of my past with hopes of a bright future. The voice: your voice, that promises me I will be safe.

With a sudden consciousness and feeling of dread, I cringe. Oh my, what have I done? Besides continuing my own abuse from your hand to my own. I have allowed you to take me there. To a place where there is no return. I have become you in my own defeat. You mock me from your unconscious state; I know you do. I know even in your own near demise you find comfort in my misery. I know I'm obsessing, maybe even a tad bit paranoid to say the least; however, seeing you laying here unconscious, I cannot help but wonder what thoughts are running through your mind. What do you see? What do you remember? What are you thinking about your family, now?

While pacing this floor back and forth; I subconsciously yet consciously try to step directly into each square dim tile. At some point, I even begin to count them. Ah, hospitals. I hate them! Heart monitoring machines beeping to remind visitors of the seriousness of the patient's condition; intravenous drip lines beeping if the bag runs too low, another machine monitoring the blood pressure and only God knows what the machine with the green and yellow cords attached to Lamont's head is for.

Every single emotion within me is conflicting with each other. I am so incredibly angry and filled with hate; well, perhaps that can be because of the level of anger. I care and do not care; guess that too can be contributed to the anger; I want him alive and dead; okay, anger as well. I stomp my feet on these hospital tiles. Damn, I hate it when I analyze myself. I just want to be angry and hate the man lying in this hospital bed almost dead; even though he is my children's father and the only love I have ever known. With nothing else to do, I scream into the cup my hands form, trying to get it together and praying for my mother to show up.

Beyond the machines, I hear the police radios in the distance. Oh boy, here they come to question me, again. I am not sure how many times I can tell the same story the same way. Mother always told me lies have no memory. Huh? Then please tell me why, why, do I keep repeating the same story the same way over and over again? Eventually, they will ask the right questions and that is when I will find myself struggling with my truths.

I watch all the CSI and the First 48 TV episodes; surely I have learned something. One thing is sure; I will not offer any information. What they do not know, they just do not know. What the hell am I thinking? How is any of this my fault? Lamont's neglect of his family is solely on him, whatever choices he made that landed him here is also on him. My aftereffects - I am blaming on him as well. Every action has a reaction, right? *Oh, Rietta get a grip!*

I must think. I must think and not say too much before my family gets here. Let's see, think Rietta, think. I am trying to make sense of it, but the police radios coming closer are distracting me. I cannot seem to think past last night's dinner or beyond this morning's breakfast, let alone this morning's catastrophe. Okay, I do not want to think, and I surely do not want to talk to any more police.

Too late. A deep Kentucky Southern long drawl accent invades my over-thinking thoughts. "Excuuuse me, Mizz Harper, Mizz Ray-etta Harper?"

I look up to see the same tall-slender-dingy-irritating-more than a little annoying-smacking-on-probably-the-same-old-sugarless-gum-detective that questioned me three times earlier today. Just why is he calling my name as a question; as if he does not know who I am, is a mystery to me. The way he is chewing on that gum makes his jaws look like they are grinding some hard substance in his mouth and he has the nerve to be smacking on it as if it's the best thing he ever had in his mouth his entire life. Two uniformed police officers accompany him. I guess I am safe for now since their handcuffs are still holstered to their belts.

Confidently, I respond. "Yes. Hello. Forgive me, I forgot your name." Actually, I am quite aware what this old-creepy-looking-stale-gum-chewing-man's name is.

He reaches out to shake my hand; I oblige. "De-tec-tive Glen Mayfield." Before I can release our handshake, he asks his first question. "How is ya husband coming along?" Mayfield's head tilts to peer pass me, while he looks directly at the bed where Lamont is laying. I want to say something fly mouth, like what does it look like, but I will not.

Hospitals always feel cold and dirty to me. The color on the walls is not white, not beige but somewhere in between. Either way, they are ugly and depressing. The best chairs in the room are tweed blends of the wall color and a darker brown. I wonder where they get their design ideas from. One should think to add some brightness to such a gloomy atmosphere. A brick wall of the other side of the hospital is the scenery outside of the window. I guess the architect did not see any need in caring about what was on the outside of the window any more than inside the rooms. I mean, why should that be a concern when a hospital visit is usually not a good thing. I would think the importance is for therapeutic purposes; you know the mental and emotional suggestion of colors can help in the healing process. *Okay Rietta, enough.*

I glance over to the bed where Lamont lies still. In my mind, I feel he got exactly what he deserves. My heart does not agree. I have loved this man for more than ten years, I bore his children, cooked his food, and made the best love to him I possibly can. No, no, I may be angry, but this is not how things should be. I roll my eyes to my own self; just cannot stop analyzing me.

Looking back at the detective, while answering him, "He's still the same. We are waiting for his MRI. There may be some bleeding in the brain. We just have to wait and see how he weathers through the day."

I assume the piercing stare the detective is giving me is one of contempt or perhaps question. I can admit I may be a little assuming, as usual. Here he is, the Caucasian detective looking down his nose at the half-breed with the white husband. I know that look anywhere; I have seen it all my life.

While growing up in a white home, with my white mother and her white family, all I can remember is the name-calling and the harsh looks. Out of three children, I am the only one whose father is a black man. The first two fathers I guess did not measure up to Grandmother Catherine's expectations either, although they are white. Let grandmother tell it, my mother, Irene is a big disappointment.

Ha! I know when mother came home with my black daddy and a big belly, the family cemetery plots were busy with rolling over dead bodies and shifting tombstones. I may not have been there to see it but after growing up in this family, I know some of those tombstones split into pieces! Hating people just because they are different is ridiculous. It is what's inside a person's spirit that makes the personality, not the color of their skin. Okay, I can admit my family is color struck. First on the color green then on white. Yep, those are the favorite colors in this family.

Although I was only five when my daddy left, I remember quite well how he fought for me to leave with him. When I saw his bags packed and piled up by the door without bags for me or my mother, my heart felt like it was trying to force a hole in my chest. I remember the tears rolling down my face and my little body shaking out of control. Not knowing what exactly what was going on, I just knew it was not good.

My father was such a good daddy. He paid attention to my every need and even did his best to accommodate my sisters as much as he could. I never went to bed without him telling me a story or giving me some life-changing instructions that only a five-year-old could understand. He was the kind of father I wished for my children.

Grandmother speaks in an authoritative tone she has mastered quite well. Her Kentucky Southern accent has no power over her prim and proper diction. "Ben, you are not taking that child with you. I will not hear of it. You need to regain your composure and leave before I make a call to Douglas. I am sure he can find a suitable way to handle this unfortunate situation."

I understand Uncle Douglas always had hatred for my daddy. Daddy has nothing to worry about when Douglas is alone. But. truth is, Uncle Douglas is never alone. Tyrone and Melvin are always underfoot. They love trouble and hate my daddy. I overheard daddy say to my mother that Tyrone wants my mother.

Daddy yells at grandmother without hesitation or show of concern. "Woman, I am not afraid of your son, his friends or your threats but I tell you this, if Irene wants to stay here, it is on her but I'm taking my child and leaving."

Mother is crying, begging daddy not to go. I was not too sure what the straw was that broke daddy's-camel's-back; however, I do know daddy put up with some degrading treatments. I experienced some of those unyielding mistreatments for just being a little too dark and I am a blood relative. I can only imagine what daddy went through. A little girl's nosey ears hear way too much for her mind to comprehend at such a young age. As an adult and after going through the struggles this family can inflict, I can understand how hard it must have been for my father. Stories I overheard about him not being good enough or the nerve of him thinking he would ever be accepted into this family. Stories of great grandparents' evil actions towards people of color. Stealing property and rigging elections, even some talks of murders. Yep, way too much for the young mind to handle.

The real deal is my grandmother's biggest weapon is not Uncle Douglas. It is her long-old money and last names. The Richardson's money and power go back a long way here in Kentucky. My great grandfather was the Governor and so was his father. The Richardson's own most of the coal mines in Pike County along with many oil rigs. They also have some of the best racehorses in the state.

Grandmother married into a powerful and wealthy family. The Mason family's money and name stand on its own merits. Their monopoly on the grandest real estate in Barren County is immense. They capitalized on racehorses as well. From what I understand, Thunder Over Louisville, (the opening ceremony for The Kentucky Derby Festival; the largest fireworks display) is their family's legacy. Next to my grandfather's wealth, the Mason family is equally matched. Could not be any other way; money matches or exceeds the money one already has. Keeping the power relies on the way you learn to play the games of the family and it is always about the green and the white. Either you are in all the way, or you are an outcast.

Once you are cast out of position in this family you stay that way. Unless you want in so bad, you do not mind getting your hands dirty for the sake of the prestigious keeping theirs clean. Using what is deemed the least in this crazy circle of life is this family's way of life.

According to grandmother, "It is axiomatic why we have those less fortunate living around us; they were born to do our dirty work." Such unethical bullshit, to live by; nonetheless it is what it is, and people make the world go round.

Both families have some of the finest cattle and tobacco farms in the country. When grandmother married into The Mason Family, she continued an unbreakable chain of power. Her parents could not have been prouder. Grandmother has always been at the top of her game and she loves every single bit of the process it takes to keep her there.

The marriage between my grandmother and grandfather was pre-arranged. The power and money were to be continued and controlled. Grandmother has good backing and even greater bank. Hear her tell the story; she has never loved any man or thing more than her power and money. I believe her!

When grandfather died 20 years ago, she never even thought about marrying again. Although grandmother confesses to being in her sixties, I think she is over seventy. She looks nothing like either. She can easily pass for a woman in her late forties. I am sure she thinks I do not know she plays and pays very well for her private enjoyments. From the young pool-man to her even younger personal trainer, grandmother gets her freak on.

Lady Catherine is in great shape. With her personal trainers, chefs, and gardeners to make sure she keeps it that way. Her skin is smooth and clear of blotches. Her hair is fiery red with natural curls that touch her shoulders. Her perfectly sculptured body matches her perfect five-foot, seven-inch frame. All her curves are firm and perfect. Quiet as it is kept, with that rocking body of hers, grandmother may have something else besides snow-flake blood. Booties like that only come in black. Okay, just joking; she has enough money for cosmetic work.

Grandmother swears she has never had a bit of surgery. Her passion for a long healthy life drives her to be persistent about what she does to and with her body. Her eyes are a beautiful green color. There will never sit a pair of reading glasses over them; however, she does wear contacts, to see. Shush, no one is supposed to know. My grandmother is a beautiful woman. She is a pro at flaunting all her assets, money, status, power, beauty, and wit. She has it all, and knows it; without a doubt, she wants everyone who associates with her to know it as well.

Mother, although an exact replica of her mother in appearance, is a disgrace and embarrassment, at least to her mother. How dare she bring home a black man! Although my daddy is educated and was a law student at that time; he could never measure up to The Richardson-Mason standards. Besides, if my grandmother were as smart as she thinks she is, she would have done a little research on my father's family. Who am I kidding? She probably did; it just did not matter.

Doing some research of my own, I found out his dark skin is because he is a descendent of the Shawnee Tribe of Indians that settled in Kentucky way before the White settlers got here. Ah, look at that, the real natives of this land. I'm not going there. His family also owns some land in Bluegrass Country. Their money may not be as long or as powerful as hers, but they got a little somum' somum' going on. Now grown, I of course do, from time to time, divulge that wonderful information to her as often as I can. Not that it makes a difference, but it sure makes me feel good. Oh, back to my story. Mother grabs daddy's arm as she begs, "Please Ben don't go, please. You know I cannot leave Danna and Kristy again. They will have no one if I leave, please stay with me, please."

Danna is the oldest of my mother's daughters and then Kristy.

Grandmother stands on her feet and grabs my mother by the hair. I watch in horror as my mother's head jerks back and forth from grandmother's tugs. I pray silently for Irene to get angry enough to kick grandmother or slap her as hard as she can; anything to make her let her go. However, she does not, she does absolutely nothing but accept the abuse, like always.

"Girl stop being so naïve!" Pointing at my father, "that man can never measure up to this family, let him go!" Then she throws out as a second thought, "And what on earth, do you mean, they will not have anybody? What in the world am I? The whole time you chased behind this insignificant portion of a man, I have been here for those children. I have been the epitome of all they ever needed and will ever need."

Daddy stands still, waiting, looking at my mother; I am sure waiting for her to say something. She does not, all she does is cry. From what I understand now, my grandmother has always had custody of my two sisters, mother was young, rebellious, and looking hard for love. Now knowing my mother so well, she was simply trying to find her own way and escape this family's hold on her life. I must admit, her way of doing things made her an incredibly young mother and caused fingers to be pointed at her that refuse to bend. But Irene is such a wonderful mother and a great person. I guess time can grow every seed to its intended state of maturity. Each time mother would try to get my sisters; grandmother pulled the custody card.

Well, she does not, nor has she ever had custody of me. But she has more power and political pull than my dad could fight. By the time daddy and I get to the front gate of the estate, three sheriff's cars are waiting. Although the sheriff's department is not around the corner; one can wonder how in the world did they get there so fast. Besides believing somewhere during the conversation, one of the employees must have called anticipating an issue. Notwithstanding, the distance from the main house to the gate is about two and a half miles.

As a little girl, the house, and the grounds seemed so immense. The foyer enormous, being half of a basketball court. The floors are a beautiful marble grandmother imported from Italy. That marble extends outside through the huge two solid oak 13 feet high doors, with the most elegant hand-painted stain glass in the center of them both. Once outside, the expensive marble covers the balcony that has two wide sets of steps, one on the right and the other on the left. The handcrafted, beautiful thick barriers extend from the end of one staircase to the other. Stepping out the front door, I needed to tippy-toe or peer through the design of the barrier to see the landscape. Speaking of the landscape; there cannot be another layout like this one anywhere.

The huge Thuja occidentalis "Smaragd" (better known as the Emerald tree) lines the outer barrier of the entire 200 acres. The marble extends all the way to the driveway and front part of the yard. The spiraling fountain is an extension of the marble as well. The lights in the fountain make the water look a gold color. The marble covers the frontcourt. In the center of the marbled circle is an assortment of roses: red, yellow, white, even blue roses, with small smooth marble stones on top of the dirt they are rooted in. There are three sets of pink Sioux Crape Myrtle trees shading the three marble benches, which is shaped like love seats. There is a beautiful array of flowers and bushes throughout the landscape.

◆

Until this day, I do not know what they said to my daddy. The tears in his eyes did not agree with his decision to leave me. Here he is a grown well-developed man, strong in appearance and extremely intelligent; yet, crying like a baby. Snot running down onto his quivering lips and tears falling from his face, daddy reaches into the car, picking me up and holding me so tight that even now I can close my eyes and feel that last hug.

He cries into my neck and tells me, "Baby-girl, your daddy loves you and I will never forget you and one day I will come for you."

Once I turned 18, I begin searching. I have been searching for my daddy for 13 years now, cannot seem to find him anywhere. When he first left, the phone-calls were very often. Then grandmother started intercepting them. Whenever mother answered the phone, I talked to my daddy. He promised me he would be back for me. It has been years since I have heard anything from him. I am sure he tried but the opposition is much bigger than he can fight.

The sound of Detective Mayfield's voice brings me back to my present predicament, "Um, can weeee go over the events that took place this morning once again?"

Finding my courage; very rudely I want to say to him, "hell no", but I will not. Perhaps I can try to say it differently. "Right at this moment detective, I am terribly upset, in fact, I have gone over the same story several times already. Can we please give it a break while I tend to my husband? I'm sure we can talk later; it's not as if I'm going anywhere."

Adjusting his cowboy-tan-flimsy-over-worn-I-am-sure-smelly-hat on his balled head; he takes in a deep breath and blows it out as if somewhat agitated, yet he stays persistent.

"I don't see any reason why ya can't talk to me now; it's not as if ya husband is waking up right now. I would rather get ya statement once again while it is still fresh in ya mind. My in-tent is to make this as painless as possible for ya and ya family and get this over with this as quickly as possible."

I do not know when he put that gum in his mouth but the way he is smacking on it after each and every word is driving me crazy. I glance down and notice he has on cowboy boots. His pants legs are tucked inside of them. Now I must do my best not to laugh out loud at this ridiculously-idiotically-dramatically-overbearing-visually-unpolitically correct ... dressed thing. I do not know what to conclude about this person at this moment. I am sure I will find the correct word in a minute. Trying as hard as I can to control my composure, I answered him, "I can appreciate your job and the efforts to move quickly in this matter and I am grateful; however, I have gone over the story, and I thought you took notes since you had your pen and pad in your hand. As I stated, I can speak to you some other time."

Folding the little pad, he holds in his hand, he places it in the inside of his jacket. Once he adjusts the hat on his head, he takes a deep breath and blows it out, as if trying to find some patience. He kind of reminds me of Detective Columbo from that old television show. He is Detective Columbo odd and asking questions in that atmosphere only he can bring.

Vagrant! That's the word I was missing, vagrant. He is ridiculously-idiotical-ly-dramatically-overbearing-visually-unpolitically correct-vagrantly-dressed! Ah, that feels so much better now.

"Now Mizz Harper, please don't make me come looking for ya. I know ya grandmother *personally,* and I'm sure she won't all this here mess cleared up in a timely manner."

Looking at his watch and then glancing over at my husband who's lying almost lifeless; he pulls a card out of his pocket and holds it out to me still smacking on that must-be-out-of-sugar-stale-chewing-gum-sure-his-breath-is-funky, as hard as he can. "Let's say, tomor' afternoon around three o'clock, let's say at mah office. Oh, and let's say ya don't be late, mah time is 'portant."

Taking a deep breath of my own, I decide being rude just can't be helped. For some reason, I just don't like this man. He makes me feel uneasy and his very appearance irritates me; not to mention that damn gum he continuously kills and resuscitates just to kill again.

In a voice and tone that cannot hide my irritation, I wave my finger in the air and look away from the detective as if he's invisible.

"Uh, let's say, no." Without waiting for a response from the too-tall-slender-very-old-stinking- smelling-like-stale-cigarettes-detective-killing-gum-chew-ing-man, I continue without stuttering. "I have your card. In fact, I have several of your cards, since you continue to give them to me each time you want to talk to me. So why don't you keep that one. Furthermore, I will not come to your office. I will be right here by my husband's side unless some miraculous event takes place and he wakes up during the night. Other than that, unless you have a warrant or something stating I have to come to your office, I suggest you leave me alone for now."

The look on his face tells me he is incredibly surprised at my response, not to mention he stopped chewing, I mean killing that darn gum for a moment. Well if that was surprising to him, I am not quite finished. Holding my finger up once again, "Oh, and since you know my grandmother, *personally,* as you have so elo-quently put it, then you should know if I feel harassed in any way, I will call her." Then I decide to add the family power into the conversation. "I am sure my grand-mother Catherine Richardson-Mason can assist you with any time frame you may need to follow." Feeling quite cocky, I clear my voice and continue, "Should I call her to see how far away she is? I am positive she is on her way here."

Finally looking him in the face; with both my pointer fingers in his face, waving back and forth, "Whether this matter is cleared up quickly enough to suit you or not, probably won't be your biggest concern *if*, my grandmother gets involved. Oh, wait, I mean *when* she gets involved."

Now that it's apparent I have left the dear-old-cowboy-hat-wearing-nasty-gum-chewing-irritating-detective-with-the-cowboy-boots-over-his-pant-legs speechless; I'm feeling somewhat energized. That's wonderful for me; however, this rusty-dusty-make-shift-transparent-irksome-vexing-male-child-of-some-poor-woman, may not feel so good after this conversation. Oh well, the heck with him, let him find some other form of entertainment besides my secrets.

I turn on my heels and take my place in the tweed chair right next to Lamont's hospital bed. The two officers that pretend not to be listening to our conversation are holding their heads down fumbling with the police caps in their hands. They heard us, and I'm sure if they feel the same way I do about this stiff-neck, stuck-up-rusty-old-need-to-be-retired-fake-detective, this will be the topic at their dinner table tonight for sheer comedic entertainment.

My dinner will be served right here, next to my comatose husband. I am sure sometime during the night his over-bearing sister-Linda, and wanna-be-more-important-than-she-is-mother-Lidia, will show up. I can almost stomach one of them, but only if they are not together. Oh, what the heck, such wishful thinking, they are always together; like two peas in a pod, like a finger to a hand, like an ice cube to water; ah, you get my drift.

How anal can a person be? Ms. Lidia, will never consider dating or marrying a man if his name does not begin with the letter L. Then she has the nerve to give all her children names starting with the letter L. Her sole reason for wanting to hate me is as simple as just that. My name starts with an R. I told you anal!

You should have seen the look on her face when she came to the hospital to see her twin grandchildren after they were born. I held my breath waiting for her to ask their names. With the biggest smirk on my face, I tilted my head up and said: "This is Benjamin and Charmin." She looked as if she was having a heart attack. The old hag just refused to keel over but I sure enjoyed the panic attack.

The twins are five now and she still fusses about Benjamin not having his father's name, but my dad's and Charmin's name not beginning with the notorious letter L. Yeah, I must admit, I enjoy the moments of satisfaction I get each time I call their names in front of her. It was not easy getting Lamont to agree to the names; but he was so in love with me then and would do all he could to make me happy.

Thinking of the twins, I need to call Ms. Elaine; they must be scared. They saw the ambulance and police cars this morning and all the blood in the foyer. I gave them no explanation, I'm sure they have been endlessly questioning poor Ms. Elaine. I am also sure she knows how to get their minds off the ruckus and into something enjoyable. Ms. Elaine loves the twins and she will comfort them, this I know.

I have no clue what I should say to them. This is also a great time to call my mother and grandmother. Mother has always been great at giving believable explanations to children. As for grandmother; well she's great at shoving shit; any shit, all kinds of shit, different color shit, smelly shit, soft shit, hard shit, she will shovel shit wherever, whenever she pleases. All one needs to know as far as grandmother is concerned is she's in charge and everything is going to be her way, and that way will be forever favorable to her and her family. Especially if she gets to push, pull, maneuver, create, cleanup, or make disappear, some shit.

Poor Detective Mayfield, (who I honestly do not care one straw about) I am sure I will feed him to my out-of-control-shit-shoveling-wonderful-powerful-grandmother, on an extremely uncomfortable plate. She may not have loved me while I was growing up, but she sure loves me now. The choice I made in a husband got me pushed to the top of her ladder of people to like, love or simply tolerate. I am officially the favorite by default of my two sisters. Their behavior got them ousted a long time ago. One of the greatest family rules of grandmother is never embarrass the family name, ever. However, the chain runs, I am acknowledged, and my position is much better. Grandmother actually hears me when I talk and she considers my opinion; although very little, it is yet considered.

Lamont is *proper,* according to grandmother, and rich. The Harpers are politically powerful with a line of judges and attorneys within their family's crest.

14

This is an asset for Uncle Douglas and his crew of mischievous-politically-incorrect-law-breaking-disrespectful-bandits-of-political-enforcement.

Uncle Douglas is now the Mayor, Tyrone is his righthand assistant and Melvin is the town sheriff. Speaking of corruption, it cannot get any more perfect in dishonesty if it were written in a script. Don't get me wrong there is some good the trio manages to do; however, that good seems to be extended much longer to certain people.

Ah, I will call and speak to the children first, and then I'll call the dynamic duo - my mom Irene and grandmother. They will be more than happy to play dustpan and broom to all the broken vessels in my life. I must admit, I love my mother more than anyone, next to the twins. Our relationship is powerful, and our bond is unbreakable. Besides being my mother, she is my best friend. Grandmother has my unyielding respect. I must admit, I love grandmother as well.

CHAPTER TWO

Keeping Secrets - Secret

"Is that what a devoted wife is supposed to be doing, sleeping? Wake your lazy ass up and take care of my brother."

Slowly I raise my head. Yep, it's them; the over-bearing sister and wanna-be-more-important mother. I have a stiff neck from sleeping in the chair all night, now I wake up to Yip-and-Yap.

With an arrogant look, that only my mother-in-law can give her tirade begins. "Girl, how do you know if he woke up during the night if you fell asleep? What if he can't talk or make any noise? With your eyes closed, you surely can't see him, trying to get your attention."

I ease up out of the chair and stretch out my arms. I slowly kick one of the two chairs I put together to sleep on. I slowly take the three steps over to the bed where Lamont is still in a coma, I kiss his covered forehead. As I spin on my heels to face my in-laws, "And how are you two ladies doing? It's good to see you both; I stayed up last night waiting for you to show up." In an even more condescending tone, "Did you guys get lost?" I chuckle to myself knowing this will be the beginning of our tit-for-tat conversation.

Linda takes the opportunity to answer my very-obnoxious-shallow-definitely-met-to-be-irritating-never-intended-to-get-an-answer-question. "First of all, we did not get lost. Mother called the hospital and we knew Lamont was stable. Second, we do live out of state and it took some time to get all of our things together for the trip, then catch a last-minute flight." Then she tilts her head even higher, giving me a snide smirk, in a matter of fact tone she continues, "Since we will be staying until he is out of this God-awful place so we can find out exactly what happened to him; we decided to take our time so we wouldn't leave anything behind."

One would think these two were twins. They wear the same clothes, maybe a different color but mostly the same. Lidia is perhaps one inch shorter than her daughter who stands a solid five feet six inches. What they lack in height, they sure have in attitude. Both have perfect blond hair. I say it's cosmetically blended by the best hairdressers; however, they will die with the lie that they never have their hair colored. Both have very nice petite shapes matched with very expensive boob-jobs.

In my mind, calling a truce will be the better way of handling this duo of trouble and insults. I repeat the chant I have clung to all my life; *"they are as important as I make them and they are as irrelevant as I make them, and they go into the file of unimportant."*

I move closer to hug, Lidia, my mother-in-law, kissing at her cheeks; one at a time. Then I repeat the same phony ritual with my sister-in-law. Smiling, in a very prim and proper tone, I say, "I'm sure he didn't wake up," nodding my head towards Lidia. "Since I stayed up all night. As a matter of fact, I just dozed off about thirty minutes ago."

Slightly pushing me while she passes to go to her only son's bedside, with a demeaning tone, "I don't believe anything you say, but you already know that. What happened to my son, I want the truth?"

She wants the truth, wow, and she's asking me, wow. This sure does contradict her not believing anything I say. I may as well get my nasty-snide on while I can since they will. I'm sure they will make me miserable as often as they can.

The make-up they wear is always packed on too heavy. It looks as if the skin has a smooth layer of plastic. I would love to introduce them to a better form of the facial base, but I do not like them like that. Besides, if I do that, my level of inner-laughter about Frit-and-Frat will somewhat diminish; and we cannot have that.

I like thinking to myself each time I see them how long it must take to pile all that make-up on their faces. I wonder if they do their own faces or if they do each other's. Either way, the clown faces are to be laughed at. Their eyes are always full of bright colors and long fake eyelashes. Somehow, they never manage to put that goop on the neck. So, the face is one tone and texture and the neck always their true pale skin tone. The fingernails and toenails are always polished with a glitter polish. Today, it's a purple-glittered-nails with two different shades of purple eye shadow. Oh, and light-colored purple lipstick. Clowns, I tell you, just plain clowns. Perhaps I should check to see if the circus is offering a reward for the missing clowns, their performance must be missed there because their act here is overbearing, and I want my peace back.

I take another look at the two from head to toe and I breathe, "Excuse me Mother Lidia; I'm not sure who you were directing your question to since you will not believe anything I say."

Slowly she turns and stares at me, and then she moves her stare to Linda and back to me. After patting Lamont on the arm, she comes directly in my face. She is so close I can smell her breath and feel the heat from her body. I suppose she is mad and probably very upset over her son, and she may have every right to be however, he is my husband, and I am his wife and the control over his life is mine and mine alone. I'm sure this woman does not think I can handle her since I never dared to; however, she had better be very careful since Lamont cannot save her and I am not in the mood for her crap.

Nevertheless, here she goes, "You listen to me, you half-breed piece of garbage, what happened to my son?"

There it is her true feelings. There has been bad blood between us ever since Lamont and I met. She did all she could back then to persuade Lamont not to marry me. She tried all kinds of shenanigans to trick him and falsely accuse me of things I never did. Here we are years later with two grandchildren she claims to love, and I am nothing more than a "half-breed" to her.

At one of our high school dances she invited one of her friend's daughters to attend as Lamont's date, knowing I was Lamont's date. She then tried to make him feel bad for not spending time with the girl and not taking her home. I don't know how she thought that was going to work out; one thing is certain; it didn't work the way she wanted. That night was all about me.

Taking the moment to compose myself, and wisely change the direction of this conversation, I breathe. "Mother Lidia, I honestly don't know. I was on my way to check for the paper and found him lying in the foyer, bleeding."

Over-bearing-sister-in-law takes over where her mother left off. Folding her arms across her chest, she leans to one side with her lips pressed much too tightly together. "So why was he in the foyer, did he go for the paper first? And if he did, why do you go for the same paper? Before I could answer she continues, "Just how many papers come to the house in one day, no one morning. Huh, how many?

Linda then turns towards her mother as if she just unpuzzled a puzzle; she flings both her hands out as if showing she is a winner and then rocks her head. I am speechless at this unbelievable nonsense. Taking a deep breath, I decide to put my pride on a platter. I position myself so I can see both their faces and with my hands on both hips I rock my head as well.

"No, we did not go for the same paper. Lamont was not home."

Lamont's mother Lidia grins before responding. "Not at home? What do you mean, Lamont finally got the sense enough to leave you? Ah, really?"

My insides are boiling, and I know this just gave them ammunition for their attacks on my nerves.

Linda take the opportunity to chime in, "Oh, so that's what happened. He left you and he was coming to visit his children and you attacked him?"

Rolling my eyes at them both and sucking my teeth I turn away from them and walk towards the bed where Lamont is unconscious enough not to have to witness this stupidity. Yes, he is a cheat, but he would never leave me; nope, not while grandmother is alive.

Linda refuses to take the hint and leave me alone with her ridiculous remarks and questions. She continues, "So, is that what happened? He came to visit, and you attacked him? How long have you two been separated, and what did you hit him with?"

Is this woman for real? This misfortunate-ignorant-out-of-her-mind-low-life-big-mouth-out-of-control-piece-of-crap-of-a-woman need to quit while she's ahead, or better yet while she *thinks* she's ahead.

Trying my very best to ignore them both, I attempt to turn all my attention to my husband, but the questions won't stop.

Linda strikes again. "Hhm, so you found him unconscious?"

Now that's the question the detective never asked. It's also the question, I don't want to answer.

I put my hands to my face and cry on the spot. Oh please, tell me where's the Oscar nominators; I may just deserve an honorary one for my flawless performance.

"You may not like me, you may even hate me but one thing you both know is, I love Lamont, I love him very much. Finding him lying on the floor bleeding was horrifying. It's something I can't get out of my head."

Linda comes close to me and finds a moment of compassion to comfort me. She wraps her arms around me and hugs me. My mother-in-law hands me a piece of tissue, she fumbles to find in her purse. After wiping my nose and eyes, we embraced and cried. Such a Kodak moment.

If Lamont could see this, he would dance the jig. It's not that I dislike my in-laws; I just feel like I must always be on the defense with them. I feel as if all they want to do is attack me. From the texture of my hair to my skin color, from the nanny that keeps the children to the color of my kitchen, anything that pertains to me is a target.

Our moment of bonding is disturbed by my grandmother's even-toned voice and proper speech. "Well, it must be significantly true what they say about disasters; it brings out the finest in people. One never realizes how much they have in common until a loved one is injured." Grandmother walks over to me and kisses me, then nods at my in-laws. She tolerates them well, but she shows little emotional interest to anyone, while nodding her head, "Hello Lidia, Linda, although I am delighted to see the both of you, I am genuinely sorrowful it's under such circumstances."

Turning her attention towards Lamont, she walks over to his bed. Slowly she reaches out her hand to touch his bandaged face. After a moment of silence, she turns her attention to me, "When that nasty-old-disgusting Detective Mayfield calls you again, make sure you divert him to me." Tilting her head down as if looking over a pair of invisible glasses, "Do you understand child?"

I nod my head, "Yes ma'am, I will."

Slowly with a royal stride, she walks over to one of the chairs I slept in; looks at it as if to make sure it is suitable before taking a seat. I forgot to share with you, how my grandmother has this incredible ability to know everything. All my life there was no hiding anything from her, no matter how hard one tries. I mean, there were things she should have no clue of, even down to my private thoughts.

When I was in the eleventh grade, I decided it was time for me to have sex with Lamont. We talked about it in private, nowhere where my grandmother could have overheard, or anyone could have told her. Yet that morning before I left for school she came to my room.

"Rietta," She said in a very calm and understanding tone, "Child, listen to me and listen to me good; Lamont is going to marry you. Do not rush and execute anything that will trigger him to look at you as other common, unpleasant, careless girls. You are a Richardson-Mason."

Under my breath, I said, "and Thomas."

She continued, "We are women of pride and self-respect." Patting the side of the bed for me to sit next to her, she went on staring over her invisible pair of glasses, "Now child, you have some deficiencies that will affect most up-standing gentleman of good principles from a good *proper* family, to look the other way. Therefore, do not go spoil it for yourself; keep that between your legs unbroken, until your wedding night. He waited this long, keep him waiting. He waited this long. Therefore, it is genuinely you, he craves, not the hymen."

As cynical as she sounded, she was right. Yes, I listened; I always listen to my grandmother except about my father. I haven't seen too many times where she is wrong. On my wedding night, I was a virgin and immensely proud of it.

About the god-awful-gum-smacking-stinky-nerve-racking-detective, I will make it my business not to hesitate one second to hand him over to grandmother.

We all sit and visit since Lamont is not waking up. Grandmother's presence seems to calm down the tension in the room. Everyone who knows anything about my grandmother knows not to disrespect her by disrespecting her family. Ah yes, there is peace in the room now. I'm feeling like a baby cuddled in the bosom of safety. I want to stick out my tongue and wiggle my head back and forth chanting, "nah-nah-nah-nah-nah"; however, I will simply settle for doing it in my mind as I take secret glances hoping to catch one of them looking at me so I can grin in satisfaction.

Soon the doctors will make their rounds and we will have an opportunity to ask questions. I pray all is well and my husband will recover. I just don't know how much he will remember about, well about... I didn't do anything wrong, why do I feel like this? I have nothing to be afraid of; so, what if he remembers, it's still not my fault. None of this is my fault.

After the nurse comes in and changes the bandages around Lamont's face and head, she informs us that the doctors are on their way to the room. I don't know what part of the intensive care unit I hate the most. Whether it is the machines beeping constantly or the constant trail of nurses coming in and out of the room. Part of the reason I couldn't get any sleep is because of the beeping machines and traveling nurses.

As the team of doctors enter the room, I have no chance of getting in front of Mother Lidia as she puts her hand out to introduce herself.

"Hello, I'm Mrs. Lidia Harper, Lamont's mother." Turning to face her daughter, she continues her introductions, "This is his sister Linda." Without pausing for the doctor to give his name, "Please tell me, how is my son?"

After I see him release her hand, I step in, practically squeeze my way to the doctor. I put my hand out and say, "Good morning Doctor Carswell,"

"Good morning Mrs. Harper, may I speak with you in private?"

The look on my in-laws' faces; priceless! I glance over to my grandmother and see the most satisfying look on her face. There, I'm totally satisfied as well.

I put on my sophisticated voice, "Doctor Trent Carswell, this is Lamont's mother and sister, and you know my grandmother, Ms. Catherine Richardson-Mason."

He nods his head towards each of them.

"It's perfectly okay to speak in front of them. It relieves me of the responsibility of repeating what you have to say."

Nodding his head yes, "Very well then,"

Turning to the other three doctors that entered the room with him, he introduces them.

"This is Doctor Gary Hamilton, the best brain surgeon in this part of the country. This is Doctor Drew Simmons, he is also a specialist, his field is optometry, and last but certainly not least, this is Doctor Stanley Haywood, his specialty is cardiology."

I nod and shake each doctor's hand. Doctor Carswell begins to explain my husbands' condition.

"Mrs. Harper, we found some bleeding in your husband's brain."

His words made me buckle as if I were punched in the stomach. I lean on the chair my grandmother is still sitting in while he continues to explain.

"I know this is upsetting; however, the bleeding can be controlled with surgery. Our concern is what's causing the bleeding and repairing the problem. That's why I brought Doctor Hamilton along with me. He will explain the procedure in a minute. One of the other problems we are faced with is there seems to be significant nerve damage to his left eye; Dr. Simmons will take care of that. Finally, Doctor Haywood is here to monitor your husband's heart. The extent of his injuries caused a great deal of stress to the heart. When the knife went in it punctured his left lung and the tip of the knife pricked one of the arteries of the heart."

As I try to gain my composure, the pounding in my chest suddenly deafens. My head is spinning, instead of hearing words, I can hear the wind. A wind that is blowing so hard it hurts. It hurts all over my body that I thought went numb a few seconds ago.

Suddenly I can hear my grandmother, in a forceful tone, "That child is going to plunge to the floor if you do not catch her right now."

Vaguely, I can hear shuffling feet, and feel hands clutching me as the room fades dim. In a matter of what I thought were seconds, I choke from the strong smell of ammonia sticks being practically shoved into my nostrils.

My thought process remained on target as I jump to my feet.

"His heart! What's the problem with his heart?" Without waiting for an answer, I continue my questions, "I didn't know he had any damage to his eye." I turn to point at his face and for what seems like the first time I noticed his eye is bandaged. "And please tell me what damage was done to his heart?" Now practically screaming, "I did not even know he was stabbed!"

I try to breathe and calm myself down. I can hear grandmother, "Rietta, calm yourself down, so you can hear what these prestigious doctors are saying."

Doctor Simmons takes over, "Due to the swelling of his face and accumulation of blood into the eye, the visible damage is pronounced. The problem is the nerves behind the eye, which are hard to see because of the swelling, may cause him to lose his sight in the left eye."

Holding my head down and shaking it from one side to the other, I suddenly feel sick to my stomach. Lidia can't hold her peace any longer, "I don't understand doctor, how would the nerve in his eye get damaged, and what's wrong with his brain?"

Doctor Carswell answers, "Mrs. Harper, your son was severely attacked and beaten within an inch of his life. Now, we don't know the details; however, the weapon used did substantial damage to his brain and the nerves in his eye. From the bruising, I am sure it was a bat of some sort. However, we are doing the best we can to get him better."

While Linda cries for her brother, she and her mother try to console one another. I look over to my grandmother who is sitting quietly, to find some kind of signal in her face, something, anything. Her face has a blank stare, as she takes a deep breath.

Where is my mother? She will at least talk to me and try to give me physical support. I know grandmother is not that kind of woman. She feels that showing one's emotions is showing one's weakness, and that just simply cannot be tolerated in this family.

The four doctors take turns explaining all the procedures that Lamont needs. Doctor Haywood tries to comfort us by saying; the small prick to the artery has already been stitched. He is only here now to monitor Lamont's heart and make sure he can stand the stress of brain surgery.

All the medical jargon is much too confusing to me. I need Lamont to get well; that's all I care about. However, if he remembers the last moments before he lost consciousness, our marriage and my freedom may be a thing of the past. Just as I begin to embrace the idea of being comfortless, I hear my mother's voice echoing through the hallway.

"What room is Lamont Harper in?"

Before the nurse can answer, I stick my head out the door, "Mother, we're in here."

Instantly I feel total relief, as if my blood warmed up and my strength renewed. It doesn't matter how long it took her to get to me, just if she is on point right now. I crumble in her arms. I hold on to her as if I were a baby afraid to take her first steps. I let go of all the held back tears.

Without asking any questions, my mother zooms right in place and picks up the bouncing ball right on cue. Grandmother may feel sophistication is the epitome of womanhood but it's not. The compassion my mother has is exemplary. Gently mother palms my face between her hands; she wipes the flowing tears away and kisses my lips. Squeezing me tight, as if she already knows, without me saying a word how alone I was feeling before she arrived. Now that I feel comforted, she gives me her be strong speech, "Now you listen to me, Rietta, try hard baby not to fall apart. You must find the strength you do not know you have. The children need you and whatever you feel they will feel. So, hold that head up and let's listen to what the doctors are saying so we will have a better understanding."

My mother has long beautiful legs. Her facial features are almost exact to my grandmother's. Years of living in the same house with good old granny has made my mother become somewhat of a social hypocrite. In front of my grandmother, my mother is a perfect Kentucky Bell but away from her, is the mother I love.

All the hoopla about power and money is not as important to my mother as it is to grandmother. The proper talk, the suffocated walk, the better-than-thou attitude, is only a front to appease grandmother. Irene is nothing like her. My mother loves people of all races and backgrounds. If grandmother knew what charities her money is really going to, via Irene, she would die. DIE!

Quickly, I grab my mother's arm and gently present her to the doctors. I introduce each of them to her and ask them to explain everything they just told me. My head is hurting from having to listen to all this again. Mother smiles without saying a word and then nods her head. I didn't realize I hadn't allowed mother to greet everyone in the room. In the pose, only my mother can fake, she walks towards grandmother, with a delicate smile and says, "Good afternoon mother, how are you?"

With the same stance, yet without the same visual affection, grandmother replies, "Good afternoon, Irene." Looking at the watch on her arm, with a frowned face, "Running a bit behind, aren't we?"

Mother seizes the awkward moment as only a true princess can. She leans in, to kiss each of her cheeks. While she speaks, she pats grandmother's hand,

"Why no mother, I intended to arrive at this very moment. I do apologize if you were expecting me sooner. In that case please forgive me; I must have done or said something to give you that impression."

My dear mother has played this role so long and so very well, she seems to have the all-seeing grandmother fooled. Which, by the way, is almost impossible; I'm telling you this woman knows everything. I am privy to this forged personality of my mother due to our close relationship.

She is the woman I want to be most like. Her ability to adapt is only equal to her courage. I know she has always hated it here in Kentucky with her family. After my daddy left, mommy must have been miserable. At first, she cried all the time; then one day, she woke up all right. No, not just alright but happy, as if her whole world was great.

Mother got out of her bed early one morning; pulling the shades open, which had been closed for three months. Suddenly she turns on her survival personality, and for her children, she adapts and makes herself happy with her decision to stay and partake in the raising of all her children. My sisters and I are grown and have our own lives; yet she still plays the fiddle with her grandmother. She said it's because she knows the best is yet to come. I have never seen her with a man besides my dad. All her family and friends try to "hook her up" but she won't cooperate.

Mother tells me, she is happy, secretly shoving it to her, over-bearing-very-demining-super-arrogant-old-trying-to-be-young-mother. As much as we share, I get the feeling there are secrets she keeps from me. I even feel she has someone she loves in her life. Perhaps she doesn't want me to know if she has a man in her life because she thinks it will hurt me. I can never forget my dad; I cannot stop looking for him. He's out there somewhere and I intend to find him.

Lidia speaks bringing me back to the here and now, "Well hello there, Ms. Princess." As she stares my mom up and down, her face cannot conceal her jealousy. This is one main reason I can't stand my mother-in-law. I know how she feels about my mother. Unlike me, Lamont tells all his mother's secrets.

In a very humble and sweet tone, my mother returns the greeting.

"Hello Lidia, it is really good to see you; I do wish it were under different circumstances."

Mother hugs her with compassion. The only person my mom is fake with is my grandmother. Irene has a heart of gold and she sincerely cares for people. After she finishes hugging her, she asks: "How are you holding up dear? Is there anything I can do for you?" Mother turns her attention to Linda, "Hi Linda, forgive me for being so rude and not speaking when I first entered the room. I'm so deeply sorry about your brother, I'm sure he will recover very soon."

Thinking about secrets, boy, do I have a few of my own. Right now, they rest with Lamont, I pray he wakes up, but the secrets stay sleeping.

After all the greetings and doctors' diagnosis and referrals, mother convinces me to leave with her.

"Come on Rietta, you have been here all night. You need to get some decent food into your system and a nice hot bath. I'm sure the doctors or nurses will call you if there is any change."

As soon as she feels my resistance, she says exactly what I need to hear, "Now young lady, if you don't keep up your own strength, you will be no good to your husband. Besides, I know your children are frightened; they need to see your face." With her arm around my waist, she pulls me close to her and whispers in my ear, "I'm sure we need to talk. You can ride with me; mother's driver, Mr. Charles, is here waiting on her downstairs. What do you say to a little mother and daughter time?"

Before I can answer, she continues, "After you bathe, and we spend some time with my grandchildren, we can come back."

I smile and shake my head yes. The truth of the matter is, I am so ready to get out of here, not that I want to be away from my husband. However, I'm sure his mother and sister will stay by his side for a while. I'll give them their privacy and me, some peace.

The doctors stated they don't believe he will wake up until the pressure from the blood accumulating around his brain is removed. I certainly don't want him to wake up and talk to anyone before he talks to me. I sure hope he either doesn't remember what I did or accepts my apology once I give it as heartfelt as I can. I don't know what I was thinking, I was so angry; I never meant to cause him harm. I love my husband and I want our marriage to work.

Turning my attention to my in-laws, I realize I haven't extended proper hospitality, "Mother Lidia, there is plenty of room at the house for you two to stay. The children will be so happy to see you. We can also take the time to get reacquainted."

In a surprisingly comforting tone, she replied, "I would really enjoy that. We'll stay here while you go and refresh yourself and take care of the children. Take as much time as you need."

We give our parting hugs and kisses. Mother and I walk behind grandmother on the way to the elevator. She has been so quiet; I am almost afraid. As soon as we reach the first-floor grandmother grabs my arm and practically swings me around, so I am facing her. Bringing me face to face, she peers into my eyes, as if looking for something. Finally, her silence is broken; with a stern look on her face and lips tightened, "I'm going to say this once and only once. If there is anything, and I do mean anything I need to know so I can fix it, you had better tell me as soon as possible. You better not bring shame or disgrace to this family." Then in broken words, "Do-you-understand?"

The stare she is giving me is most frightening. Her lips are squeezed together as tight as they can be. Her stare of warning is shaking me; I can feel my heart beating, no, it's pounding inside my chest, out of control.

I am afraid of grandmother, always have been. Her bark is just as bad as her bite. Believe me, she barks loud and hard, and I have never seen her back down from anyone or anything. Some people fake their power and position; this is never the case with my grandmother. Grandmother has made things happen, and I have witnessed it. She is definitely not one to take lightly; especially since grandmother seems not to have a conscience.

Tugging my arm, she squeezes tighter, "Do you hear me? If there's anything I need to know; you better be at the house tonight and tell me. If that God-aw-ful-detective asks you any more questions, you had better not speak to him; not one word. I'll have our attorneys notify him, making sure he understands that all his questions are to be diverted to our family attorney."

As she eases her grip, her face returns to its wrinkle-free state. She pulls on the hem of her blouse to straighten out her clothes before continuing with her instructions. "Don't you forget, you are first a Richardson-Mason, everything else is unimportant. You must operate like it, talk like it, and live like it. We may not be perfect but the world sure as hell does not need to know it. Now, you go with your mother and check on my grandchildren. Bring them by the house if you must; Ms. Rochelle is there, I'm sure she will not mind caring for them. Ms. Elaine must be terribly upset herself not to mention exhausted. She probably needs a break."

Grandmother leans in with her cheek to my lips. I kiss her on one, then the other. She repeats the same motion with my mother. She's right; of course. Poor Ms. Elaine must be tired as well as run out of excuses for the twins.

Although grandmother's offer is a good one, Ms. Elaine is a little overprotective with the twins. Ms. Rochelle helped raise Mother but that means nothing to Ms. Elaine. It's sort of funny to me the way she mothers the twins. I know she's not going to let the twins go anywhere, with anybody. As far as she's concerned, no one can handle them the way she does. And she's probably right.

Grandmother takes her perfect stride, and struts to her waiting limo as Mr. Charles holds the door open for her to get in. Mr. Charles is always smiling. I bet he can write a book on all the things he has seen in his forty-six years working for this family. Her walk is a perfect runway walk. Her posture is always straight and tight. Her clothes are perfectly fitting and always fashionable. Right now, she is wearing a beautiful light-colored pink blouse with a deeper pink two-piece pants suit. The jacket is long and flowing, so when she walks it sachets in the wind. Her pants hug her hips and are never tight around the legs. Her red bottom heels, purse, sunglasses, and perfume are always designer - of course. I am almost positive she has her own blend of perfume created for her since she refuses to tell anyone what fragrance it is.

From what I understand, Mr. Charles' father worked for my great-grandparents. Mr. Charles has been a part of this family since he was born. He was a young fourteen years old when he started driving for them. Although grandmother will never admit it, she's his senior. She knows she's an old fart! Well, I know she is.

Love to get the True E, story of lies, cheating, and all the hidden videotapes from Mr. Charles one day. I bet he knows all; I just bet he does. Ah, he's so faithful and loyal; he will probably die with all those secrets. I must admit, loyalty goes a long way in this family, especially since the pay is good. And that pay is not always in monetary form.

Mr. Charles is the only in-house employee that does not live on the family property. That in itself is odd since the control my grandmother loves and so desperately needs over the people close to her is extremely depleted by Mr. Charles not living there. He may just be the only person grandmother never disrespects. I mean ever, she has never disrespected him in any way.

I must admit, Mr. Charles is a good-looking man. His tall six-foot three firm frame is in perfect form for a man his age. He must work out a lot, there is no fat on this man at all. Other drivers wear hats, not Mr. Charles; his wavy salt and pepper hair is so smooth looking and always trimmed. He too has a very distinguished scent that he will not share. Ah, secrets! He does wear a uniform that is always pressed and clean. It shows off his nice physique, and I do mean nice. I wonder if he has someone in his life and perhaps that's why he doesn't live on the grounds. Let him keep all the secrets he has; I'm trying to keep my secrets a secret for as long as I can. That is going to be a full-time job for me from now on.

Mother and I head off in the opposite direction of my grandmother, and I take my first deep breath in twenty-four hours.

CHAPTER THREE

Bumps in This Road

Mother and I always have a wonderful time together. No matter how long we talk, it is never enough time. I only have two great friends and one best friend. Gwen and Lynnette are the greatest friends anyone can have. My mother is my best friend; when I find it necessary to hide things from Gwen and Lynnette, it never enters my mind to hide anything from my mommy-Irene.

Sometimes I think my mother's determination to stay close to me, is to make up for the lack of love I received from other family members. While growing up, grandmother always catered to my sisters. Her hopes for them far outweighed their hopes for themselves. You see, it is not important what we do in this family. The important thing is, if you do anything that could cause any unfavorable recognition to this family, you had better not get caught. Personally, that requires way too much work. I figure, do not do anything you cannot live with. Well, up until now.

Danna seemed to hate the entire privileged-life-style grandmother afforded us. Everything she could do to hurt this family; she has done it. When she was turning eighteen, she decided to throw a birthday party. Although Grams; (no one should tell her I call her that); was away on vacation in Paris, and my mother was in Miami, she gave her permission along with some ground rules. Regardless of what those ground-rules were, the most important thing to remember is, not to do anything to bring disgrace or embarrassment to this family in any way.

I was forcefully sworn to secrecy by Danna, concerning anything I would see or hear during this party. With the threat of an even more uncomfortable life than what I have experienced already for the past thirteen years; I promised to mind my own business. The truth of the matter is I honestly could not have cared less what my devilish sister did as long as she left me alone.

The deal was made, I could invite Gwen and Lynnette over to stay the night if we stayed out of the way of the party. So many people showed up; if we stood in the middle of the floor, naked, no one would notice. Nevertheless, I promised we would not intrude on her fun; for the most part, I kept that promise. The music is blasting and whistles blowing, while the partiers screamed and danced on top of furniture. With popcorn and soda, Gwen, Lynnette, and I watch from the second-floor foyer as my sisters' friends destroy my grandmother's home.

The irresponsible acts of my sister were almost unforgivable. My grandmother's house, including some of the priceless art, passed down to her from her parents, and to them from theirs; were destroyed. Within this house is a complete basement, where the party can take place. Down there, visitors can do all the jumping and breaking they want to. Not without mentioning, on the other side of the pool area is a party house. I'm sure grandmother was at ease thinking that was where the party was going to take place.

By six the next morning, there was vomit, piss, and bloodstains on the Victorian sofas and love seats. One of the Pinner Qing Dynasty Vases was in pieces along with a Tufft table. The carpet had holes where cigarettes and blunts were dropped or laid. Oh, and the smell of all the alcohol in the air, was atrocious. The only reason the party ended then is because Sheriff Winters received an anonymous call.

Until this day, Danna has no idea I was the one who called the police. I figured enough was enough. I'm sure a couple of girls left that night and went to the gotta-get-rid-of-this-problem-doctor a month later. I wouldn't be surprised if three days later, some of the guys went to see the gotta-itch-and-pissing-green-stuff-doctor.

They were nasty. Some was having sex on the couch, on the staircase, on the floor and even on the damn Queen Victoria dining room table. I was not the most popular child in the house, but I did and still do appreciate my overbearing-hard-to-understand-no-nonsense-better-not-cross-me, grandmother. The whole party pissed me off. Needless to say, Sheriff Ned Winters ended the party by calling parents to come to get their kids before he takes them to jail. If that wasn't bad enough, he made an unofficial report (for grandmother's eyes only), detailing everything he saw. Along with the pictures he took. Which I'm sure will only exacerbate the situation.

Every parent who had a child at that party was called into a meeting with my grandmother and her personal assistant, Nylah, who is Mr. Charles' niece. I don't know what was said but none of the party people was ever allowed into our home again.

After the totals in damages were tallied up, it carried a price tag that was well over five hundred thousand dollars. Yep, a whopping half a million bucks. I never thought the money was the biggest problem for grandmother. I heard her tell Danna how disappointed she was in her lack of respect for the lifestyle she has been afforded to live. However, before the conversation was over, the humiliation and the fact that shame was brought to the family was the last straw for the camel.

Danna didn't back down; she may be the only person who is not afraid of Catharine Richardson-Mason. It seems as if Danna gets her kicks by defying her. Danna's cantankerous-churlish-curmudgeon-foolish-down-right-stupid-careless-can-never-win-against-the-grandmother-behavior will be her undoing. Actually, I think it was the glimpse of pain she was able to inflict on grandmother that made the effort more fascinating to Danna.

With her bags already packed even before grandmother arrived back from her trip, Danna was getting as much money from the bank as she was allowed. Again, Catherine was never a fool. We each had bank accounts; however, she placed a limit on them. This way, if you left without the blessing of Catherine, you didn't leave rich.

Danna ran into my room, huffing, as if out of breath. She hurryingly sits on my bed. Although her tone with me is hardly ever calm or nice, she manages to talk in a civil tone this time.

"Hey Rey, let me get a few bucks."

Turning my attention away from the book I was reading, "How much, I think I have thirty dollars."

Jumping off the bed, she begins to pace the floor back and forth. She takes a deep breath and stops her pace long enough to hold me by the shoulders and look me in the eyes. I can see she had been crying. She appears to be extremely nervous as she bites on her fingernails. As bold as Danna's persona is, I never thought she could buckle to a point where she comes to me for anything, less more show any fright towards grandmother. She never cares what grandmother thinks or can do; until now.

She sits on the edge of my bed, then she gets up to pace the floor. She sits again and then paces. Her red hair is a mess as if she had not bothered to comb it since her party. She may even stink a little. I take the chance and take a deep breath trying to correlate my senses to my thoughts. Yep, she stinks. Stinks of alcohol, sex, weed, and cigarettes. Trust me this smell is a nasty combination. In fact, if she had to hide, her scent would give away her whereabouts; yep, just follow the smell.

In an anxious voice. "I need that thirty and everything you can get out of the bank."

Suddenly, she becomes agitated and now here she is, the real Danna. The sister I have been living in hell with my whole life has taken over the conversation. Her long deep-red hair is swinging as she paces. Her shape is odd to me since she has a flat butt and oversized tits. Her face is filled with light brown freckles, her size is medium built. She's not small but not heavy either. Her height is around five feet five inches. She may be considered somewhat funny looking but not ugly.

"Look, I don't have time; I need whatever money I can get my hands on before that old hag gets back. Now, get your ass up and put on some clothes, and get your tail to my car, and let's go to the bank and get some money."

Does she really think I would give her a dime of my money? If she does, the jokes on her. The irrational way she is acting lets me know, this is only the beginning. When she is determined to do something, most times she gets it done, even when it's not the best thing to do.

With an angry stare in her eyes, Danna looks at me with her shoulders hunched up and her hands open towards me. I turn my head away from her, trying not to look her in the face. After a few minutes of her standing there, she finally speaks, "I know you hear me, and I know you're not just going to act like you can ignore me. So, get your nappy head up, and let's go and get the money, now. You know what, just give me your bank card."

My heart is pounding, and I can feel the sweat dripping down my back. I know it's not hot in here; it must be the fear of what I know can happen next. I try to come to a rational thought that the yelling and screaming give her some sort of false power. She cannot make me do anything. I simply sit and say nothing. Without another word, she slaps me so hard my head jerks from one side to the other as the spit in my mouth spews out.

In total shock, I sit completely up and grab my face with both my hands, covering my cheeks. If I was not afraid before, I am now. She grabs the front of my pajama shirt and snatches me up from the bed then shoves me across the room to the floor. There is no way I'm going to attempt to get up, but I don't have to; Danna locks her fingers in my hair and pulls. While dragging me across the room, I try to break her fingers free of my hair but it's useless.

My hair is one of my best features; well to me, it is. It's thick, dark, and curly. My sisters' and grandmother's opinion are it's nappy but it's not, it truly is simply curly, and I have no problem combing it; neither does my mother. Danna continues to fling me from one side of the room to the other. I'm screaming as loud as I can. I know someone should be here by now. Finally, after about three minutes of her abuse, she stops, with one last shove of my head. I'm not sure if I am supposed to get up. I don't know if I should even take the next breath. So, I sit there, I sit there with my eyes in a fixed stare on her; silently praying she is done with her attack on me.

As I stay on the floor, with blood dripping from my busted lip, Danna kneels in front of me, "Now, you ready to get to the bank or give me the bank card?"

All that she just did to me does not change my mind. I slowly shake my head from one side to the other: no. Standing up she begins to rock from one foot to the other. I know to cover my face, I can almost feel her intense heat, I'm so afraid she will kick me in the face, I want to get up so that I am off the floor.

"Oh yeah, you're not? Wow,"

She turns around for a second; all I can remember is her sneakered foot coming towards my face; so fast I didn't have time to move. When I wake up,

Ms. Elaine is taking care of me. I lost my two front teeth and received eleven stitches under my chin. There is hell to pay when my mother gets home. Both my mother and grandmother returned home the same night after Ms. Elaine calls them.

The last time I saw my grandmother this mad was last year when Kristy; 15, and Kenneth 17; got caught by his mother having sex in his room. Wow, speaking of a bad time. Kristy got sent to boarding school and Kenneth to military school. I don't think Mr. Stuyvesant would have sent his son away if Kristy wasn't the granddaughter of Catherine.

Grandmother has this way of promoting self-punishment by asking you what you think she should do before she bangs down the final gavel. Either way, it's a bad time when you must face her wrath. Danna is most definitely in for the hardest time of her life. My room was torn apart, proving she was looking for my bank card. She or no one else would ever find my things. I have the perfect hiding spot. In grandmother's enormous quarters, where no one, not even defiant Danna will dare to go.

Not only does she have to answer for the out-of-control party, all the damages, and the great embarrassment to the family but there is a price to pay for physically abusing me. Crazy as it seems; my grandmother did not accept any excuses from anyone for putting marks on me. Calling me names and causing me mental discomfort is acceptable to a degree; however, visibly causing me harm is placing a different name in a different category on the treatment of the black sheep; and we cannot have anyone thinking I am being abused under this roof. I am still her granddaughter.

Yes, she, herself, is abrasive. According to her logic, she has paid the cost to do so. However, she never hits; her money, influence and extensive vocabulary are too powerful to have to. Although I'm bi-racial, I have an exceptionally beautiful light brown tone that easily shows burses. Grandmother used to say; in a matter-of-fact-sophisticated-tone, "Do not bruise that child, people will think the inconceivable. The chatter all over this municipality will be that we are abusing her because she's unique."

This caused me to feel special in an odd sort of way. Hey, one takes what they can get.

Once my mother and grandmother return home and see my face along with the report and pictures from Sheriff Winters; a family meeting is called. This is a sure sign that things are not going to turn out good for whomever is facing the family. Frankly, I honestly do not know why Danna stayed around for this. She should have left. Oh, perhaps she was lacking the funds to do so. I do not know. One thing I do know is, trouble now has her name permanently attached to it.

Staring at grandmother with the evilest look, Danna folds her arms as grandmother read her the riot act.

"There is no proper diction, I can afford in my lexis that can define how disappointed I am with your actions. You really should be ashamed of yourself."

Standing before the entire family can have its advantages and disadvantages. The advantages are there are some witnesses who can be potential allies. The disadvantages are you may find yourself pissing off the entire family and then no one will defend or stand up for you. By the stance alone, Danna is headed for the latter.

All tribunals in this family are conducted with all the family members present. As I stated, this has its advantages and disadvantages; all of which depends on attitude. If your attitude stinks - like Danna's - well you get what she gets, discharge papers.

Still, with the look of defiance all over her face, Danna allows her mouth to express clearly how she feels.

"Look, just say whatever you want to say, so I can know what I need to do. All this talk is not going to change what happened, so, what's next?"

Uncle Douglas was and still is many things, but disrespectful to his mother he never will be. I don't think it has much to do with inheritance, he genuinely loves his family.

Uncle Douglas stands up, points his finger in Danna's face and speaks. "Have you lost your mind? That's my mother and I am plenty more grown than you. Never have I spoken to my mother in such a manner. Have you lost your mind? Or you have decided your untouchable?"

The hostility I saw in Danna's face is now replaced with surprise and I think I see a tad bit of fright. I must admit, it's not just what Uncle Douglas is saying; it's the threatening tone and finger gestures he's using.

Without waiting for her to answer he continues, with his hand raised pointing his finger, "Don't even attempt to answer; I know you have gone crazy. Would you like to see the bill for your little shin-dig? A bill you can never afford to pay?"

It's so quiet in between Uncle Douglas' words; I'm sure if a pin dropped, we could all hear it. With an after-thought-suggestion, he continues, "Oh, I got it. You're the privileged granddaughter. You got it like that. See that's where you got it all wrong. Your position in this family is contingent upon your ability to never bring open shame to us. What do you think naked people, drunken teenagers, broken family heirlooms, destroyed furniture and doctors' visits; not forgetting to mention the abuse you wroth on your sister, have done? These things do not constitute your understanding of these contingencies."

Danna scanned the room with her eyes. Once she found my mother's face; she stares at her. Taking a deep breath, she speaks with quivering in her voice, "I do apologize for my actions; I hope you all can find it in your hearts to forgive me."

Turning her attention to my grandmother, "Grandmother, I ask that you please accept my deepest apologies for disrespecting you and for destroying; *your* house. It will never happen again." The way she emphasized YOUR HOUSE was sarcasm at its finest.

Even now, I can still hear the contempt in her tone. Although I think she realizes the position she's in, I don't think she is sincere at all. No, her tone and facial expression is too cynical. Grandmother crosses her legs and folds her hands together on her lap. With that straight-back-perfect-posture, she clears her throat. Even when she's angry she speaks with such poise and eloquence.

"Oh really; well that's good to know. I guess I can easily throw this implausible character you've demonstrated under a rug somewhere. Perhaps I can even purchase the memories of all the families whose children attended this fiasco of a party. Perhaps I should let this matter slip by just one more time. Huh, what do you think child? What should I do?"

Hey, I know she's not expecting an answer. I'm sure Danna knows that as well. I also know Danna knows she has ripped-her-drawers with this family. So, I guess in her mind this is her last stand. I can only assume with what came next;

she has settled with the fact she wants out and before she leaves she is going to say everything she feels she can get away with.

Danna stands up and fumbles with her shirt. Pulling on the hem as if straightening it out, then patting her hands on her jeans. She smacks her lips together then takes a moment to glance the room again. Danna walks over to my mother and kisses her on the cheek.

"You are weak, always have been. Never have I seen you stand up to her. You're like a little girl. Whenever she speaks, you may as well whimper like a wounded puppy."

Uncle Douglas makes a move towards Danna, Irene stops him, "No Douglas, let her say her piece."

Clapping her hands in Irene's face as if congratulating her, "Oh, my goodness, you have a voice. I never heard it before. Well, mother, I am not like you, and I am not afraid of this woman. This family has done nothing short of destroying whatever life you may have had. Did you forget how you were the disgraced daughter because you allowed a black man to access your royal muffins?"

Danna seems to have found her strength and no one is stopping her. She leans back on one-foot looking Irene up and down with her lips turned up and face snarling. Pointing her finger in my mother's face, "I will never be the whimpering puppy to this woman as you have been."

Moving around the room, she fixes her attention on grandmother. I cannot believe the audacity she has to disrespect our mother, no, my mother and then turn her vicious tongue on grandmother. My heart is pounding, and I am deeply saddened. She takes a few steps towards grandmother but don't get too close and continues her verbal assault.

"I know you want me to grovel and beg but I won't, not today, not tomorrow, and not ever. What's done is done. Whatever you're going to do, do it, and just get it over with."

Wow, I could never, I would never, and no one would ever be so face-to-face-defiant. I know now she has lost her mind. I mean usually when she does something; and she has done lots, she falls into place. I cannot for the life of me imagine what's going through her head.

Grandmother has a visible grin on her face. Almost as if she's satisfied or proud. I am so confused.

"Well child, are you finished?"

With nothing less than total sarcasm and contentment, Danna releases her tongue of furry. Moving her head back and forth and waving her finger around,

"No, not quite. I don't want to be in this family any longer. I am done with all the social limitations and guidelines. I'm done with all the conservative pretense and avowed secrecy. Oh, and the mundane insurmountable obligations placed upon every family member with the knowledge that failure will result in repudiating your membership."

Now, grandmother is smiling and clapping her hands. As she stands to face my-poor-lost-now-in-more-trouble-than-her-big-mouth-can-chew-sister; I hear a very unusual sneaker escape from grandmother's mouth. This cannot be good.

"You know darling, I am rather amused that you have an extensive vocabulary. This gives me immense delight on one hand." Holding one hand higher than the other as if a scale. "However, on the other hand, you have proven to be quite an intellectual travesty and a fool."

Danna motioned as if she was going to speak and Grandmother raises her hand for her to stop.

"You've said enough, and I do mean enough. Do not think for one minute, because you have been allowed an opportunity to speak your mind, it was the right opportunity to take. Before I am complete, you will see it would have behooved you to maintain that nasty tongue." Grandmother looks at Mother and asks, "Would you like a scotch, my dear?"

Irene, shaking her head yes, "Absolutely, Mother and would you like one also?"

Maintaining that grin on her face she nods once for yes, "Absolutely, I'm with you. How about you, Douglas, would you like a scotch?"

"Yes, ma'am I do, and I will go get all three of them."

I swear Uncle Douglas looks as if he's practically running for the bar.

Grandmother turns her attention back to Danna. With her finger up as if trying to remember something, "Now, where was I? Ah yes, I remember; that massive mouth of yours. You see dear granddaughter of mine. This family has been afforded a marvelous existence. Absolutely nothing you had to participate in to create. All you did was be born and the rest was provided to you. Well, I'm sure that makes you feel privileged and probably somewhat powerful; both of which you should sense; however, not parallel to me."

Uncle Douglas returns with the drinks in record time. I'm sure he gulped down one or two before coming back. This family meeting is intense. Grandmother takes a small sip of her glass of scotch, while mother gulps as much as she can fit in her mouth at once.

All eyes are fixed on grandmother as she returns to her seat. Danna is displaying nervous movement. I'm sure she's not in control of less more conscious of. Once seated grandmother gets to the grand finale of this meeting,

"Well dear since you're eighteen I cannot very well send you away to boarding school. Therefore, I have come up with two alternatives for you. Once you allowed your rebelling mouth to seize the entire consciousness of due respect; my first thought is you have gone insane and probably need to be committed. However, that will cost this family more money and further public shame. Your relentless mouthy attack is justifiable of nothing this family can render monetarily on your behalf. Oh well; too bad. The other is what's left and probably more adequate."

At this moment I wish I can have a scotch, straight up. I'm not the one on trial here but I sure feel like I am. My palms are sweating, I have a nervous twitching in my left eye, and I feel nauseous. In my mind I'm yelling to the top on my lungs; get this over with, please. I mean if you're going to kill her and bury her next to the family plot; where I'm sure there are bodies other than family, restlessly decaying; then say it. Let's just get it over with.

Danna has stood before the family for a number of infractions, but nothing like this. This is when she should have been the humblest but instead, she's allowing her pride to test the waters. Perhaps she does not understand the unchartered waters are full of man-eating sharks; each has grandmother's teeth.

Grandmother continues, "You will vacate this house immediately. You will not be welcomed back into this house until you have demonstrated yourself to be worthy."

Did she say demonstrated to be worthy? Hell no, no one can prove themselves worthy of this family. The bloodline is our heritage and mistakenly Danna thought it served as her right. But it doesn't, it simply serves as an opportunity that we were born into; nothing more, and nothing less. Like any other opportunity, it comes with advantages and disadvantages. One just must recognize and understand the invisible limitations and play fair.

A heightened tone in my grandmother's voice brings me back into focus.

"You will depart with that single suitcase you have already packed. Sink or swim, the choice is yours. I can only hope with that sweltering vocabulary, you've managed to acquire some common sense too. At the very least, more than what you have so brazenly displayed here tonight."

Still, without a conscious realization, she has no power, Danna makes the mistake of speaking yet again. "Fine, I will be happy to go."

For the first time since this meeting started mother speaks directly to Danna. "What has gotten into you, child? Do you not understand the predicament you're in?"

Turning to face mother, "What predicament mother? I'm eighteen and that means I'm grown. I can make my own decisions. Besides, I know grandfather left us all a good inheritance. So, if I'm leaving, I will gladly do so with my money in hand."

The look on my mother's face; is of total shock. However, another look, and I see the tears falling down her face.

"Nepotism, is that it? You thought you had personal-privilege-and-favor to some money because of your name? So, you throw your family to the curb? You allow your childish stupidity to cost you more than you can imagine."

Without a glimpse of remorse, Danna continues to show her fangs. "Look who's talking. You don't think I know the only reason you stayed here is for the money, your inheritance, your piece of the pie?"

Mother gets out of her seat and begins to pace the floor while she continues to unleash some much-needed parenting. "You poor wretched child; you played cards you never had. All that mouth and you have absolutely nothing in that brain of yours; you are clueless and empty of any kind of logical thinking." As mother is talking, she is moving closer and closer to Danna, so close their noses are almost touching. "I stayed here for you and your sisters. Not for money because unlike you, I have my own money and plenty of it. You, on the other hand may have bitten off more than you can chew, and now you will choke on it."

Turning to grandmother, Irene walks over to her and says, "I agree mother, do as you need to do. I will be upstairs; there is no need for me to sit through the rest of this."

Uncle Douglas follows my mother out of the room.

Grandmother calls out to Ms. Rochelle who enters quickly, "Yes ma'am."

"If you don't mind would you please be so kind and have Charles pull the car around to the front."

"Yes ma'am, right away."

As Ms. Rochelle leaves the room grandmother turns her attention back to Danna, "Just so you will never make such a grave mistake again, listen to me. I am the matriarch of this family. *My* husband has left every dime of his wealth and monopoly matters in my power. Including and definitely not limited to, all inheritances. Do you honestly think we didn't see rebellion coming? While you're exploring yourself and being *grown,* try to speak less and learn more self-control."

Finally, that defining moment must have hit Danna. The look on her face tells the story. The tears accumulating in her eyes are now falling. She is fidgeting from one leg to the other. With a shaking voice, "What, what do you mean?"

With a very satisfied look, grandmother finishes this meeting. Reaching on the table next to where she was sitting, grandmother retrieves a bank card. Handing it to Danna, "This is your inheritance, for now, my dear. I will deposit two thousand dollars a month into this account. That is all you will get. I truly hope you have good friends, because the lifestyle you so recklessly flung away, has come to an end. You may now vacate my home that appears to disgust you so much. Charles will drop you off wherever you want to go; however, he is on loan to you for only an hour, make it count. Good-bye, my dear."

With desperation in her tone, "Grandmother, wait! Are you serious? What am I supposed to do? How long do I have to stay gone?"

"All of that depends on you. Take this information with you; this world is broad of people that live on significantly less and learn valuable lessons on saving and investing in their future. I suggest you do the same. Bye, my dear."

Holding her hand out for me to follow her, "Come, my child, let's get those bruises looked at. Ms. Rochelle will make a dental appointment for those teeth to be replaced as soon as the swelling goes down."

Grandmother couldn't send Danna to boarding school, so she did the next best thing. After all was said and done, Danna, was sent packing. With one suitcase, a bank card and good advice, Danna left the premises.

Mother was so upset when she saw my face; I don't think she even thought about the consequences Danna had to face. Grandmother made deposits, without any increases until Danna turned twenty-five. Danna never attempted to mend her family relationship and grandmother stopped expecting her to. It took that long for Danna to understand, there is a big difference between being committed to the integrity of this family and the false delusion that money alone can buy you respect.

So glad the "bad-seed", *me,* managed to stay out of the kind of trouble that would have cost me a position in this family. Even with all that bad-blood.

Well, I may be too grown to be thrown out of this family; perhaps I may have enough money to keep me in. What I'm not sure of is, if I can get the forgiveness I'm going to need from my husband.

As long as my mother is by my side, I know I will be okay. As much as we talk and as much as I share with her, I just can't find a way to tell her what happened with Lamont.

CHAPTER FOUR

Twin Love

*A*s we stepped into the house, the twins run and jump on us as if we have been gone for months.

Together, as if practicing a song,

"Hi Mommy! Hi I-Mee!"

From the very beginning Irene stated she is not to be called grandmother, granny, Nan-nah, nanny or anything that will reflect an aging old wrinkled, although cute and cuddly, grandmother. When the children were little babies, she dubbed herself I-Mee, which I think is cute.

I'm glad to be home and happy to see my babies. They make me smile no matter what's going on around me. The way they jump up and down while holding onto me, makes me feel as if nothing else is important. I can always rely on Benjamin's charming personality and a more than pleasant smile to comfort me. He seems to always know when I need special attention. Charmin, although she is just as lovable, is daddy's little girl. Once Lamont enters the room, no one else exists. Daddy was Charmin's first word at three months, and the last one she says each night. If Lamont isn't home before bedtime, she will continuously call him on the phone until he says good night to her. If she can't reach him, there is no sleeping in this house until she does. Needless to say, I've had many sleepless nights in the past year.

Lamont is never just daddy; he's *my* daddy according to Charmin. Even when she talks to Ben, she refers to him as *her* daddy; as if she's speaking to someone other than her brother.

I dread the questions ahead. When I spoke to Ms. Elaine, she stated the children were asking her all kinds of questions. While grabbing me by the neck, Charmin is peeping over my shoulder; no doubt looking for her daddy. And the questions start, "Where's my daddy? Huh, what happened to him?"

I squeeze a little harder and try to get as many kisses as I can before having this conversation, I know I can't avoid. I'm trying to get my composure under control. Mother and I talked about this while we were out, yet I lost all the confidence I seemed to have mustered up before arriving home, to face my yet so innocent and delicate children.

Like only Irene can do, she steps in using her impeccable timing, "Hey, hey, let your mommy get her shoes off and give her a chance to sit. She's been gone all night; don't you know she misses you?"

Charmin releases her hold on my neck. As she's taking a few steps away from me, she has the oddest look of frustration on her face. With her arms folded across her chest, and her eyes squinted, "I want to know where my daddy is, I-Mee."

With a smile on her face, my mother reaches her arms out to Charmin. As cute as can be, Charmin, has a lovely head of light brown hair that is naturally curly, reminding me of Little Orphan Annie's hair when it's wet. It takes some special care but somehow, we have managed to find the right combination of products to manage her beautiful hair.

Ms. Elaine always has the twins dressed as if they have plans for the day. Charmin has on one of her favorite two-piece orange and white polka-dot outfits with orange, white and black hair bows, and barrettes. Benjamin is like a little gentleman, very independent with a smooth charismatic character - as long as he is not upset. Once upset, the temper-tantrum will have to play itself out because there is no reasoning with him. He also has a head of light sandy brown hair. Thank goodness the barbershop is always available. We keep it cut short with just enough on top to show off his curly mane. He is wearing a brown pair of slacks with a pullover three-buttons tan Polo shirt. He loves to put his hands in his pockets and loves, even more, to have coins in the pockets so he can jingle them.

I take a deep breath as Irene takes control of the twins so I can get a moment to bathe and change my clothes.

"Come on dear, your mommy is going to tell you all about it, just as soon as she gets a little comfortable. Do you think you can wait for a few more minutes?"

Slowly relaxing her arms and shaking her head up and down, Charmin relaxes.

"Yes ma'am, I can."

Under my breath, I whisper, "Oh, thank goodness."

Ben kisses me on the cheek, "Can we get in your bed and talk?"

Kissing him back, while nodding my head yes, "Sure, we can. I'm going to take a quick shower. Why don't the both of you get the ice-cream, four spoons and meet me in the bedroom, with your I-Mee," I close one eye as if I need to think; "in about twenty minutes - okay?" While I was growing up, no matter what kind of problem I was having; it never seemed as bad once I was lying in mommy's bed.

Then there are the smiles of approval I needed to see. Mother holds out her hands for each one to grab hold. Off into the kitchen, they go for the ice-cream. Up the stairs, I go, for the shower and a quick prayer.

Ah, the shower is amazing, I feel as if I've been dirty for weeks. For some reason, the hospital can make you feel dirty. Yucky. It seems like the place you go to for your health is the nastiest place to sit.

After drying off and massaging every place I can reach; I find the most comfortable pair of pajamas and put them on. My hot pink pjs with Betty Boop's face all over them. I enter my bedroom to face the music. It's no surprise to see all three of them sitting up in my bed. Mother on one end, with the twins in the middle, I climb on the other side. Ben's hand is holding one side of the gallon, while Charmin's grip the other.

My explanation to my children is just like the one I gave to everyone else. I found Lamont lying in the foyer, bleeding and unconscious. Other than that, I can't say how he got home. The one thing I can say is he didn't come home the night before...again.

While we eat ice-cream together, I casually change the subject from Lamont to my grandmother's house. The twins love going over there. Grandmother may act like she's sucking on lemons all the time, but the twins seem to add all the sugar she needs.

There may have been some hard times for me while growing up in her house; however, somewhere along the line, I have found the tender side of her personality. Notwithstanding her audacious character, which holds firm to the family business and her matriarchic position which exemplifies her controlling approach to life. Now that I understand her, I wonder if understanding means I lowered my values or raised them. All in all, when it comes down to it, right or wrong, Catherine Richardson-Mason has done everything in the name of this family's survival. For that, I must appreciate who and what she is.

Those are the kinds of conclusions I know we're supposed to come to while making decisions. The conclusion that no matter how we do a thing, it had better work out for what's best for the family. No matter why, it had better make the family look good in the end. I'm afraid I may not have considered that unwritten rule yesterday morning when I found Lamont.

I am afraid. I'm afraid that my husband may die. I'm afraid that if he doesn't die, he won't wake up from the coma. I'm even more afraid that if he does wake up, he will remember all the things I said and maliciously did before the paramedics and police arrived.

Leaving all the hoopla behind, I relax and enjoy the solitude with the three people that matter to me the most. Everything else can wait its turn in the line of all the troubles awaiting my undivided attention.

CHAPTER FIVE

The Fears that Find Me

*A*lthough the beeping machines are driving me insane, I'm happy being here with Lamont. I'm even happier Lidia and Linda are at my home visiting with the twins, which of course, allows me time to be alone with my husband. Notwithstanding, away from them is probably the best deal of the day.

There's a duel going on in my mind concerning my husband's recovery. Part of me wants him to wake but I don't want anyone else here when he does. I want the suffering of his loved ones to end but I want to be the only one here when he opens his eyes. I must find out how much he remembers about that morning.

Dr. Carswell has confirmed that Lamont will need surgery to relieve the pressure on his brain. All the assurance he gives does not evict the butterflies that have taken up residency in my stomach. I trust that Dr. Hamilton will do his best.

I decide to go down to the cafeteria, not because I'm hungry but it gives me a break from the morbid atmosphere of the room. Just as I step into the hallway I glance up and who do I see? No, no way, there is no way this undeniably-irritating- got-to-find-something-better-to-do-with-his-life-gum-smacking-no-doubt-need-a- woman-detective, is back to talk to me.

Well, it doesn't look like he spotted me yet. No, he's too busy being nosey in other people business; glancing in rooms and checking out the nurses. So, I duck behind the nurses' station and practically crawl to the elevator.

As I crouch here, I almost snicker out loud at my behavior. I just can't be bothered with this man today, or any other day for that fact. Finally, the elevator doors open, and I make my dash for it. No sooner than I enter the elevator I hear him call my name.

"Mrs. Harper. Mrs. Harper."

Here he comes waving his hand in the air, and I press the button. I'm sure he can see the smirk on my face as the doors close in his face. Yeah, I know he will either be right in the same spot when I return, or he will find me in the cafeteria. Damn, why can't he understand English? I guess grandmother's attorney hasn't called him yet.

As the elevator doors open to the basement level, I step out and there he is smacking on the gum. I sure hope it's a new piece. He seems rather attached to the one he was chewing the other day. I swear, if he tries to hand me a business card, I'm going to smack him with it.

"Good morning Mrs. Harper. I tried to get to you before the elevator doors closed; I guess you didn't see me."

He cannot be serious. I mean he just cannot be serious, how in the world did this idiot pass any test less more a test to become a detective. I, I don't even know what to say, I really don't.

"Mrs. Harper, I just need to ask you a few..."

I instantly cut him off. I am not listening to anything he has to say nor am I answering any questions. I throw up my hands.

"No, Detective Mayfield, you may not ask me any more questions. I have answered all the questions I am going to answer for you. So, if you don't mind, I'm headed to the cafeteria."

As I attempt to walk past him, he steps right in front of me; still chewing on that damn gum. He is so close I can smell his funky-stale-cigarette-smelling-nasty-dog-poop-breath, no, I don't think he changed that gum, his breath smells too bad. Reaching into his jacket pocket as if I said yes to his request, he pulls out his note pad. Clearing his throat, he proceeds, "Mrs. Harper, where did you say you found your husband?"

Really, I mean is this man really going to totally ignore my request for privacy? No one can be this stubborn-egotistical-over-bearing-obnoxious-need-to-get-a-woman-quickly-to-do-something-with-all-this-time-he-apparently-has-on-his- hands-idiot.

Well, guess I'm going to have to pull grandmother's card to get this man off my back.

"Stop! I guess you are hard of hearing, so I will talk a little slower and louder for your understanding." I'm extra rude and probably very wrong, but I mimic sign language as I chastise him. "I'm-not-answering-any-more-questions-so-put-your-notepad-back-in-your-pocket! I will not take another one of your cards; I will not talk to you. However, if you need to talk to someone, my grandmother said to divert you to her." I put my finger on my chin as I prepare to feed him his words, while using my fingers as quotation marks. "Now, if I remember correctly, the last time we talked you said you know my grandmother personally, right? So, you should have her number, I suggest you call her. She's waiting excitedly for that call."

I turn on my heels and walk away, leaving Mr. Detective standing there holding his pad in his hand. I refuse to turn around to see how long he stands there. I must admit I feel quite exuberated.

Calling grandmother and letting her know to expect a call from this so-called-detective would be too nice. I'd rather let him make the call without giving her the heads-up so he can feel her wrath. I'm not sure why I don't like this man; I just don't, and I want him to know I don't like him, so he will leave me alone.

What I wouldn't do to hear the conversation between grandmother and Mr. Stiff-neck-annoying-yuck-faced-detective first-hand. Well, if he does know grandmother personally; let's hope that works for him, while she bites into that ego of his. Poor fellow, perhaps he'll catch her in a good mood, and she gives him her nice-nasty demeanor, that way he'll scratch his head, wondering if she just told him off or not. Or he may catch her in a mood where she has no time for pampering his feelings. If that be the case, he will be in the full effect of emotional pain while she rips him a new asshole; metaphorically speaking, of course, grandmother would never touch someone's asshole. Metaphoric or not, it will be just as painful, he won't be able to tell the difference.

I set my eyes on a banana-nut muffin and a cup of hot peppermint tea. It's better than nothing although I still have no real appetite. I make my way back to the side of my husband's bed. Lamont looks so helpless; I truly hope he pulls through this. Ever since this happened, I think how horrible it would be to not have him. I love him, I may not like some of the things he does, but I do love him. While I get comfortable in my chair right next to his bed, I reach out to hold his hand. Reminiscing about our lives, I can see where there have been more good times than bad. Things didn't get bad until about two years ago. I wish I could pinpoint why.

My deep thoughts are disrupted by a light knock at the already open door. As I look up, I see an unfamiliar face. In the doorway stands a voluptuously built woman. Her eyes are green and hair long and blond. Her make-up is perfectly applied, just as perfect as the pants suit and matching shoes she's wearing.

"Hello, my name is Robin, may I come in?"

I clear my throat and answer, "Uhm, ye-yes. Do I know you?"

I get up from my seat to greet her half-way in the room. I reach my hand out to shake her hand. As she reaches out, she says, "Please excuse me for intruding; I am a co-worker of Mr. Harper. I hope it's okay that I came. I-I-I just wanted," Her words are cut off by the choking sound of her fighting back tears. Who is this woman, I never heard of her, I never met her before? Why is she here? As if she can read my mind, "I am so sorry, for my intrusion; I have been working with Mr. Harper for over a year now and I heard about his accident. I truly hope I haven't upset you by showing up without any previous communication. I did try to call the number listed as a home number, but I didn't get an answer."

Well, she could be telling the truth. Ms. Elaine does not answer the house phone since we all communicate through cell phones. Still, I don't know anything about this woman and frankly, I am upset. Perhaps jealous since I have never met her. Did she say she has been working with my husband for over a year? Really, over a year, and I haven't heard of her? And she is drop-dead gorgeous on top of that. I suppose I'm being somewhat rude, I guess I can at least answer her and relieve her of the discomfort I am sure she's feeling. However, there is a nagging deep feeling in my gut, which tells me this woman is trouble.

"No, come on in. You're not intruding; I'm Rietta, Lamont's wife. How are you? I'm pleased to meet you."

I know I'm lying I am not pleased to meet her. Well, perhaps I'm just not pleased she's been working with my husband and I don't know her. I walk in front of her, leading her to Lamont's bedside. Yeah, that sound was choking back tears, because now she is crying without holding back. Covering her mouth, Robin cries almost uncontrollably. All I can do is look at her, in puzzlement.

Now I must play nurse to someone I don't know. Am I expected to show her some kind of sympathy or something? Here standing right in front of me is a woman dressed to perfection, with long-legs, blond silky hair, a fresh manicure, expensive perfume, with the smell of mistress stinking all over her. Not to forget to mention the bold nerve of this woman to show up here and have a conversation with me, his wife,

I want to ask questions. I want to scream. I want to pull her silky hair and drag her across the entire floor and dirty that Versace suit, break the heel on just one of her Gucci shoes, smudge her make-up, hit her in the head with her Gucci handbag and break all her fingernails. But I will contain myself. She may turn out to simply be a co-worker. NOT! Lamont owns his business; he doesn't have co-workers, he has employees.

Putting my hand on her shoulder, "Don't worry Robin, he's strong and will pull through this."

As I do all I can to resist acting unseemly, she turns to face me, "Does anyone know what happened to him?"

"No, no, not yet; when I found him, he was unconscious and unable to talk."

I reach for the box of tissue on the nightstand and offer it to her. She takes a tissue from the box and wipes her nose. Sniffling as she pats the tissue on her face, "May I ask you what the doctors are saying about his condition?"

Just in case I haven't made it clear, I don't like this woman. When the hell, no, what the hell, no, who the hell does she think she is, coming up in here asking questions about my husband's health? I guess my silence, and probably the expression on my face is telling the story I haven't allowed to escape my mouth, yet. Robin looks at me, takes a deep breath and touches my arm, "Oh, please excuse me Rietta, I don't mean to pry. It's just that I'm concerned about Lamont and I just want to know if he's going to be alright."

What? Okay, that's it! Did she just call my husband Lamont, not Mr. Harper?

"I don't know you and have never heard of you; frankly, I am a bit confused about your presence here. Not to mention your questions and emotional reactions. Just who the hell are you and what was that last name you neglected to tell me? And don't tell me you're my husband's co-worker."

Suddenly her grief expression turns into the most cunning smirk. She walks on the opposite side of Lamont's bed; with one hand, she pats his chest and with the other, she rubs his bandaged head. I can feel the blood in my body boiling, I want to explode but I can't. I am so shocked at her demeanor, I can't move. I stand at attention, ready to find the words that would express my feelings; however, right now I can't find any. I feel as if a truck just smashed into my chest.

This woman dressed in her two-piece, pastel shade of peach suit, still with that smirk on her face leans over and kisses Lamont on the forehead; then turns to walk out. Once at the door, she turns back to face me.

Her voice takes on a most seductive and catty tone. "Oh, you're almost right, I don't work with him at the *office*, but I guess you can say I'm his co-worker. I'm sure if he got a whiff of my, I mean *our* favorite perfume, he may even wake up."

Before I can say a word, she dashes out the door. I can't seem to move fast enough. I gaze at Lamont and then at the door. Finally, I find movement in my legs and head for the door. I will be giving this fake-preppy-Bobby-doll-two-bit-home wrecking-out-of-her-mind-piece-of-shit, a small piece of my mind as soon as I catch up with her.

She must be headed for the elevator and so am I. As I make a mad dash in the right direction, I don't see her. There is no way she could have caught the elevator that fast unless it was there when she got to it. That's fine, I'll find out who that hussy is. With my chest pounding in sync with the headache I suddenly got, I power-walk back to Lamont's side; full of determination to get some answers. As soon as I enter the room I realize, I won't get any answers, not here, not now.

Robin may not even be her first name, and I darn sure didn't get her last name. Oh, I'm so freaking mad; the nerve of that, that, that piece of, that tramp. That's okay, I will find out who she is, and when I do, she can either give me information the easy way or the hard way. After all, I am Catherine Richardson-Mason's granddaughter, and I know some stuff.

I look over at Lamont laying there, looking so defeated, so helpless; suddenly, Robin isn't that important. I will not allow her to distract me from doing what a good wife should and shouldn't do. I should focus on my husband. One thing is certain, I shouldn't go woman hunting, no, not at all. Not when I have so many options at my disposal to hunt for me.

The name alone gives me access to the hospital's security tapes. Perhaps I'll ask mother to assist in this endeavor instead of grandmother. Minimizing my embarrassment will be hard enough, and I definitely don't want my in-laws to know about this, less more my grandmother.

CHAPTER SIX

Panic, Pressure, and Patience

*A*lert alarms jolt me from my sleep. Before I can awaken completely, the room is brightly lit from every light being turned on. Nurses are in the room snatching pillows from under Lamont's head, while the bed is being lowered to a flat position. I don't know what to do. Looking up at the wall clock, I see it's almost 2:30 a.m. Perhaps I should call my mother; she and Lidia left together a few hours ago. As I reach for my cell phone, I hear Doctor Carswell say, "Get the crash cart, stat."

Asking myself, crash-cart, crash-cart for what? Then I realize the alert is because Lamont's heart has stopped. Oh no, I-I-he-he can't die, he just can't. With the phone in my hand, I cannot seem to remember how to use it. I can hear myself screaming, as my knees crumble under me, I feel them as they hit the floor.

Ms. Taylor's, the Caribbean night nurse, yells above the commotion, to another nurse who's on duty her accent bouncing off the walls, while she points towards a chair in the corner.

"Cynthia, geet she, she done ett the floor; just move she ova dere."

I feel hands grab me and help me to my feet; practically dragging me to the chair that was pushed in the corner on the other side of the room. There are so many people gathered around Lamont, I can't see anything.

Dr. Carswell yells, "Take her out of the room and call the family."

I can't speak, but I can hear my voice screaming; *'no, no, this cannot be happening.'* The only reason to call family is if my husband is dying and he cannot die. As soon as I take a step, my knees give out and so does my consciousness.

I wake up on a gurney and to Irene rubbing my face with a cold wet towel. As I slowly come to full consciousness, I look around the room. And here, here is everyone, with tissues, red eyes, and runny noses. Lidia and Linda are comforting one another; grandmother is here with Nylah and Mr. Charles by her side. As I focus, I see Uncle Douglas, Tyrone, and Melvin! Dread floods my soul, but my speech has left me and is too frightened to return. If Uncle Douglas is here, it has to be bad, really bad.

The question in my mind is right on the tip of my tongue, but I dare not ask. I'm too afraid to ask. Oh, but I need to know. My heart is pounding, I feel as if I will explode if I say one word. Damn, I wish someone, anyone, would just say it; just tell me what I need to know without me having to ask.

Here it is, Irene, my mother is always on time, she is so in tune with me. She sits on the gurney next to me.

"Rietta, how are you feeling? Are you okay? Dr. Hamilton rushed Lamont into surgery. The bleeding on his brain caused him to have a stroke. The bleeding needs to be stopped. I know it's hard baby, and I know you're frightened but you have to try to stay strong."

Although I am not speaking, I can hear myself speaking, it must be within my mind because no one can hear me, no one can hear me screaming as loud as I can. My mother can feel what I cannot say, and she comforts me as if I were still her baby. She rocks me in her arms holding me as tight as she can. Like the baby I need to be right now, I cry and bury my face deep as I can into her arms.

Since no one can hear my heart's words, I pray. I pray to God, that He would give me another chance with my husband. I pray, he will let Lamont live, I pray we can survive all this and fix whatever is wrong in our lives.

Oh God, I'm not angry anymore, I'm just in love with my husband.

If there are no previous nail-biters in this room, they have all been converted. Nails are being bitten, hair is being twisted, fingers bent, marathons walked in small circles and lots of crying. However, no one is talking; it's so word-quiet, it's deafening. I wish someone would say something, anything at all.

Nurse Taylor walks into the room with bottles of water and coffee on a pushcart.

"Me figure, ya not eat nuth'in, so me bring ya some wata and coffee. Me got some cookies and cake fa ya too. Try and poot som-um on ya belly, ya ear me?"

No one moves towards the cart, so she walks to each of us; me first. As she hands me a cup of coffee, "Now Mezes. Arper, if ya not eat nuth'in ya can't be strong fa ya man. Now try to drink dis eer coffee, and bite on one-a cookie or so. If ya want somum else me get it fa ya. Just let me know now dear."

Mother reaches for the coffee for me and grabs one for herself.

"Thank you so much, nurse. I'll see that she drinks the coffee and eats at least a cookie or two. You're so kind."

For the first time since I sank into my mother's bosom, I attempt to sit up. Mr. Charles comes to my assistance and tries to help me get comfortable. After he manages to accomplish his goal; gently but parenting he asks, "Mrs. Harper, would you like for me to go and get something hot for you to eat? I know no one wants to eat but the nurse is right. If you all don't eat you can't keep up your strength."

He stands up straight and looks around the room at each of us. "All of you need to eat. I'm going around the corner and get pizza and a bucket of chicken. It looks like it's going to be a long night."

Mr. Charles then looks at grandmother and says, "Catherine, would you like something different? Or would you like to ride and get some fresh air?"

Did he just call my grandmother Catherine? Nah, I must have been hearing things. Catherine? I thought I knew but now I know. And she's not correcting him; she has a look of tenderness, sort of endearing on her face. What; let me find out. Now, this got my mind in a different place.

Now, I can feel the hunger and just that one little slip of the tongue snaps everyone out of whatever hole we were buried in. Now everybody is giving an order. Lidia is the first, "Um, Mr. Charles, Linda and I will have pizza and chicken. Thank you."

Mother seconds that motion for us, Nylah, and Uncle Douglas also agree.

Grandmother is the last to decide, and Mr. Charles doesn't wait for an answer from her. He walks over and takes her hand and leads her up from the chair she's sitting in and takes her by the arm and leads her to the door.

Once in the doorway, he turns around, "We will return in a few minutes."

Am I the only one who just witnessed this? What is going on with those two? Okay, I won't be embarrassing, just in case I am tripping, I will ask my mother secretly. As I lean over to whisper, Lidia rushes as if she is expecting us to have a conversation, she is not privy to. In her hastiness, she starts the questioning.

"I don't mean to pry but isn't that Mr. Charles your grandmother's chauffeur?"

In a tone that would suggest her question is stupid, my mother answers, "Sure, why do you ask?"

Now her face is turning slightly red as if she realizes she's talking about my grandmother and not some loose woman in the streets.

"Oh, nothing, it's just that I heard him call her by her first name. He also seems somewhat comfortable; you know personal with how he handles her. What's with that? I mean isn't he the help? And I hope he doesn't get my order wrong."

Now, Irene takes a deep breath and prepares to let loose her nice-nasty persona. Poor Lidia doesn't know my mother. Irene stays her distance, so she doesn't create a more difficult relationship between myself and my in-laws.

"Well, it depends on how your mind works. See your perception is strictly based on the information you have. Sometimes that information is not enough to come to a complete intelligent conclusion. Now, I'm not too sure what your real question is, so I'm going to answer you how I took it."

As if Lidia understands she crossed a line, she attempts to apologize for the question. But it's too late, she's going to get the answers she needs so she doesn't make this mistake again.

Mother straightens her back to sit up straight, clears her throat and speaks in a clear and slightly raised tone. I know this is so Linda can hear also.

"Mr. Charles has never been the help. He is family, that's why he's here in this hospital room. The help would have been waiting in the car for a phone call." She then looks at Nylah before facing Lidia again. "This young lady right here, is family. Now granted, they do work with our family; however, they are so much more than hired help. They work for themselves."

Lidia puts up her hands in a stop position, "I do apologize; I didn't mean anything by it."

Irene puts her hands up as well, "Oh, sure you did. Now, we are here because your son, my son-in-law, Reita's husband is not doing too well. Now my question to you is this: Would you rather concern yourself with questions about whether or not my mother is sleeping with Mr. Charles or how Lamont is doing?"

The agitation in Lidia's face is quite visible. She blows her breath hard and folds her arms. However, my mother is not yet finished checking her.

"Whatever Mr. Charles and my mother's relationship is, is none of our business. They gained the privilege of privacy when they became adults. But for the record, that man loves and respects my family, and we love and respect him. His presence in this room is because he has earned that respect. As for your food order, he's not going to get food because he must, he's not a waiter; he's getting food for us all out the kindness of his heart."

Lidia is still holding up that finger as if she is in church trying to be excused. However, Irene is just about done, and that finger will either fade away to her side or thoughtlessly remain in that stuck position.

"My mother is a woman of dignity and self-respect and whatever she decides to do, reflects those qualities. She has earned the right to do whatever she desires, without any questioning from her family, or anyone else."

Standing and fixing her clothes, my mother turns to me and smiles, "I'm going to the bathroom, my love. Are you good?" I shake my head yes. "Good," she turns towards Lidia. "Are you good?"

Rubbing her neck as if it's stiff, Lidia closes her eyes. Shaking her head yes, "Yes, yes I'm good. Please forgive me; you're right I know I stepped over the line."

Mother, being the wonderful person that she is, gives Lidia back her dignity. She reaches out and pulls her into her arms, "Darling, we never know what's going on between those two and we just gave up trying to figure it out. You just had the nerve to ask out loud when the rest of us whisper about it."

Then she winks her eye and laughs. Everyone bursts in laughter. Suddenly the room seems much brighter. I declare I feel the closeness between us all. Laughing together truly does well like medicine.

Irene goes to the bathroom and Lidia hugs me; she really hugs me. Linda comes over to us and adds her arms and warmth. That's my mama, she seems to know just how to fix the things that appear to be broken.

By the time grandmother and Mr. Charles return the mood in the room has taken a turn for the better. Without saying a word, everyone will keep the small, teeny-tiny misunderstanding between those of us in this room. Grandmother will never hear about it neither will Mr. Charles. Well, we know grandmother has the ability to just know some things. So truthfully, there is no telling.

We all eat and even laugh a little. Lidia and Linda reminisce over Lamont's childhood and the quirky teen experiences we all grew up with. I share our family's happy times and never allow a negative word to escape my lips concerning my husband. Grandmother even joins in on the conversation by adding her uncanny ability to know things before they happen. Everyone laughed as she told about Lamont and I trying to sneak off and be together before we were married. I was almost embarrassed, even feeling somewhat ashamed, until grandmother showed me her softness..

"Yes, Rietta believed she was prepared because she was so in love with Lamont. I am so extremely proud of her reaching the right conclusion. She remained a virgin until she and Lamont were married. She kept herself pure because of the integrity she has." Taking the time to look right into the faces of the Bobbsey-twins-Ying-Yang, grandmother continues, "Lamont is truly an incredibly lucky man to have a wife who has certainly not been touched by another. Rietta, is indeed a prize of honor."

Wow, did my grandmother say all that? With my ego inflated and my strength renewed, I breathe deeply and smile, as a tear of gratitude escapes my eye. That ability grandmother has is the one reason I tried my best to be as good as I possibly could be. The fear of her disapproving of anything I do has always been more than I could bear. It was bad enough that I felt somewhat pushed aside because of my bi-racial heritage; however, truth be told, I earned the respect of this family; respect I can only hope is filled with true love.

Anything I could do to make her love me is what I did. I need her approval and her love. This is not taking anything from my wonderful mother; she will love me no matter what. Whether I am a good girl or not, mother will always see me as a diamond. Grandmother, on the other hand, works on a merit-system; you earn it, you got it, you don't, you won't.

After the rising of the morning sun and what seems like days on top of hours, Dr. Carswell accompanied by Dr. Hamilton enters the room. Suddenly all the laughter and conversation cease, and everyone is at attention.

Dr. Hamilton finds me in the room, approaches me and begins to explain, "Hello Mrs. Harper. We had an awfully close call, but we've managed to stop the bleeding in Lamont's brain. Although this gave us quite a scare, it turns out to be a particularly good thing. Because of the stroke, it demanded our attention much sooner than we anticipated. This is good because if we didn't have to operate tonight, we would not be able to tell you the good news."

Good news? I thought. While I stand here practically not breathing even though the news, I'm hearing sounds good; mother takes the lead, "Hello again, Dr. Hamilton, thank you for this good news. Please continue."

"Yes, apparently what we thought to be bleeding of the brain was actually a blood clot that formed from the blunt force trauma to the head. From the force of the hit it created a clot that appeared to be directly on the brain when in fact it was wedged between the skull and the brain."

Lidia is excited and obviously ready to ask questions, I still cannot ask. I keep holding my breath, waiting for the bad news to come but so very thankful none is coming.

With tears of joy flowing from her eyes, "Will he wake up soon, is my son going to be okay?"

Pointing toward Dr. Carswell, Dr. Hamilton turns the question over, "I'll let that question be answered by his primary doctor."

With an open hand, he motions towards Dr. Carswell and slightly bows his head.

"Well, I don't want us to get ahead of ourselves but from the looks of things, the prognosis is looking favorable. However, we still have a few concerns, much of which rely on how long it will take for Mr. Harper to wake up. Our consensus is that the blood clot is the reason he stayed in the coma. Since has been rectified we will patiently wait for his eyes to open."

I cannot contain myself any longer, with tears flowing and my heart bouncing all over the inside of my chest; I ask my first question, "So, you do expect him to wake up soon, right?"

Dr. Carswell continues to answer the questions posed. "That is what we are all hoping for, but Mrs. Harper let me caution you, waking up is only part of the issue. We do not know if he will have all his memory, or just parts of it; or for that fact any of it at all. We also do not know if he will have the activity of all his limbs. We have no way of knowing what kind of damage he has suffered through this ordeal until he wakes up."

The sadness has returned to my soul; just as I bow my head grandmother speaks up.

"We appreciate both of you, Doctors' Carswell and Hamilton, and we realize you are performing your extremely finest expert effort. I'm sure you can appreciate our position as family. How difficult it is to expect the best and remain optimistic when the visual appears so dismal. Nevertheless, we will do our absolute best not to squander faith and maintain a positive outlook for and with each other. Thank you."

For one moment I forgot who my grandmother was and redundantly I proceed to reintroduce her.

"Oh, excuse me Dr. Carswell;" I raise my arm towards grandmother. "This is..."

Interrupting my introduction, "No need for any introductions, we all know Ms. Catherine Richardson-Mason quite well. Her contributions to this hospital along with her strong presence on the Board of Directors speak volumes to her generosity and deep concern for the people in need of this facility, not forgetting the people who are employed here."

With a smirk on her face that screams; proud of myself, grandmother nods in agreement.

"Thank you very much for your support and we will continue to do our absolute best for your love one. Now, are there any more questions we can answer for you at this time?"

I wait for a moment and when no one asks any more questions, I excuse the doctors after thanking them once again.

"Thank you, Dr. Carswell and Dr. Hamilton, for all the hard work you are putting in, we really do appreciate you. We are good for now; I know you are available for any future questions we may have. The only thing I need to know is when can we see him?"

Doctor Carswell, answers, "Right now, my suggestion to you all is to go home, get a good-night's rest. Mr. Harper is in recovery and will be there for the rest of the day and night. Relax your minds; if there is any change in either direction, we will call you. For now, he cannot have visitors until he is out of recovery."

If I could just see him for a few moments I would be able to rest but I know I won't if I don't see him. Before I can get the nerve to beg my grandmother intercepts my thoughts. She's getting as good as my mother.

"Dr. Carswell, perhaps Rietta can glance at him if she promises not to touch and disturb him so that her mind is set at ease; do you think that will be possible?"

Nodding his head in agreement, "Sure, I'm sure that can be arranged. Give me a few moments and I will send one of the nurses from ICU to get you. After that, this doctor orders all of you to go home and rest. I don't want to see any of you until tomorrow."

Wow, I'm happy I will have the chance to see Lamont, but it will be hard to stay away. I guess I have no choice; besides this will allow me to spend some much-needed time with the twins.

Much sooner than I thought the nurse comes in and leads me away to see my husband. I wondered as I walk down this brightly lit, yet dim hallway; do all the walls have to be this god-awful beige color? Each step, the sounds of the machines seems to create a symphony of rhythmic noise. I glance in each room I pass. We get to the end of the hallway and the nurse presses for the elevator; once in, she presses for the third floor, just one floor below us. The elevator stops and opens slowly. The nurse walks off and I follow her closely and anxiously. Although it has only been moments, it feels like too long. Finally, we come to a double-door and the nurse waves her badge at the sensor, it beeps and the doors slowly open.

There are several beds in a row with intravenous drips and heart monitoring machines. Yep, more beeping machines. We pass a nurse's station and I can see Lamont in the second bed from the station. I promised not to disturb him. As much as I want to reach out and touch, no hold him, I know I cannot, not right now. I must make seeing him be enough for now. I slowly look at each machine, small tubes are leading from the bags hanging on the pole and disappearing between the bandages on his head. There's another tube in his mouth hooked up to a big machine with a pump going up and down. It reminds me of a ukulele.

The visit is short but very satisfying. By the time I go see Lamont and return to the waiting room, grandmother is gone along with her entire entourage. Leaving strict instructions that lunch is at her place for the entire family. When Catherine decides family lunch, whatever was on your private agenda has then been rescheduled. I'm happy we are having lunch together; it's about that time.

Mother hugs me tightly and gives me one of her amazing smiles that say a thousand words without sound. Lidia and Linda are going with me, I can only pray that everything stays as calm as it appears at this moment.

Whispering in my ear, Mother asks, "Do you need or just want me to go home with you."

Hell yes, I do, but I think I need to try the alone thing with my in-laws. I whisper back, "Yeah, I do. But I know I need to get a grip and deal one-on-one with the other side of my family. I know you are only a phone call away. "

Smiling, Irene looks at me as if examining me for something out of place. Walking around me shaking her head up and down, now allowing small snickers to escape her lips, "Ah, well, I see, we are growing up. Pretty soon you will be all good on your own huh? "

Laughing at her very loudly, pointing my finger, "Now I didn't say all that. I'm simply good for a few hours before lunch at grandmother's, only. Don't be so quick to deem me as all grown-up. Besides I kind of enjoy being your baby. That will never change. Even when I'm old and grey, I'm going to call my mama as much as I can."

We laugh and walk out of the room together. I honestly don't want to leave Lamont but I'm sure things will be okay. I heard the doctor say he doesn't know if Lamont has all his memory. If he lost any part of his memory, I pray it's the last thing I said, and did.

CHAPTER SEVEN

Good Things Sometimes Comes to those Waiting

*H*ours have turned into days and days into weeks; tomorrow will be an entire month since Lamont's surgery and two months since this ordeal began. We have noticed movement in his fingers, and he squeezes my hand when I ask him to. Although his eyes are open, he hasn't spoken yet.

I wonder what is happening in his mind, I wonder what he's thinking, or even if he's thinking. Each time I enter his room, my heart feels as if it's flipping over.

My in-laws have begun a very productive relationship with me. It's almost hard to remember how difficult they used to be. Ah, I don't know; sometimes I feel that Lamont's accident is a blessing in disguise; then again, perhaps not.

This is so tormenting to me; sitting around biting my fingernails, afraid he will start talking when I'm not in the room. One thing is certain, I understand the old quote: *"What a tangled web we weave, when we practice to deceive."* My intent was not to be deceptive; it simply turned out that way. Now that the ball has already begun its roll, there is absolutely nothing I can do about it except wait and see how things will turn out. Oh hell, I just want to scream!

The twins finally will get a chance to go see their father in the hospital. I waited for all the swelling to go down in Lamont's face and headfirst. Besides the swelling, his face was purple, red, and blue, I was afraid it would frighten them. Although Lamont is not talking, the children need to see him, if for nothing else than to comfort their curiosity. Charmin keeps asking why her daddy left and won't come back. It's enough to break my heart. Little Ben seems to go with the flow. He will ask about his father, if, he hears his sister asking, as if it's an, oh, by the way thought.

I hear Lidia talking to the children pumping them up for their visit. I think we all are equally as excited as the twins are, for them to finally see Lamont. Having to answer questions and repeat the same old story each day is not easy.

Ms. Elaine seems to have her hands full, from the sounds of it. Poor woman, having to deal with the twins is bad enough, now she has been dealing with a grandmother that wants her proper due and an auntie that feels privileged and entitled. I never interfere; Ms. Elaine knows how to handle herself. This woman helped raise me. Ha! Where do you think my mother and I learned the nice/nasty approach? I believe her grandmother raised my grandmother. Therefore, we never call family, the help. After being a functional figure in this family for so long there is no way Ms. Elaine can be labeled the help. She has a voice and active power to make decisions for, and with this family.

I know Lidia means no harm and I'm sure that's the only reason why Ms. Elaine hasn't lit her up. I'm enjoying watching my family come together, we all will be alright. I feel as if we are simply learning how to work together.

As if Charmin is running from a ghost, here she comes screaming, "Ma-ma, ma-ma, tell Auntie Linda I can wear my pink socks and pink shoes. Please tell her, please. She's not being very nice to me."

The look on Charmin's face is priceless. Her face frowns, lips poked out and her arms folded across her chest. I suppose I need to express how serious the color pink is to my child; if it's not pink, it's orange.

Before I can get my thoughts together to help in the situation, here comes Aunt Linda, "Charmin, get in here and put these clothes on, right now."

I don't want to interfere, but I must, I guess to save face for both of them I need to do an Irene. Still smiling I tell Charmin to go into her room and wait for her aunt to come. I then take the opportunity to gather Linda and Lidia together in my room.

"Hey guys, I should have told you this so please forgive me for not thinking about sharing this with you before. There are times when Charmin won't wear anything that is not pink or orange. At this point I have no idea why, but I feel since she must wear clothes, then she is the one that needs to be comfortable in what she's wearing."

Oh boy, it looks as if I have offended my dear sister-in-law. Her face is frowning almost as bad as Charmin's face was when she came in my room pouting about the clothes.

"Look Rietta, I honestly do understand the fact you allow the children to explore their own way of doing some things; however, I went shopping for them both and I spent a lot of money on her clothes. Please tell me what I am supposed to do with them if she refuses to wear them?"

This will not turn into a bad situation; I refuse to allow it.

"I totally understand your point and it is well taken. Perhaps if you can just consider the fact that the children have been going through some of the same feelings we have been dealing with for almost two months. I'm sure once she sees her father, she will be much easier to deal with. Besides, he can get her to do almost anything; including wear different colors."

Okay, I know this is a temporary fix, but who has the time right now to disassemble the fight for power between a slightly dysfunctional adult and a precocious child? Certainly not I!

Linda gives me a slight smile, "You're probably right, I'm sure once she sees Lamont, she will be easier to deal with. I apologize for not thinking. The last thing I want to do is create a wedge between me and my niece."

Further indulging her, "You know Charmin is a Drama Queen not to mention spoiled rotten, thanks to your brother, and all the rest of us. It's her way or the hard way."

We all laugh and call it a truce. Linda is pacified and Charmin does what she does best; gets her way.

I see Auntie with a comb and brush in hand. Now I know this will not turn out good no matter what I say or do; therefore, I will do Charmin's hair. Linda will not be able to survive the hair-combing-challenge. Charmin hair is a lot like mine. Thick, curly and the texture; I'm sure, is not what Linda is used to.

I stop my sis-in-law and explain I'd rather be the one doing Charmin's hair. I further explain that because of its texture it may be hard to handle. She buys it and the problem is solved before it becomes a dilemma.

The trip to the hospital is not so quiet. Ben is unusually noisy; most times he is so quiet you can almost forget he's in the car. I find myself telling Ben to take a seat continuously. He's pouncing and flipping back and forth from one seat to the other.

Lidia doesn't seem to be bothered by her over-excited grandson. Linda, on the other hand, is not so happy about having Ben's feet hit her in the head. Our Lexus SUV is roomy but I'm sure the manufactures didn't have bouncing kids in mind.

Finally, Linda can't hold her peace any longer, in a very snappy tone and with a grab of Ben's arm, "Boy that is enough; sit your tail down and don't get up again until we arrive at the hospital. Do you understand?"

Not only is Ben taken by surprise, so am I. As I look into the rear-view mirror, I can see tears accumulating in my son's eyes while he looks directly at me as if he is waiting for me to say something.

Frankly, I think Linda is in a mood today. First, it was her and Charmin, now her and Ben. Well, my thought is she may need a few minutes of time-out. However, I cannot say that; I must be the diplomatic one and keep the peace between my children and their aunt, and myself and my in-laws.

This time Lidia steps in and defuses the very delicate situation.

"Linda, he's just excited about seeing his father and like a child he can't sit still. Try to be just a little more patient; we should be pulling up to the hospital in about ten more minutes. And do me a favor and keep your hands off my grandson."

The look of frustration on Linda's face doesn't change in the direction it was anticipated to. Instead, Linda looks even angrier. As if she's the child, she folds her arms and blows out her breath hard, not even trying to hide her anger.

I suppose my chuckling is not making the situation any better; so, what I wanted to avoid, I inadvertently opened the flood gate. With a quick adjustment of the eyes, Linda is looking right at me, frowning.

"Do you find something funny?"

Quickly losing the smirk on my face, "No, no, Linda, I am not finding this funny. I know you're frustrated and not used to having bouncing children around. I know the children can be somewhat difficult to deal with."

Okay, so I thought I was helping, it is now apparent that all I can do in this situation; that seems such a small thing to me, is make it worse. Linda readjusts herself in her seat and gives me the most hideous look.

"What are you trying to say? Are you assuming I don't know how to deal with children because I can't have any? Is that what you're saying Rietta, because if so, let me tell you something..."

Just in the nick-of-time, Lidia intercepts, "Linda! Stop that, now we are all excited and probably a little nervous. I think secretly we all are hoping the visit with the children may cause Lamont to open his eyes. Anticipation is not a settling feeling but despite all the emotions we are feeling, we are family and we will conduct ourselves as such. Now Rietta didn't say any such thing, and I don't believe she even insinuated it. Just relax and calm yourself, I'll keep Little Ben still."

Wow, she actually said Ben's name. Usually, she calls him Little Lamont. I guess things are changing for the better. We continue the ride in peace. Mother is meeting us at the hospital. Oh, and I want my husband to open his mouth, but I don't want him to remember everything.

In the short few minutes, it takes for us to arrive at the hospital, Ben falls asleep. I guess sitting still relaxed him too much. Linda rushes to carry Ben; I'm sure in hopes of taking this as an opportunity to mend the damaged bridge between her and her nephew.

Children are so resilient when he wakes up; he probably won't remember the arm snatching or the harsh tone he experienced. Especially since that is not what he is used to coming from his auntie; or anyone for that fact. Linda kisses Ben until he wakes in her arms, and just as I predicted, like the male child he is, he indulges himself in the kisses and extra hugs. I smirk and I'm glad.

There is the face that lights up my day. Mother, as usual, is right on time, waiting for us in the lobby. This is where I revert to a child getting the hugs and kisses, I need. Oh, I love my mother!

"Hello everyone."

Mother takes the time to kiss the children and hug them before focusing completely on my in-laws. Shaking Ben's legs that are dangling from Linda's arms,

"Hey, big boy, what's going on? Are you the baby of the day, having your auntie carrying you?"

With the eyes of a big-eyed cartoon character and the tone of a spoiled child, he responds by shaking his head up and down, "Ah huh."

Still not finished with his Academy Award-winning performance he buries his head into Linda's neck and squeezes her neck so hard she hunches her shoulders for some slack.

Mother smiles and says, "Well, you go right ahead and enjoy yourself, if you like it like that."

Charmin is not so easily calmed from her ordeal and she lunges at the opportunity to tell.

"I-Mee, Auntie Linda has been very mean to me and Ben all day, I-Mee, all day. She was yelling at me and trying to make me wear an ugly blue dress. Then she hit Ben and hurt his arm and yelled at him. She is very, very mean, I-Mee, very mean. I-Mee, she didn't want me to wear my pink clothes. I-Mee, please tell her I do not wear blue."

As if telling isn't enough she has exaggerations and then the face. Oh my, she has the extra face. Her eyes are filling with tears and her head drops to her chest and now she is holding her arms up towards my mother to be picked up. Now, I know this is way overboard, even for Charmin.

Mother is mother, and she never acknowledges the accusations but instead picks Charmin up and gives her all the kisses she wants. We all smile and laugh and head for the elevator. The ride upstairs is quiet until the doors open.

Charmin waves her hand in front of her nose and frowns up her face, "I-Mee, what is that smell, pew, it stinks in here. Is my daddy in this stinky place?"

I guess Charmin having such an extraverted personality may turn out to be a good thing later on in life; if she can control her impulses to leave out the lubricants.

Planting one more kiss on her granddaughter's forehead, mother says, "That's the way hospitals smell because all medicine has a different smell of its own, but all mixed together, it stinks." Holding her nose and making a stinky face, "Pew, you are right it does stink; but I bet once you see your daddy, you won't smell it anymore."

Ben suddenly is fully awake and joins in the conversation. "Daddy, where is daddy, I-Mee? I want to see daddy too."

Linda bounces Ben in her arms, "And you shall, we are headed to his room right now."

It's good seeing them so excited, I, on the other hand, am excited yet nervous. As we step into the room the bed is empty. No Lamont, no sheets, no respirator. The room is practically empty, and my heart just stopped beating; I feel faint. No one says a word, I mean; no one. We all simply look at each other and I declare everyone is holding their breath. Then a familiar voice fills the room,

"Ah, me bet ya sir-prised, da man of yrs don wake-up tah-king em ead off. Em give da doctors rah fright ya know. Em wake up fussing, where me wife, me pintnies, what appen ere? Oh, em tahlk, tahlk, tahlk, dem doctors take em down for rah brain scan. Em be bock soon ya know."

My head is spinning, all I can hear is talk, talk, talk. What was he talking about? Of all the days, he wakes up wanting to talk when everyone is here. I'm trying to compose myself; I just don't think I'm doing a good job of it. Linda and Lidia are ecstatic. Mother is in tears, then she looks at me and I cannot fake anything with her. There is no fooling her at all. As thoughts run through my head, I know I'm panicking, I'm happy my husband is alive, awake and even talking, but I cannot help it, I'm scared to death. Mother reaches for me and pulls me to her. Some of her words are whispered, and others are out loud for the company we are with.

Whispering, "Now, I don't know what it is you have not told me but before this day is out, we will have that talk. Do you understand? "

I shake my head, yes.

Out loud, "Girl, you better not faint because if you do, you're hitting the floor this time. Take a seat; I know this is a huge surprise you look like the blood drained from your face. Do you want something to drink?"

Shaking my head, "No thank you, mother I'm, I'm j-j-just so happy and shocked." Turning my attention towards Nurse Taylor, "Why didn't anybody call us and let us know about Lamont's progress?"

With her hand on her hip and a smile on her face, "Gal, that hubby of yas' wa-nun let no-one make a cake. Em say em ungry and dat em noo ya be ere soon. Dem doctors take em right down to see what appen in em brain. But a good sir-prise fa ya now. Me noo ya appy, em be bock soon, me check and see fa ya. Me be bock."

Linda looks at me and says: "Do you understand what that woman says? I can only get bits and pieces. I can't believe they let someone that cannot even speak English properly work in such an important position."

Seemingly very frustrated she blows hard and bounces down in the chair. I take one look at mother and I know she is on edge of rebuking Linda and correcting her foul way of thinking. Instead, mother taps my hand and suggests we take a short walk down the hall. I always welcome any time I can spend with mother, except now. My stomach's butterflies have begun movement; it feels as if there's a war going on in there between different butterfly families. I feel punches, kicks and turning over, ugh!

Oh, I feel sick. However, this is my best friend and I knew today was coming; I may as well get this over with. So, I agree, and we leave the twins with Linda and Lidia and begin our walk; our longer-than-I-can-stand-to-think-of walk.

Without asking, I begin to tell everything. I told, all the lies I didn't admit to. And she did what she does best, listens and comforts me; never accusing me of anything wrong.

After our talk, I wondered why I didn't have this conversation long before now. I guess we continue to live and learn. All I know is once grandmother finds out my truths, I'm not going to receive the same treatment. She asked me to tell her if there was anything she needed to know. I denied everything and told her nothing. I have broken the number one rule of this family. Never bring any shame upon this family or its name.

I'm very sure the fact that my actions were not planned and spontaneous will have no bearing; it will not count for anything. The worst that can happen is the worst I can't tolerate. Oh-my-gosh; help me! Mother holds me tight and reassures me of the fact that no matter what, she will stand by my side. From where I'm sitting, I will need her to do just that.

By the time we begin our walk back to the room, the elevator door opens and there he is sitting up on the gurney smiling. My heart is flooded with happiness and love. I'm not sure if I should run and hug him or stand there waiting for an invitation before I can decide, the decision is made for me.

With his arms stretched out, "What are you standing there waiting for, an invitation? From what I've been told you have been here for two straight months hugging and holding me when I was incapable of hugging and holding you back."

Wiggling his fingers like an impatient child, he stretches out his arms further, reaching for me to come. "Get over here baby."

And I run, I run into the arms of my husband who is showing me nothing but love and kindness. *"Oh God, thank you, thank you for hearing me, thanks for allowing me another chance to love my husband and him to love me."* I ride back to the room sitting on his lap on the gurney.

We enter the room to excited children and relieved adults.

The children ask questions Lamont can't answer. Lamont asks questions no one can answer. Finally, when all is said and done, we are all happy, and we never mind the small stuff.

CHAPTER EIGHT

Darkness Comes to Light

With the entire hospital ordeal behind us and we are getting on with our lives. Lamont is back to himself, no, no, I take that back. He's not back to himself. He is better than he was before his injuries. The husband that went into the hospital was a man that had little to no compassion for me. Now, he shows me his love and compassion all the time.

Dr. Collins said he may never remember what happened or he may wake up one day and be able to tell us everything that happened to him. The bits and pieces that he doesn't remember haven't seemed to disrupt any important parts of our lives.

After the two and a half months stay in the hospital and the two months home recovering, Lamont is ready to get back to work on Monday morning. That's three days from now, that does not give me much time to find that skanky-hoochie-think-she-can-hide-from-me-Robin. I did not forget about her. I want some of that ass.

When Lamont first comes home, I intercept the first of many special delivery packages for him, from Robin. In one of the small and neatly wrapped jewelry boxes; as always, a handkerchief smelling of the very same perfume that wench had on when she showed up to the hospital. Favorite perfume my ass, I will find her.

Once I told my grandmother about the little encounter with the mysterious woman, she was more than happy to put Uncle Douglas and his goons on the detective squad on her trail. If it smells like trouble, Uncle Douglas, Tyrone, and Melvin will be in the front to make sure the trouble stays within the guidelines of our family rules.

Linda and Lidia said their good-byes a week ago. I honestly began enjoying our visit. There is no doubt Lamont has lost some of his memory, he acts as if the wonderful way we all get along is normal. Perhaps, it is now, and no one is talking about how it was before. This is the perfect example of how something bad can cause something good to happen. My family is closer than we have ever been. Even grandmother is different. She has loosened up a lot, perhaps a little too much.

The other day, grandmother and Mr. Charles went out to dinner. Now, that may seem like a small thing, but they went out together as if on a date. Well, not that I'm calling it a date but I'm just saying that is not like my grandmother. First of all, although Mr. Charles is a real family friend and we consider him family and all, the fact remains she has a problem with color and money boundaries; so, what is really going on with that.

My father was not welcomed into this family because of his skin color and financial status. My mother and I were deprived of having him around, just because he didn't measure up to her standards; whatever those standards were or are. Strange how the strong convictions that created pain for others are the same convictions tossed aside for personal satisfaction. Don't worry, I will try my darndest not to allow my pain to disrupt grandmother's or Mr. Charles' happiness. I did say I will "try".

Grandmother has shown great signs of change, and she is not as difficult as she used to be. Nonetheless, this is still a very drastic change. Living under her roof was ridiculously hard, mostly due to my darker skin tone and who my daddy is. If not for the color of my skin, most people would never have known I was a black man's child from the hairstyles to the fancy clothes and private schools. But I will never hide that fact, I am proud of who my father is, it's my heritage. I haven't permed or straighten out my natural curls since Charmin was born. We both rock our natural curls very proudly.

There were invisible yet tangible prices that had to be paid for that change to be developed. Not to forget to mention, the fact that the bigot way grandmother used to think has caused lots of pain and unforgettable memories, I will never forget. Nevertheless, I have had a wonderful life despite mean sisters and racist relatives. Everything seemed to have worked out very well.

Sometimes in my private thoughts, I wonder if I married a man of the Caucasian persuasion just because it was the only true choice I had. After all I clearly can remember the results of my dear mother's choice of a black husband.

Irene has been lonely; there is no way she can't be. I'm close to her and we talk about everything, yet we never talk about her personal life and why she doesn't date. I have never seen my mother with any man, none whatsoever. I want to ask her how to find my dad, but I don't want to hurt her feelings. She has never hidden the fact she still loves and misses my dad. It's almost as if she is waiting for him to walk through the front door. Huh, good luck with that; especially since her front door is still considered the entrance to grandmother's house. And why does she still live there?

Whenever we mention the name Benjamin, it's because we're talking about a busy six-year old. I don't know how Mother would take it if I were to ask her about my dad, the Benjamin we both miss. I guess I won't know unless I get the nerve and go ahead and ask. I mean what's the worst that can happen. She can tell me she has no idea where he is and not to ask her again. Or she can burst into tears, run out the room, and say how cruel I am for mentioning him. Perhaps, she can collapse in my arms and say, she has been waiting for me to ask about him so she can tell me. Who knows?

One thing that's certain, I need to know more about my dad and the only way I'm going to know more, is to ask the one person that may know: my mother. I guess there is no point in wrestling with this within my mind any longer; tonight, is the night. I'll call her on the phone and ask.

Knowing about my bloodline can help me understand why my hair is crinkly-curly as if it's struggling between the two textures with no conclusion of which it should be. Part of it wants to be straight, the other part nappy, so somewhere along the line, it settled for in between and stayed curly. I love it. Anyway, I want to know about my father and his father and mother. I want to see pictures and hear stories; I want to see if other family members look like me or if I favor someone. Yep, tonight is the night I ask all the questions I need to ask.

The ringing doorbell startles me. I swear, if that is another package from that piece of crap-home-made trash-slimy-more-than-a-slut-poor-excuse-of-a-woman-Robin; I'm going to become a detective myself and find her and put my foot, no, both my feet in her one asshole, at the same time.

I peep through the curtains; oh, wouldn't you guess it, it's not the female headache, it's the male headache. Rolling my eyes and breathing deeply I try to prepare for this very unwelcomed visitor before I unlock the door. I find myself completely agitated by the thought of him smacking on gum. Sure enough; I open the door and he's smacking gum. Now I must wait for him to get his fill of chewing before he can say a word.

In between smacks he manages to extend his hand, "Mizz Harper, how's ya doing today?"

I don't care how long he holds his crappy hand out; I'm not shaking his hand. I don't like him, not one bit; there is no need to pretend. While he stands in the doorway with his hand still extended, I rest my hands on my hips.

In a tone that clearly sounds my dislike, "Hello Detective and what brings you here?"

He takes a step closer as if I'm going to move out of the doorway and invite him in. I don't get it; he must know how I feel about him. I mean come on, he's a freaking detective; if he detects good enough he should detect I don't like him. How in the world is he going to solve any case being so dumb?

I stand my ground and don't budge. As a matter-of-fact, I close the door a little, squeezing myself in the doorway. While blowing my breath, I ask, "Can I help you, Detective Mayfield?"

With a look of confusion on his face, his head drops as he removes his hat from his head. This may be the only time his chewing, um I mean smacking on that gum ceases for a moment. In a slow drawl, just as irritating as smacking on gum, he speaks.

"Why yes, Mizz Harper; I would like to speak with ya husband if ya don't mind. I tried to wait a while to allow him to get settled back at home before intruding on his recuperation time. Is he available?"

I guess if it's not today, it will be one day. Perhaps I should just get this over with. But, nah. I'm not feeling that good. Well, at least not before I instill the fear of the Richardson-Mason Family in his heart.

"Uhm, did you have a chance to speak with my grandmother's attorneys before coming over here, and did you call first? Perhaps I missed your call."

Now putting his hat back on his head and smacking on that gum even worse than before; in a tone of humility almost in a whimpering voice, "Please forgive me Mizz Harper, I honestly forgot the instructions I was given by ya prestigious grandmother. I mean no disrespect nor any harm. I will completely understand if ya refuse me the permission to speak to ya husband."

What, what is that? Does he really think I will fall for that weak-emaciated-foolish-pompous-rat poisoned excuse? Really, I mean what kind of new approach is this; "prestigious grandmother", and understanding my refusal, what? Oh, it is stupid but funny as hell. Too bad he won't see me burst out laughing at him. No, I'm trying hard right now to save that for after I close this door in his face. However, oh my goodness, it's killing me holding it in.

Folding my arms, I just look at him. I don't even have a response. All I can do is give him the mother's look of, really? This is going to get really uncomfortable in a few minutes because I'm not going to say another word. I am just going to stand here staring at him. And I hope he sweats. I am trying to hold back the laugh that is tickling in my belly. I have to hold my breath trying not to laugh.

Clearing his throat, "Huh, Mizz Harper?"

I'm still staring at him without blinking or moving, stiff as a board I'm still staring. I need to clear my throat, but I won't, I'm not going to make a sound; just keep staring. The tangled words he used trying to spin a web for me only spun one for him. Although I'm leaning on one leg while the other is available to pat, I won't move. After a few moments, he is reaching inside his pocket for a handkerchief to wipe the sweat from his brow.

Oh yeah, I think he's getting it. He's switching from one foot to the other. I bet he's thinking about that ridiculous statement he made and if he could, he'd kick his own ass. He should ask me to do that for him, and then I will find it in my heart to speak six words: *yes, turn around and bend over.*

Fumbling with his hat, "Mizz Harper, do ya think I can speak to ya husband, or if today is not a good time when do ya think I should come back?"

Still staring, not talking, and not blinking.

"Mizz Harper are ya going to at least answer me? If I said something wrong please forgive me, okay."

Still staring, not talking, and not blinking. Just hoping my body is not jerking from laughing to myself.

"Okay, Mizz Harper, I get it. I understand."

Blowing his breath, in obvious defeat, he fumbles in his jacket pocket. If this man hands me one of his out of date-black-and-white-smelling-like-spearmint-stale-gum-which-I-have-enough-of-my-own-business cards; I'm going to...

Yep, that's exactly what he's doing. As soon as he extends that arm out, offering me that card, I slam the door; without breaking my stare, talking, or blinking. Now, let him go back to his office and write that in his report, stinking-old-cockroach.

Once the door is closed and I'm far enough away; I burst into laughter. I laugh so hard I cry while crossing my legs so as not to pee on myself. Boy, do I wish my mother could have seen that. No sooner than I make my way to the kitchen to check on Ms. Elaine and dinner, the phone rings. Funny thing is it's the house phone. No one uses that phone; I wonder why we even have it.

Ms. Elaine reaches for the still ringing phone. "Good evening, Harpers residence, how may I help you?"

Almost instantly, she frowns and her free hand rests on her hip. I hear her speaking in her strong native accent, "Excuse me, I think you got the wrong number; have a good evening."

It rings again. As if she's expecting it, she stands in the same spot. Snatching the phone from its cradle; without the proper greeting, she just begins to talk.

"Look, I already told you to stop this nonsense; what do you want? I thought we came to an understanding yesterday. Don't call here anymore; there is nothing here for you."

I watch as Ms. Elaine begins to point at the phone as if the person on the other end can see her pointing.

"You know what, I put a trace on this phone yesterday and the police will find you. And let me tell you something..."

She begins to speak in Spanish and she's talking much faster than I can keep up. I do understand all the four-letter words she's using before she slams the phone down in its cradle.

I wait for a moment until she stops cursing out the hung-up phone and seems a little calm, then I asked, "What's all that about, Ms. Elaine?"

Giving me the non-of-your-business-look, "It's nothing that you should concern yourself with, just let me handle it. It's one of my relatives getting on my last nerve."

Now, that's strange; because I know all her family and they do not get on her nerves. She has one of those families movies are made of. So, why is she lying to me? If that phone rings again, I'm answering it.

It doesn't take long before I get the chance to race for the ringing phone, but she beats me to it again.

"Hello!"

Now, she won't talk, all she does is make noise just to let the person on the other end know she is still on the line.

"Ah-huh, oh okay, uhm, yep, well alright then you have a good night, I will pass that information on."

I stare at her waiting for her to say something but instead, she avoids eye contact with me. I ask, "Who was that? Ms. Elaine? And don't tell me a relative because I know better."

Vigorously stirring a pot of mash potatoes, she looks at me, "Now, didn't I tell you not to concern yourself with my problems?"

Ms. Elaine helped raise me; I think I know her as well as she knows me. I got my hind-part spanked by her a few times. She has always been family to me, and I know she is trying to protect me.

"I don't think that was about your personal problems. Who was that on the phone? Was it that woman?"

With a look of surprise on her face and her hand resting on her hip, Ms. Elaine sucks her teeth. Most of the time you cannot hear her strong Latino accent; however, make her angry and you can hardly understand her English.

"You know about that woman? This Robin tramp?"

I shake my head, yes. Although I know about her, I had no idea she was call-ing my home. Once I confirm I know about Robin, Ms. Elaine opens up and tells me how Robin has been calling every day since Lamont came home.

The nerve of her. Better yet the real question should be: just how serious was my husband with this woman, that she feels entitled to call my home? Ms. Elaine assures me; she intercepts all of the calls and Lamont doesn't know anything about them.

Her final word on this topic before setting the table for dinner is, "I don't want you to have no trouble and I know she is trouble for this house, and I'm not having it. Whatever she wants, find out and get her out of your life. Do you understand Rietta? She is nothing but trouble."

Shaking my head, yes. I know it's only a matter of time before Uncle Douglas and his friends find her. Just to make sure they are on their job I think I'll give him a call after dinner tonight.

I try to compose myself before calling the rest of the family down to dinner. Trying to be okay when I am not is hard. All the things that have transpired from the day I found Lamont laying in the vestibule have not been easy to handle. However, I think I'm doing a fairly good job. Robin is not making this any easier on me. Not that I think she intends to do anything but make my life hard.

Ms. Elaine realizes I am upset, puts all her cooking utensils down for a moment to comfort me. While holding me she whispers, "You know you are like my own daughter, and I have been here with you your whole life. Do not worry about this thing. This woman will be gone soon. Your husband loves you and that's all that matters right now. Forget the past, it is over. She had better hope someone else finds her before I do."

She takes a moment to wipe the tears from my face. Like she did when I was a child, she holds my cheeks in the palm of her hands and kisses me on my fore-head then on each cheek. Then she continues, "Remember, you are Mrs. Lamont Harper and the mistakes in-between does not matter, now matters and Lamont Harper loves you. Don't let this thing mess with your happiness. I talked with Douglas and he is working on it. Now, you don't worry. Okay?"

While nodding my head in agreement, I realize she is always on the job. I ask her, "What did Uncle Douglas say?"

After giving me that, what did I just tell you look; she points her finger at me, "Okay, I'm going to tell you, but you are to let us handle this thing." Shaking her finger fast and hard as if she's going to shake it right off her hand, "Do you hear me? Do you understand you are not to do or say anything besides enjoy your life? Okay, my Rey-Rey?"

Wow, she hasn't called me that in years. I shake my head in agreement. Now the hard part will be to do as she has instructed me. I know she is right; all I can do is bring hard emotions into this and all that can do is hurt me more and jeopardize my newly-mended marriage. I run to the bathroom to make sure my face shows no trace of the tears and I put on the happy face and call everyone down for dinner.

We enjoy dinner - as usual. Mother is such a pleasant welcomed face when she comes over. Not only do I enjoy her company but the children love having her around. Lamont and Irene have a wonderful relationship also. As close as I am to my mother, I kept most of the problems between Lamont and I a secret. Keeping the peace between two people I love is of the utmost importance to me.

After dinner is done and we all retire to our own space; the twin's race for their I-Mee to give them a bath and read them a bed-time story. I relax with Lamont in the family room. We cuddle together on the long, extra wide sofa in front of the television to watch a movie together and sip on red wine. I enjoy these moments with my husband. Right now, it's hard to remember how uncaring Lamont was before the accident. Since he's been home, he has been the loving and devoted husband he was when we first got married. Our marriage was exceptional for the first eight years. I don't know what happened and at this point in our lives... you know what; I don't care; enough of that thinking.

There are still some things Lamont cannot remember, I guess whatever it was that was causing him to not love me is one of those lost memories and for that I am happy. The movie we are watching holds our attention long enough for the twins to finish their baths and come for their goodnight kisses. Benjamin runs in first; full of energy he flips over the back of the sofa and grabs hold of Lamont's neck.

"Daddy, I love you so much. Come on and tell me a long story so I can go to sleep."

Before Lamont can answer, Charmin jumps right into her father's lap; squeezing her hands between her brothers so she can grab Lamont's neck.

"Daddy I want a bedtime story too."

Lamont stands up with both children swinging from his neck. He wraps one arm around the front to hold Charmin and he puts his other arm behind him to hold Ben. Up the stairs, they go, but not before my dear husband smiles at me and blows me a kiss.

In his bad imitation of actor Arnold Schwarzenegger, he assures me, "I'll be back."

Mother sits by me as the three disappear up the stairs. Nudging me gently, she asks, "So, what's up? Are you still getting those mysterious packages?"

Shaking my head up and down, "Yep, I am. But guess what? Now she's calling every day; about three or four times a day."

"You still haven't mentioned it to Lamont?"

Shaking my head from side to side, "Nope, I have not. Actually, I'm not sure if I should mention it. I mean, what if he doesn't remember her, and my mentioning her brings it all back? Then on the other hand, what if he does remember and he's trying to forget all about her and put her in the past? I don't know ma, help me."

I lay my head on her shoulder and like only she can do; her words of wisdom – which are always good – pour out.

"Well, let's not worry about telling him right now. I suppose we can wait until Douglas finds out who she is. Only time will tell. Until then enjoy your husband and children without the added stress."

When my mother is around everything feels better. I enjoy her just as much if not more than I did when I was a child. She has always been my comfort. I remember when I was twelve and needed braces. Grandmother was never one for tact or considerate to one's feelings. It either is or isn't, no shades of grey. After going through all the pain of having the darn wires placed in my mouth; my wonderful sisters had a field day; every day, relentlessly teasing me. I cried and yelled, "Stop! Leave me alone!"

It seems like the more I cried and yelled, the more enjoyment they got. Finally, I'd hear my grandmother fussing as she stomped her feet coming towards us. In my heart, I hoped she would make them stop. For some reason, I felt for once perhaps she would show me some kindness and sympathy. Needless to say, that is not what happened. As grandmother got closer and closer to the door, her rambling became more and more clear. She wasn't fussing because they were teasing me; she was fussing because I was crying.

"All of that wailing and for what? What is the dilemma? Your skin is much too weak and way too dark. In this family, it is behooving to pull it in and strengthen it up."

Now instead of just having my sisters hammer my feelings, grandmother joins the group. But not for long, almost immediately my mother shows up in the doorway. I don't know where she came from; all I know is, that was the end of all the pain, instantly; both physically and emotionally. After clearing her throat to get everyone's attention, she places her hand on her hip and with the other hand, she points her finger.

"Oh really? Really? I didn't get the memo on how drastically the rules changed. How foolish of me? I was still under the notion we protect the family and stick by one another. So, correct me if I'm wrong, we are now teasing and hurting those we call family?"

Even grandmother grew quiet. This may have been the first time I saw my mother stand up to my grandmother; but it certainly is not the last. Later that night I heard them talking. Mother was very clear when she told her no longer would she allow me to be treated like I was beneath them. The conversation between them went on for an awfully long time; I stopped snooping and went to bed; however, I heard enough to know there was a new deputy in town. Not sheriff, grandmother still reigns, she just became less difficult to live with.

It wasn't too long into my thoughts before Lamont returns with a sexy smile and a look of total satisfaction on his face, popping his collar. Ah, I think; to my-self; my here and now is so much better than my past.

Lamont continues his bragging rights on his fatherhood, "Being the fantastic dad that I am, both of my pride and joys are sleeping."

Licking his lips as if he sees something good to eat, "Two down, one to go."

Mother quickly jumps up from next to me and extends her hand for Lamont to sit right next to me.

"Well, I'm going to get out of you two love-birds way and go home."

Mother has a room here; I don't know why she leaves all the time. I guess that's the pleasure of having more than one place to call home. We walk her to the door to say our goodnights. Although I'm feeling a high rise in my sexual passion; which may call for as much privacy as possible; I still extend the invitation,

"Mother you know you don't have to leave. The children will be looking for you in the morning. You sure you don't want to stay?"

With a smile on her face, "You know I do have a life outside of you and this family."

Lamont covers his mouth, "Ooooo really; wow, yah don't say." Doing an awfully bad impression of W.C. Fields, he puts his fingers to his mouth, pretending to play with an invisible cigar, "Well then my little chickadee, do tell us about this other life you have."

Grinning she leans in for a good night kiss from us both. "Love you both, have a good night. I have plans."

Lamont holds her by the waist, "There you go again, acting like you have a life outside of us. Go ahead enjoy yourself and don't stay out too late young lady."

Waving her hand and laughing, she leaves out the door. Lamont turns his attention to me. In one swoop he picks me up in his arms and carries me to the family room. Kissing me gently yet passionately, he lays me on one of the giant pillows on the floor. There are four giant pillows each big enough for an adult's entire body, lying in front of the huge fireplace.

As I lay there, Lamont runs to turn on soft music, turns off the lights and lights cinnamon-scented candles. On his way back to my waiting arms, he stops at the bar to get a bottle of rum and a bottle of coke. I intend to run and get some grapes, strawberries, and ice but I don't have to. By the time I get the thought in my head, Lamont is coming back with all three in his hands. With the biggest smile on his face, he leans down towards me for a gentle kiss on the lips.

After all these years, my body still craves him just as I did when I was a teenager. Right now, I'm nervously but anxiously anticipating his touch. I gaze into his eyes and fall in love with him all over again…again. I know one of the purposes I was birthed, is to be this man's partner for life.

"I love you, Lamont."

"And I love you, Baby. I love you with all my heart and I know I will always love you."

He gently takes me in his arms and kisses me with a passion that sets my loins on fire. I will surrender to him, all of me, unconditionally, without any exceptions. I moan, encouraging him not to stop kissing and caressing me. I collapse my body in his arms as his kisses move from my lips to my neck, to my breast. He gently rests my back on the pillows as he begins to remove my clothes. Once I am completely naked, he kisses every inch of me; turning me over to kiss my back, from neck to toe.

I close my eyes and forget there are other people in this world. Now that he has satisfied his desire to excite me, he turns me on my back. The look on his face is so warm and loving. Yet I can see the beast behind the hunger, and I want to feed him, I long to satisfy him completely. Sitting up, I reach up to undo his shirt, kissing every part of his body I can reach. I gently push him to lie down as I unbutton his pants. He is such a good-looking man.

Standing six feet-one inches, his frame is firm, stomach flat; Lamont's shoulders are broad, and he stands and walks with a strong assuring posture. His sandy brown hair is always neatly cut, and his face clean shaven. Oh, and my husband has excessively big hands and feet; that is not reserved for the darker brothers only. And his smell, oh my husband smells like fresh air. Okay, I know you may not understand that but to me, it's a fresh clean smell with a hint of musk, which is such a turn-on.

With my eyes closed, I kiss the inside of each thigh. Taking my time, I kiss and gently lick his hanging sack. I tease him, blowing on the tip of his manhood, which is already hard and throbbing. As I open my mouth, he stops me. With his finger up he moves it from side to side in a no motion; then says, "Uh-uh not yet, we have all night and we are going to use every minute of it."

He reaches over to the table where he placed the fruit and drinks. He fixes two drinks and places a strawberry in each glass. He puts a grape in his mouth then picks up the glasses and hands me one. Before I could take a sip, he leans in with a kiss while giving me half the grape in his mouth.

We drink and touch each other everywhere. Words can't be understood above the moans and groans of pleasure. But we don't complete the satisfaction;

we continue to take one another to a place of total surrender. Saying and doing everything that comes to our minds without prohibitions.

Finally, Lamont stands up and reaches for my hand. Pulling me to my feet he holds me as close to him as possible. We embrace and dance to Faith Evans', "Kissing You"; from The Waiting to Exhale soundtrack.

I can't breathe normally. I can't swallow either. I feel like a virgin ready to give up her jewels. The pulsating between my legs ache; it aches with the anticipation of pleasure.

Lamont whispers in my ear, "I have a surprise for you. Are you ready to follow me?"

I nod, yes.

He takes me by the hand and leads me up the stairs. On the first landing he tenderly eases me down on the last step, as he kneels between my legs, he gently pushes my back to rest on the mid-landing. He explores my private part with his wondering fingers; oh goodness, yes, he's in the right spot. Just before I can explode, he stops and guides me to the second landing.

Once we are on the second landing he stops and sits me down on the top step pulling me to the end of the step he kneels between my opened legs. With one hand he holds my back and with the other, he guides his swollen penis into me. He never moves his gaze from my eyes. As he slowly pushes every inch of his manhood into me, I close my eyes and raise my hips to meet him. I am ready to give him my pulsating vagina. Just as I try to grind my hips; he stops me. He removes himself from me and stands. Still grinning, he reaches for my hand and pulls me to my feet.

We continue to the bedroom. I am so excited; I can hardly contain myself. As we enter the bedroom Lamont leads me to the bed, without a word, he seats me on the edge and then drops to his knees. He uses one hand to open my legs and the other he places on my chest, pushing me back on the bed. My chest visibly moves up and down from the deep breaths I take in. I can feel his warm breath as he moves closer to his expectant goal.

Oh, I feel as if I'm going to explode from the anticipation alone. Kissing my inner thigh for a moment he wastes no time opening his mouth and kissing me down there as if he's kissing my lips. I moan and rotate my hip to his rhythm.

With my back arched, I moan louder, this is it. Oh, my goodness, I can't hold it, I don't want to hold it. With tears of total ecstasy streaming down the sides of my face, I grab his head proclaiming him as my big daddy, who just found the golden ring. I explode. I explode with total satisfaction.

Lamont's smile is that of a conqueror. He stands to his feet, "The night has only just begun my lady. *This* will be the night you will never forget; *this* I promise you."

He leaves the room and goes into our bathroom. I hear him turn on the water to the Jacuzzi. As he reappears into the doorway, I brace myself on my elbows; smiling; I ask, "So, is that the bath I hear?"

He answers, "Why, yes, it is." There he is with that W.C. Fields impression again. "My little chick-a-dee, you know how much I love the bubbles."

He rushes to the bed and bends over to place a hasty kiss on my lips once again. Like an overly excited little child trying to keep a secret, he runs towards the bedroom door and disappears. I patiently wait and before I can wonder where he's gone, he reappears holding the bowl of fruit and the rum and coke we left downstairs. Ah, my super sexy husband has added whip cream to his menu, and I know this is going to be a long night. One that I will enjoy and just as my big daddy says, I will never forget.

As for Robin, she is forgotten tonight, and no doubt will be tomorrow morning as well.

CHAPTER NINE

Unchained Skelton

*L*amont has been back in his office for a couple of months now and it appears all is well. Each night when he comes home, he takes the time to tell me all about his day. He implements a new system in our lives. At the end of the month, he sits me down and opens his briefcase and shows me everything he has done, including the financial books for the month. This is a complete difference from how things used to be. I now feel as if we are truly one family, joined in every way. He has made me a part of who he is, and I am loving it.

The husband that went into the hospital was cold and totally evasive towards me. That husband didn't hold me or make me feel wanted less more needed. That husband said cruel things to purposely hurt my feelings. That husband was no doubt a cheater and a liar. That husband kept secrets about his business and finances. The husband that left the hospital is warm, gentle, and loving. The husband that left the hospital is passionate and connected to me in the way he was when we first were married. This husband is not mean and says the most charming and complementary words to me. This husband is determined to keep his family intact. This husband I know is deeply in love with me.

There have been no phone calls, no packages, nothing from the Robin person. I understand her obsession; I really do. She apparently feels she and Lamont have some sort of future together; or had. I'm upset with her because she crosses the line, penetrating the *home boundaries*. Even after unanswered calls, no responses to her little gifts, no, oh-I-haven't-spoken-to-you-in-awhile-and-I-need-to-hear-your-voice-calls from my husband; she still easily can become a repeat offender.

Funny thing is, I haven't spoken to Uncle Douglas concerning her. Maybe I'll call him just to see if he knows anything about her. I don't want to wake any sleeping dogs, but I don't want any jumping out the bushes to surprise me either.

After I kiss my husband at the door before he leaves for his office; I head for the phone. Just as I pick it up from the table it's ringing.

Oh, it's my dear mother. I answered, "Well good morning, my favorite dear mother."

In a pleasant voice I am so accustomed to hearing, she replies, "Good morning my wonderful, dear, darling daughter,"

I clear my throat and wait before I say another word. She knows what I'm waiting for. I hear her snickering on the other end. Finally, she laughs, "Oh, excuse me, good morning my wonderful, dear, darling, favorite-who-can-never-repeat-that-to-anyone, daughter. Now is that better?"

I match her laughter and reply, "Uh yes, that's much better. And don't worry I know you love all three of your children very much. I just pull at you more aggressively, demanding more of your attention."

She answers, "Well as long as you know how much you mean to me that is all that counts. What are you doing today?"

I peep over to my calendar and hit myself in the head as if I forgot something. Overly enthusiastic and without thinking about the fact, this is my personal secret; I blurt out, "Oh ma; I forgot; I have an appointment to see a building for the new community center."

With surprise in her tone, she quizzes me, "New community center? What and when? I mean you didn't tell me about this."

I honestly was trying to keep it quiet until I was sure this over-privileged gal can pull it off. I want to get this project off the ground all by myself. Everything has been given to me although I went to school and graduated top of my class. My accomplishments are a marriage, two beautiful children and a great last name. Although these things are socially important; personal accomplishments that give back are spiritually and morally important and beyond what money or a prestigious last name can buy. I want to do something that counts outside the confinements of my privileged-private world.

Since Mother is on the phone and I mentioned it, I may as well tell her.

"You know one of the things I have always wanted to do is counsel youth and build a center that can facilitate programs that can help constructively guide youth. Helping them to channel their energy and focus on their future and how to make it work for them is one of the main goals."

Mother is not saying a word. I call out to her, "Ma? Mother> Are you still there?"

After a few more moments, she responds. Her voice sounding a little shaken, "Yes. I am here baby."

"What's the matter, Irene? Did I say something you don't approve of, what is it? Do you think I can't or shouldn't do this?"

She finally jumps into the conversation I thought I was having alone and babbles on without stopping to take a breath.

"Oh, no child; are you kidding? I'm just speechlessly proud of you. Your father will be also since he has the same passion. Part of his going to law school was to learn of ways to help the youth, especially troubled youth. He uses his position to do just that and I am so surprised and ecstatic to hear you following in his footsteps without knowing."

I gasp and look at the phone. Did she just speak of my father and did she just do it in present tense? I know what I heard, and she is going to have to give me some answers. In a very professional and overly sophisticated tone, "I never knew that mother. Please tell me more about him. You never speak of him to me. It's fascinating to me, hearing I think like my father. Please do tell me more, dear mother."

She pauses for a moment, "Oh, I-I, got a little excited and carried away; for a moment you sound so much like Ben. It took me by surprise. Come on, tell me all about what you're doing."

I knew it! I knew she would change the subject. That's fine, I'll get her to go with me and then she will have to talk.

"What are you doing today; why don't you come with me so I can tell you all about it. I think it will be good to share it with you. Perhaps you can help me get all the kinks out."

Instantly, she accepts the invitation. "I'd love to go. I'll be there in about an hour." She quickly ends the conversation on this note, "Love you, see you shortly."

She hangs up the phone before I can return the sentiment. I know what I heard her say. I was listening noticeably clear. She mentions my dad as if they talk now, not in the past tense. That's okay mother-dear; we will have a nice long visit today. I head upstairs to get myself ready.

Lamont doesn't know I started my own non-profit corporation. I know I have no idea about inner-city youth, but I do know about pain and disappointment. That does not come on just one side of the track, or one shade of skin color. I know I am extremely fortunate and more blessed than I can say, and I make no apologies for that. However, I do feel because I am blessed and because I can do more, I should. Besides, I cringe at the fact many youths don't have an Irene to rescue and protect them. Before Lamont's incident, I started this project and never included him in any plans. I think now that we have a better relationship, I can share them with him. I will know the best time soon.

It does not take mother the full hour to arrive; I hear her coming through the front door as I'm coming down the stairs. With her arms extended, "There she is, my wonderfully intelligent daughter."

We embrace and head to the kitchen. I haven't eaten anything yet, so I offer her some breakfast, "Would you like a chicken biscuit? Ms. Elaine makes them from scratch."

As she's picking up one, she replies, "Are you kidding, yes I want one of her famous chicken biscuits; I love these things. Where's the coffee?"

Pointing in the direction of the coffee pot, I realize she's only making nervous small talk. Because there is nothing in this house, she doesn't know where to find. Knowing Irene, she's going over that conversation we had on the phone a thousand times. Somehow, I need to help her relax.

We know each other well enough to know we will have that conversation about my father before this day is over; however, it can and will wait. I love and trust my mother and I want her to be comfortable, not on pins and needles. I do not point out her obvious nervousness; instead, I change the mood of things by abruptly throwing the one question that will change her train of thought.

"Hey ma, what do you think about me having another baby?"

Almost choking on her coffee; she looks up at me with a look of surprise. Placing her cup on the counter she walks close to me and places both her hands on my stomach. "Wow, are you expecting?"

Before I can answer she's dancing around in circles and yelling at the top of her voice, "Oh, my goodness, oh my goodness! Oh wow! WOW! Yes! How far are you? Yes! Yes!"

Ms. Elaine comes running from the back of the house, yelling, "What is going on in here? What is happening? Are you okay? What's wrong?"

I was only trying to break mother's uncomfortable moment. Now she's dancing around in a circle and since Ms. Elaine now sees nothing is wrong; but it's an obviously happy moment, without knowing why, she joins Irene dancing in a circle. It is priceless.

With a tee shirt in her hand, (I'm sure she was folding up the laundry), Ms. Elaine is waving it above her head as if she's listening to rapper Petey Pablo. Irene grabs her free hand and swings them both around in circles as if square dancing. An incredible sight to see; it's a shame I'm going to have to burst their bubbles and totally ruin their choreographies but not before I video this moment on my phone.

Finally, Ms. Elaine, still dancing, asks, "What's going on, why you so happy Irene? What is it we are celebrating?"

Mother answers without breaking their dance routine. "A new baby in the family, your little Rey-Rey is expecting."

Oh, no she didn't! Now both have upped the excitement level to plum scary. And crazy is here too. They are whooping and hollering and swinging each other around like mad women. It's time to end this display of; whatever it is. I have more than enough on the video to blackmail them both. Slowly I move closer to the duo and join in the dancing and do a few twists and kicks with them. I begin to sing in a childish tone, "Ha-ha-ha-ha-ha, I'm not pregnant, ha-ha-ha-ha-ha, there is no baby."

Repeating the line a couple of times I decide to keep singing and dancing with them until one of them actually hears me. I wish I had someone else here so we can bet on who will hear me first. My bet is on Ms. Elaine.

We go on and on for a few more verses of my song, "La-la-la-la-la-la, yawl not listening, I'm not pregnant, fa-la-la-la-la-la, yeah…"

Each time I get to the "yeah", I twist my hips harder and throw my hand up in a fist. Finally, Ms. Elaine tries to join in with the singing. It takes two or three fa-la-las before she abruptly stops dancing and puts one hand on her hip, while still holding the tee shirt in the other.

She looks at me then at Mother. With her eyes squinted and her finger almost on my nose, she slowly turns to Irene; (which is where I think she should point). "Uno momento young lady."

Mother, still not knowing why the celebration has come to a screeching halt stops dancing; while regaining her breath, she reaches for me to come closer to her. I move closer and she taps me on the stomach. I smile and look over at Ms. Elaine; who's now twisting up her lips, with that hand on her hip. Ms. Elaine puts her finger to mom's forehead and tilts her head upward. It's all I can do not to laugh because I know she is trying to think of a way to say what needs to be said. And I am just waiting for it to happen.

We both look at my happy mother as she continues to baby talk to my stomach and rub it as if she is a first time-grandmother. "Yeah, grandmother's li'l-bundle of joy, I can't wait to meet you. Yeah, my boogie-woogie-woo, I-Mee loves her baby-boo."

Okay, it's almost sickening but funny as hell. Finally, Ms. Elaine can't take any more, "I-yi-yi, you not having another grandbaby? That's it, it's over."

Coming closer to Irene with that finger pointing right in her face, Ms. Elaine squints that eye and says, "You know when you were a little girl, you never listened. No, no, no, once you had something in that head, you hear nothing else. Everything goes right out the window and all you know is what you want to know. I-yi-yi, what am I gonna do with you? What is Rey-Rey gonna do? Huh, I know, just continue to love you. That's all we can do, so I love you, but you are so hard-headed. "

I'm cracking up. Irene's face is filled with confusion. Her eyes are going from Ms. Elaine to me and we both are laughing hysterically.

As if someone hit her in the top of her head, she puts both hands on her hips, stomps her foot and yells, "There's no baby? You're not pregnant?"

Slapping both her hands together, and stomping her foot Ms. Elaine yells, "Bingo, you got it. Now stop so much fuss and get on with your day."

Irene looks at me snarling like I did something wrong. With a very tiny grin on her face, she says, "Is that supposed to be funny? You told me you were pregnant."

Shaking my head, no, "Oh no I didn't."

"Yes, you did, I heard you!"

"Uh-uh, that is not what I said." I can't help but laugh, "You heard Ms. Elaine."

Mother glares at both of us before giving both of us her back and sashaying away, "That's alright; I know what you said."

Ms. Elaine, still holding that tee-shirt, swings it around her head on last time and walks away while giving mother one last piece of her mind, "You can't help it; I know. You hear a little something and run with it. You've been like that ya whole life; I don't expect to see any changes now. Well, at least I got in a workout today. When you come back you can rub my legs down; they gonna be hurting later from all that dancing around like a knucklehead."

All three of us laugh. I hug my crazy mother and we head out for our day of business. Of course, I replay the video for her once we get in the car. She is cracking up with laughter. Each time I think about this, I will laugh, and laugh hard. Well, at least it did the job and relieved mother of her nervous energy. We ride without mentioning my dad. We cannot talk about anything but the project and the video.

The realtor has four properties for us to look at. Since I've been working with her, I made it perfectly clear how large the land and space needs to be since it will be a multi-functional facility. Therefore, I have my fingers crossed; hoping she has met my requirements.

Diane is right on time. She is pulling up to the first property just as we are. Wow! This place is breathtaking. There is plenty of outside space, and the building is absolutely beautiful on the outside. It looks big enough for what I have I mind. We all exit our vehicles at the same time. As Mother and I follow Diane to the entrance; Irene begins to ask questions.

"When did you put all this together? You didn't tell me about these plans."

Hunching my shoulders, I answer, "Before Lamont's stay in the hospital, I realized I am totally reaping the benefits of who I married and who my mother is. My worth is based upon the people I'm surrounded by not upon my own abilities. If it weren't for that I would be just like far too many young ladies, lost and trying to find my way. I need to do something to give back into my own existence besides raising my own beautiful children and spending the fortune I was *given*."

I look over at my mother who has a smile on her face and a tear running down her face. She shakes her head up and down and wipes her face. Clearing her throat, she says, "I cannot tell you how incredibly proud I am of you. Finding yourself is one of the most important things you will ever do in this lifetime. I am so happy you have arrived at this point; there are so many privileged people that never do."

Taking a second to reflect on the moment; there is silence. Then mother asks me the second most important part of my decision. "So how do you propose to implement your vision?"

Putting on my sophisticated-business tone, I answer quickly, as if I was waiting for that very question. "I am highly creative, and I want to use that to create a facility that will provide structure. Not just giving information but have programs that will assist in direction and providing the necessities that can lead to success. With a complete theater, studio, a total performing arts center, with after school programs, career preparation classes, family counseling and free-talk sessions, I think we can make a good start. There will be summer programs as well."

I pause just for a moment; allowing that portion to sink into her mind; then I continue.

"I have tons of money, so getting started is not an issue; however, I've had meetings with the juvenile court system and a couple of school superintendents. This program will be used for youth who commit non-violent crimes as an alternative to detention centers and boot-camps. The school system has agreed to use us as an alternative to kicking some of their students out of school.

We will put together a structured plan, requiring the assigned youth have a schedule and mandated hours to complete the program they are assigned to. Now our program is not limited to troubled youths, this youth program is open to the entire community."

Mother takes a few moments, and then she shakes her head from one side to the other. She's looking somewhat puzzled; I hope she can understand and feel what I am trying to do. I don't need her approval, but I would sure love to have it.

Finally, I see a smile taking the place of her puzzled look. Reaching her arms out to me I move right into her embrace. As our cheeks touch, I can feel the tears running down her face. She whispers, "I cannot tell you how immensely proud of you I am. You are just like your father and he will be so proud of you. This is just the kind of facility he wants to establish. I'm sure he would…" Abruptly stopping and changing the direction of her conversation, "Do you have help, does Lamont know? I mean how are you going to implement all this alone?"

I move back just enough to see her face; she looks away from me. I know I am not stupid. Mother is talking about my father as if he's a present figure in our lives. She is not getting away from the questions this time.

There is no way I can confront her while the realtor embracing this moment with us; but you can bet your bottom dollar I will confront her as soon as I get rid of Diane. Therefore, I answer her questions, "Gwen has her degree in child psychology and social development. She's one part of my partnership investment plan. Lynnette is a Professor of Sociology and she conducts a self-awareness mentoring class at Kentucky State. She also wants to become a partner. And as you know I have my family law degree."

Mother nods in approval as we continue to walk the property. After we finish our tour, I turn my attention to Diane. "This place is perfect; the location and the size are exactly what we talked about. You definitely understood my wishes and I am pleased to tell you this is the one."

A look of satisfaction covers her face, "I am so happy you are pleased, Mrs. Harper! However, I do have a couple of other places I lined up for you to see. Are you sure you don't want to take a look at them?"

I span the building, turning slowly to take it all in and respond, "No, I don't want to see anything else. I knew I would know the place the moment I laid my eyes on it and this is it. I don't want to see anything else. All I need is the paperwork so my attorney can go over it and we can set up closing date."

Diane pulls me into her arms. It's not hard to see how happy she is; the commission on this place is retirement worthy. "Mrs. Harper, it's been a pleasure working with you and I will have those papers on your attorney's desk by the end of the day. Fumbling through the big manilla folder tucked under her arm, she pulls out a business card. "I have his number right here." Taking time to read the card, "That's Mr. Craig Wycemen; I will have a courier take the papers to 706 Multurn Avenue, second floor, suite C-1. I'll give him a call so he will be expecting them."

Sounding my approval, we shake hands before mother and I leave the building. Once out the door, I just peer at my wonderful mother; she totally ignores my stare. But that's okay, it won't be long mother dear, it won't be long.

We do a little shopping then drive a little way from my new business site and turn into a parking garage of a nice restaurant for lunch. Once we are seated in a comfortable corner booth; I order a nice soft Merlot to go with our charbroiled salmon lunch. Now that I have her nice and relaxed, it's time to dig in with the questions.

"Alright Irene, out with it."

Patting her lips with her cloth napkin, she gives me that look of surprise. Turning her head around as if she's looking for the person I'm talking to; she finally looks back at me and pats her chest while clearing her throat, "Huh, are you talking to me? Out with what, Sweetie?"

Unh, unh. I'm not playing this game with Ms. Prissy. She knows what I'm talking about. I should use a better approach, "Mother, please, let's not play coy. I need to know about all those comments you were making about my father."

She picks up her glass of wine and gulps it. Then lifts her hand, wine glass in it, for the server to refill it. I don't say a word. I just give her the mother stare.

After the server fills her glass, she has the nerve to tell her to leave the bottle. I am still quiet. We both know I'm good at this. Remember stinky-stale-rank-detective-whacha-ma-call-him? I just stare. Mother takes a couple of looks at me and continues to chug-a-lug her wine. Tilting my head to the side, I lift my glass and sip slowly. Oh, I can see she's getting uncomfortable and that's good. I'll just keep staring and sipping my wine, waiting for our meals to come. Besides, I'm driving. I'm only having one drink and we will leave when I'm good and ready. Hope she doesn't have any other plans; I possess the keys and an undefeated stare.

Finally, after Irene's third glass of wine, our meal comes. We will not be having a nice lunch conversation over this wonderful meal. Nope, not us! I will not lower my stare. As the server places the meals before us, I never take my eyes off my sweet, dear mother.

Lifting my hands and placing them in a praying position, I pray; yep, with eyes wide open staring at her.

"Dear great and awesome Father in heaven, I want to thank you for everything you have so graciously done for me, *all* my life. I thank you for my family and my wonderful mother, who is my best friend. Thank you for Mother Dear, and how remarkably close you have allowed us to be. So close we sometimes know each other's thoughts.

Now God, I know you're not going to allow her to play the Lucile Ball roll on me with the *I-dun-know* crap. So please, you know she's keeping something from me concerning my father that I deserve to know and I'm begging you to deal with this woman. I trust you will, like you always do, work it out and let her be honest with me. Make her spit it out, all of it! Oh, and of course I thank you for this wonderful meal you have allowed us to be able to afford. Amen. Amen."

I pick up my fork without removing my stare and begin to eat my salmon and continue sipping my wine. Placing one hand on her forehead as if she has a headache and the other one on the table, she takes a deep breath and exhales hard. With the hand on the table, she begins to tap. Still staring without saying a word, I decide to change my approach and look out the window while I eat my meal - quietly - and it's good.

After a few moments, she finally speaks, "You know Rae, you are truly my daughter and I know that tactic you're using and I'm sure God appreciates your gratitude. I must say it was quite amusing, to say the least."

I'm still looking out the window and sipping on that same glass of wine. Hhm, guess I'll slurp it just for the heck of it, she hates when I do that. I want to laugh, but I refuse to. She will give in and give me the truths I need.

Mother picks up her glass and finishes the last drop in her forth glass; then continues her single conversation. "You know why I hate getting so excited? Without thinking, I talk way too much. You know how that is, right Rea? Okay, you win! There is something I need to tell you, but this is not the way I had it planned. I feel forced into this before I have everything in place."

Without turning my face away from the window, with raised eyebrows; I quietly wait for the rest of the confession.

Seemingly a little agitated mother shifts in her seat and continues, totally uninterrupted by me. "Can we talk about this later or at home?" I slowly roll my eyes back to the window and chew another full fork of my rice pilaf. "Okay Rae, enough of this. Come on, I'm going to tell you everything. Now you know I won't lie to you; I may keep some things from you, but I won't lie to you. Do we have to talk here? Can we go someplace private and talk?"

Turning my head in her direction, trying ridiculously hard not to smirk, I show my expression of victory. Slowly I take the last sip left in my glass and answer her. "Where do you have in mind mother?"

Sucking her teeth, she responds, "A little cabin is the only place where we can be alone and uninterrupted."

"A cabin mother, wow, this must be huge. Okay, let's enjoy the rest of our lunch and go to the little cabin; sounds good to me. I'm game."

Mother slowly picks up her fork and attempts to eat her meal, but she can't. I know I pushed her to commit to having this conversation with me, and I'm trying hard not to feel bad about being such a brat; but hey, whatever works.

Mother pays for the lunch and we head for the car. Once we both click our seatbelts, mother speaks, "You know I love you and the conversation we are going to have will change your life. I pray for the better and I also hope you understand." Fumbling in her bag she pulls out her cell phone, "I need to make a phone call; we may as well get this all over with."

As I sit in silence, I can feel a chill come over my body as if something big is getting ready to happen. The feeling is good and bad at the same time. You know, like sour and sweet candy; it's good but surprisingly very sour before the sweet comes in to completely make it worthwhile. Taking deep breaths, I try to calm myself; however, my body is responding to something I cannot explain, my hands are shaking and I'm sweating. All I can do now is wait to see what's happening next.

Mother speed dials someone. I hear a man's voice on the other end. Did I just hear him say "Hello Sweetheart?"

Mother answers, "Hi, we have a situation. Rae and I are headed for our special getaway. Can you meet us there in about 30 minutes?"

Their special getaway? What the heck is going on? But I won't say a word. I will not open my mouth, not yet. All I can do is wait and I will wait. The voice on the other end agrees without any questions. Turning her attention to me she tells me where to head. We continue to our destination without saying another word. I refuse to allow my mind to even think, so I turn up the volume to Mary J Blige's CD and I rock to one of my favorites by her, "Take Me as I Am."

Irene reaches into her purse and pulls out her emergency pack of calm-me-down-and-help-me-to-think-cigarettes. She keeps a pack on hand for those occasions her nerves are frayed. The only time she smokes is when she's *very* uptight, which is not often. She keeps a pack until they are stale; then she throws them away and buys another pack. I feel somewhat responsible for her agitated nerves this time. I may have been a little too harsh, somewhat demanding, probably a little spoiled and bratty. Okay, I was down-right way too dramatic; oh, alright I should be ashamed of the way I acted. I pull over to a parking spot before we reach our destination, turning to my mother.

"Ma, I'm so sorry for acting so ugly. You do not deserve that kind of treatment from anyone. Please forgive me. Whatever it is you have kept from me I know it had to be out of love. I could have and should have waited for you to pick the time to tell me whatever it is. I'm so sorry, please forgive me, please."

She meets me in the middle of the seats, and we embrace. I can feel the tears running down her face. I feel her body shaking. I cry with her. I can feel her emotion although I have no idea why we are shedding tears. These tears are of something other than happiness or sadness.

We hold our embrace for a few minutes without saying a word. She releases her hold and I do the same. She holds my face with her two hands, looking into my eyes, her voice trembling, "I love you very much, and I have tried to protect you from all the boogie-men that appeared in all your nightmares. I did all I could to save you from all the real-life monsters that lived right up under our noses. Making you feel and know you are special is so important. The secrets we have kept were for your own good. Why so long? Ah, I am not so sure if that was the best decision. It just seems as if time flies, without digesting how much time is actually going by. Well, I cannot make any excuses; however, what's done is done."

Looking into the face of my best friend, my strength, my mother, I realize how fortunate I am and have always been. My heart is so conflicted. I don't know if I should be happy or sad, but I'm feeling both at the same time. This anxious nervousness is exciting and painful all at once.

I lean in and kiss my mother on her lips and try to give her an unbreakable assurance, "Ma, I love you more than I can say. You have been an exemplary mother and friend. There is no one on this earth I owe so much to. There is nothing you can tell me that can or will change that. I could never have gotten a better pick of a mother if I had to pick for myself. I'm sure God is pleased."

We hold each other tight. Mother takes a deep breath and tells me to go ahead on to our destination. Another long thirty minutes and we are in Jamestown; about seventy-five miles from where we started this morning. I can see why she uses the term, *getaway*. It's beautiful. I've never been out here before. Pulling into a parking space in front of the resort office. we get out of the car and walk towards the entrance. Mother looks around as if looking for someone. Once inside the lobby she is greeted by a young lady, who practically runs to hug her.

"Hello Ms. Irene. How are you? So good to see you again. Your place is ready. Will your husband be joining you?"

Without any noticeable concern for what I am hearing, mother answers the young woman. "Hi Andrea; it's good to see you as well. And yes, he should be here shortly. I actually thought he would beat me to here."

With a little chuckle, she responds, "Knowing that husband of yours he probably went to buy you some flowers or something. He is such a romantic. I don't think I ever saw him come in without something special for you. You are truly blessed."

I cannot believe what I'm hearing; this is not real. Irene is essentially carrying on a conversation about a husband I had no idea she had. Her tone is smooth without a trace of nervousness now. Without being given a key, mother thanks the woman and walks out the door and back to the car. I follow, with more questions than I had hours ago. Now I feel sweat running down my back and I'm feeling lightheaded.

This time mother walks to the driver's side and gets behind the wheel, "I can take us the rest of the way."

I lean against the car trying to catch my breath, but I cannot shake this feeling. My knees are trying to buckle from under me. Irene must have found the strength she needed because she is no longer nervous. Feeling the need to bend over; I do so while holding my stomach. Tears stream down my face. The thoughts running through my mind are going so fast, I can't focus on one thought at a time. I'm dizzy. I want to pass out. I'm trying desperately to hold it together. How can I? I heard the woman mention a husband. All this time I thought she was lonely - all alone. I slowly get in the car and sit down.

Mother starts driving down a small road towards the lake. Just as I begin to unravel, the car stops in front of a beautiful cabin. As I get out the car my legs feel weak, so I lean up against the car trying to hold myself up. I feel the gentle touch of my mother as she takes me by the waist and leads me to the door of the cabin. Removing a key from her purse; she steps to the side for me to enter first.

All the decorations are exactly what mother would have in her own place. There are pictures of the entire family. I begin to take my time to look at the pictures: my children and husband, sisters, and grandmother, Uncle Douglas, Ms. Rochelle, and Ms. Elaine. I gasp at the huge picture over the mantle, it is of my mother and father on their wedding day. She's stunning and he's so handsome. They seem so happy. As I continue to look at all the pictures on the mantle, I see more pictures of my dad; they're older pictures. He and my mother are together in many of them.

As I approach a picture frame with a picture of them hugging, I notice the outfit she has on. When we went on our last shopping spree I picked it out for her. Just as I turn to ask the biggest question, I hear the door open and shut. The footsteps are coming closer. I hear them stop short of turning the corner into the living space where I'm viewing the photos.

Mother goes to greet the person coming in. Trying to listen, I barely hear the gentleman ask, "What and how much did you tell her?"

Mother answers, "Nothing! Nothing at all. I figure we should do everything else together. Are you okay?"

He answers in a very gentle and loving tone, "I'm very good sweetheart and don't worry/ Let's go in there and have this long-overdue conversation."

There is a pause and then I hear the sound of a kiss. I want to run. I want to run to anywhere but here. I cannot explain this crazy feeling of fear and excitement all at once. My insides are flooding with happiness for my mother, while I feel as if I am about to jump off a cliff.

The footsteps begin again. I see mother with her hand extended behind her holding a hand. I see his foot first then his hand holding mother's. For some reason, I save his face for last. His stomach is flat, arms muscular; on his wrist is a gold chain matching the one around his neck, visible under the causal Armani outfit he has on, with matching alligator shoes.

His scent, oh his scent, is amazing; the smell of his cologne reaches my nostrils with each step he takes. He is a smooth dark-skinned, six-foot-two handsome man, with a perfectly trimmed hairline. His close hair cut doesn't hide the detailed waves that seem to glide into the fade he's sporting, along with side-burns that are trimmed neat joining his beard and thin mustache together, which is brushed with hints of gray. Showing beautiful pearly white teeth; this perfect specimen of a man reaches for me, "There you are, my baby princess, Rae-muffin."

No one, I mean absolutely no one calls me that but one person, one person only. As his arms wrap around me, my knees no longer can do the job of holding my legs straight. They buckle and I fall into the waiting arms of my daddy, my father, the first man I loved, and I lose consciousness.

CHAPTER TEN

Dropping the Bomb

As my eyes slowly open, I hear voices. One sounds like my husband, Lamont, the other Irene. Then I realize I have not been dreaming, because I hear the same distinctive voice I heard right before I passed-out. Sitting up on my elbows, I swallow hard and take a deep breath, then blow it out with force. I want to call out to Lamont, but I realize calling out to him will bring all three of them and I need just a few more minutes. The thoughts flooding my mind are too much. I'm trying to answer my own questions without having any of the information I need to make an intelligent conclusion.

What-the-fuck! That's my father in there! My father! What in the world can they possibly tell me to make this sensible? What? Was he in a coma for years and didn't remember anyone but mother? Or was he prisoner of war in the Army for the past twenty-five years? Hhm, let's see - he was held captive by spies from another country. Oh, I get it, he is a spy and he couldn't put his family at risk, so he stayed away.

ARRGGHH, not only do I want to scream and cuss like a freaking-drunk-en-out-of-my-mind-sailor-whose-woman-is-screwing-his-brother, but I want to fight, goddamnit! Okay, I'm going to try and calm down. It's apparent they are in there having a good time getting to know each other. The only one in here alone is me. Shit, how long have I been out? When did Lamont get here? He must have been here for a few minutes; he already sounds acquainted with my father.

I hear Lamont say, "I'm going to check on Rietta."

I quickly lie back down on the couch and close my eyes. As Lamont's steps come closer, I feel my body tensing as I try hard not to move my eyelids. I can feel his presence close to me. He kneels next to me and whispers in my ear, "Hey, I know you're awake. I can feel you. Why do you think I came in here?"

I open my eyes as tears fill them. Lamont holds me in his arms and kisses my cheeks. A hard-silent cry shakes my entire body. "Shush. All I can say is, you need to hear what they have to say. It's a lot to swallow and more to try and understand. Irene loves you with all her heart; this you know; that's why she called me. After talking to that man in there, I am positive he loves you the same way." I bury my head into Lamont's chest, and he holds me tight.

"Before this is over with, you will see how blessed you really are and how much you are loved." Pulling me away from him enough to look in my face he says, "I'm going to get you a wet towel for your face and then I'm going to let your parents know you are ready to hear what they have to say. You don't have to say anything, just listen. Okay?"

I shake my head okay. Mother knew I needed him here and I am so glad she called him. After wiping my face, I sit up and take a few deep breaths. Then I nod my head for Lamont to go and get my parents. I realize I have two parents, two. A mother and a father, wow!

My mother peeps around the corner first and moves towards me with caution, not offensively or defensively, just slow. I still can't talk. I know if I try we will spend too much time trying to get me to stop crying. My dad follows close behind her with a huge smile on his face. Lamont moves last but beats them to the couch where I am sitting and sits next to me.

With an undeniable amount of excited energy and a huge smile, Irene holds my hand and says, "Honey, I want you to meet the only man I have ever loved; your father."

There's that feeling again. The room is spinning, and I feel as if I can't focus. As I feel the warm arms of my dad wrap around me and I smell his wonderful scent, I gasp, holding on with every bit of strength I have. I hold on as if I'm afraid to let him go. I hold on tight for all the years I needed to hold him and couldn't.

When the silence is finally broken, I hear his voice, "Hello Rae-muffin, it is so good to see you." Releasing his hold on me, he looks at me from head to toe, "Wow, look at my little girl all grown up."

I still cannot speak, there are no words forming in my mind to say. Irene takes the opportunity to explain without the questions being asked.

"I have been with your father all this time. We were not sure when or how to tell you. It seems like each time we thought the time was right, something else would happen in this family that prevented us from doing so."

Did she just say, *"All this time?"* in the nick of time Lamont speaks.

"Excuse me, I-Mee, you just said you've been together all this time, just how long is that?"

My father decides he would be best to answer the question, "Irene and I have never been out of communication with each other. We are still married, and I have shared your life through her eyes. I was at your wedding and at the hospital when you gave birth to my grandbabies. Many times, you were so close I could have reached out and touched you."

With a trembling voice, I ask, "Wh-wh-why didn't you; why didn't you reach out and touch me? Why didn't you let me know you were so close?" Standing up, "I needed you so much, I thought you were dead or just didn't care. Why now? Why did you let so many years go by, why?"

Mother reaches for my hand and attempts to kiss my face, but I move away. "Now you know that I love you; more than any words can say but the decision not to tell you was mine. Many days and nights your father cried to hold you and begged for the opportunity to be a part of your life. It just seemed each time we thought the time was right, something else was happening in this family and I felt we needed to wait a little longer."

In disbelief, I listen to the only person I have never doubted, the only person I have completely trusted all my life, tell me she decided to keep my father from me. The one thing I felt was always missing, the one thing I felt would make me complete. With my mouth open, I am yet unable to form the words that will commit to my feelings. The tears won't stop flowing. I look at my mother as if she's a stranger; I feel as if she's a stranger. I look around the room for Lamont and when my eyes are fixed on him, I scream, *help me*. Then I realize I am screaming inside; no one can hear me.

I need to run and get away from all the new strangers I just met. Yet, the biggest part of me wants to stay and forgive them for such a betrayal. While trying hard to gather a clear thought, Lamont grabs me just in the nick of time. He holds me close and tight. In my ear he whispers, "I love you with all my heart but we both know I have made some bad decisions and horrible mistakes. However, it never changed the fact I love you or your love for me. This woman standing here in this room has more love for you than anyone can ever have. No one has to tell either of us this, we know it. Now, I cannot say why she chose to handle your life like this, but I will say whatever her reasons, it had to be because of that love. Give her a chance to explain. Most of all give your father a chance to know the wonderful woman I am married to and love."

I can't stop shaking nor crying. I still can't find a space to understand. Lamont just holds me tighter. Irene comes close and does the same; before I know it, my dad is part of this embrace and I no longer care why. All I want is to know this man and love him.

Oh, please do not get it twisted by thinking they are getting away with keeping such a huge secret from me. I will know why this loving, wonderful, very comforting, darn-near-perfect-mother of mine kept the other element of why I am who I am, from me. May I add, he is so darn good-looking.

We spend the next couple of hours talking. Daddy can tell me about my entire life and show me the pictures to prove he was always with me. Hearing his voice brings back memories I thought I was too young to remember. It's as if his scent, as well as the sound of his voice, has never left my memory. I can feel the familiarity between us as we take the time we need to bond. Perhaps now I can be complete.

Now that all the formalities are over, I need to know why they kept such a thing from me. I glance over at my mother who looks so incredibly happy; I'm almost afraid to spoil the moment. However, before we leave this room, I need to know. I reach for my parents' hands, "You have to explain to me what happened and why you guys didn't tell me you were together. "

Irene answers first, "After your grandmother put Ben out, we stayed separated for two years. He went back to school to finish his law degree. After that, he came to the house to see me. With his degree in hand, he knocked on the door."

Daddy holds up his hand to interrupt Mother, and he continues the story. "When I knocked on the door, it was as if your grandmother was expecting me because she answered the door herself. I held up my degree in her face and asked her if Irene was home. She chuckled and grunted, then said, *'If you imagine that piece of paper makes a difference, permit me to burst your bubble once again; it does not.'* I asked again if your mother was at home and could I at least see you, my daughter. She slammed the door in my face, before yelling I better hurry up and leave since she already called the sheriff."

With tears in his eyes, he pushed forward, "All I could think about is the last time she called the sheriff on me. Your mother didn't know this at the time, but I spent almost a month locked up. My family didn't know where I was. Every day while I was locked up, I was beaten and threatened. I was told if I made it out alive, I better not ever come back to the house."

I interrupt, "What? Beat? Who beat you?"

With tears in his eyes, his answer comes as no surprise, "Your uncle and his goons came to jail like it was a paying nine to five job. By the time I was set free, all I wanted to do was disappear. Not only did I need medical attention, but my heart and pride were torn apart. A stray dog got better treatment than I did. Most days I didn't eat and had no water. I barely survived broken ribs and a concussion. My father reached out to some powerful attorneys he knew and because he would not be scared off, they finally let me go. They almost killed me."

My mouth can't close. I cannot believe what I'm hearing. I look in my dad's eyes and I can see the pain; I can hear it in his voice. I know he is telling me the truth. My heart is broken; how can the people who say they are my family do such a thing?

He went on, "I stayed in the hospital for two weeks. As far as I knew; at the time, your mother didn't even know I came to the house."

Mother fills in from her perspective, "I found out about the incident when I overheard Douglas and his friends bragging about what they did to Ben. I went to mother and asked her about it. She tried to deny knowing anything about it at first; however, after I found Ben and he confirmed the story, I confronted her again."

I interrupt to ask, "Did she finally admit it? And did she tell you why they did such a thing to my father?" The rage I feel is immense. I can feel my heart pounding fast and hard against my chest. I want to hate everyone that was involved in treating my father like this.

Irene answers my question with answers that only infuses my anger, "Yes, she did admit to not only knowing about it but ordering it."

I hold my stomach and gasp. Lamont reaches for me at the same time my dad does, and all my strength is drained from the pain I now feel. My mother tries to finish. I guess she feels I should have all the information now.

"Mother felt that Ben wasn't good enough to be with me…"

I interrupt, and yell, "No mother, she felt he was too dark to be a member of her prestigious-precious-uppity-fake-full-of-shit-family. I want you to tell me everything, but I want nothing but truths. I think I have lived with enough lies." Looking in her eyes I continue in a tone that expresses my pain and anger, "Don't you think I have had enough lies told to me mother? Don't you think I deserve the total truth?"

With tears in her eyes, she looks at me in the same loving way she always has, and she responds, "Yes. Yes. You are right; you deserve all the truth, no matter how ugly it is. Your grandmother was a very evil and prejudice woman back then. She felt she was doing me a favor; that's how her mind worked. Ben stayed away from you because he was told if he came around, she would make you disappear. Neither of us doubted her words so we kept our relationship between us and kept your dad out of your life."

I hold both my hands to my eyes and cry out loud, and hard. My dad holds me in his arms and tells me repeatedly, "I'm so sorry. I'm so sorry. Please forgive me for not being here for you. I love you and always wanted to be with you. I wish I could have been stronger for you."

After a few more minutes of everyone crying; including Lamont; we all dry our eyes and I realize what my mother actually said. Make me disappear. My grandmother threatened to make me disappear. I can't believe this; I cannot believe she could be so hateful just because someone is different.

We don't get to vote on who our family will be, or our color, or nationality. We don't get to vote where we will be born or in what part of the world or what side of the fence we land on. We are taught without questioning what religion we should believe in. We don't get to pick and choose the most important matters in our existence; those choices are made by The Creator; so, if we hate people because of race, religion, nationality or financial status then who are we really hating; each other or the one who created and made those choices for us all? This is the behavior of a lunatic; a self-proclaimed-to-be-intelligent-wealthy-high-minded-overbearing-self-centered-think-she's-better-than-everyone woman.

Enough private thoughts: I stand in the center of the floor and speak. "I hate what she has done to you daddy, I hate what she has done to you mother, and I hate what her decisions have done to my children, my husband, and to my life. Because everything she has done has an effect on my entire life and everyone that's a part of it."

Again, we find ourselves physically supporting each other and our tears, this time in the spot I stand. Lamont heads to the bathroom and returns with tissue and wet towels for us to wipe our faces.

I now ask the other important question, "Did you guys get married again?"

Daddy looks into Mother's eyes. He pulls her to him, then answers without removing his gaze from Irene.

"No baby, we didn't have to; we never got divorced. We have been married and faithful to each other all this time. There is no other woman in this world for me but this one standing right here in front of me."

Lamont smiles and looks at me. While moving closer to me he holds his arms out; and says, "I know what you mean. I didn't understand that once, but I do now and there is no place I'd rather be than with this woman right here."

The rest of the evening we spend reminiscing and catching up. I find out my father is not just an attorney, but he owns one of the top law firms in Frankfort, which means grandmother knows all about him. Oh, and he has his own wealth; his family has always been wealthy.

We don't mention grandmother again all night. Lamont calls home and we speak to the twins and Ms. Elaine; telling them we will not be home tonight. Home will be the first place we all go tomorrow. I can't wait for the twins to meet their grandfather. When we leave this place tomorrow, my father will not be a secret any longer and grandmother will pay for what she has done. This I promise.

CHAPTER ELEVEN

The Fat Lady Can't Sing Here

*O*h, my goodness. I peep towards the clock sitting on my night table; the flashing red numbers are 7:30 a.m. It's Saturday-late-sleeping-get-freaky-busy-with-my sexy-hot husband-morning. What is that ruckus I hear?

Sounds like the twins are jumping on the beds; trying to create a new way to get downstairs. I look over to my right side; oh no, no, no Lamont is already up but I'm ready to get freaky!

I know what this means; dad is here. Those two; no, those four; nah, those five, yep, five have been almost inseparable for two months now. I bet Irene kicked Ms. Elaine out the kitchen and is fixing that scrumptious smelling breakfast I smell. Ms. Elaine doesn't mind, nope, she is enjoying this just as much as the rest of us. Ah, oh well, I might as well jump my-hot-horny-ass up and take a quick cold shower.

Once out the shower, I can hear everyone in the kitchen. The little stinkers didn't even come and get me for breakfast. I walk downstairs right into the kitchen refusing to speak to any of them. I go straight for the coffee pot. Pouring a cup of joe as if they aren't even there. I'm really not upset at all. The way this family has bonded is so much more than anything I ever dreamed of.

Daddy is the first to speak, "Well, well, well, did we wake you Rae-muffin? And was the side of the bed you slipped out of in another world?"

I spin on my heel while putting my cup to my lips; trying to hide my smile. I take long slurping sips while moving my eyes from one of them to the other. Lamont hunches his shoulders, picks up his fork, and continues to eat.

Li'l-Ben follows suit. Daddy looks over at Lamont and he dives his fork into the hot cheese covered grits. Mother grunts and sips on her coffee, Charmin raises her arms, hunches her shoulders, and says, "Oh well mommy, I guess no one is going to pay you any attention. Get a plate and sit right here next to me and we can eat together." Looking over to her grandmother she continues in her sweet innocent tone. "Right I-mee?"

Mother is laughing; she places her cup down and hugs Charmin, "You are so right, baby."

Laughter fills the room. I fix my plate and take my assigned seat.

"Later for you all; why no one came to wake me for breakfast?"

Lamont stops eating long enough to answer, "I did sweet-ums; you were in the shower, so we knew you would be down shortly."

Oops, I didn't think of that; guess the egg is on my face. Changing the subject, I ask, "What are you guys doing today?"

Daddy answers, "We are going with you to the youth center. We know you've been working hard trying to get things ready for your opening day; therefore, we are putting on our gloves and helping with the last bit of cleaning and decorating. Besides, we have something for you to place in the center." Putting his hand up as a last-minute thought, "If you like it that is."

Wow, these wonderful people I have the privilege of calling my family are just great. I take my time hugging and kissing each one of them.

"I'm sure whatever you guys have will be perfect."

Ms. Elaine raises her hand and shouts, "I'm coming too."

I kiss and hug her as well, "Of course, you are, we won't be complete without you."

After we are done with breakfast, we all head upstairs to dress for the day. Daddy and mother have their own space here for whenever they stay over. They have actually been here more often than not; I know my dad needs as much time with us as he can get. We need it as well.

Once we arrive at the youth center everyone gets busy sweeping, dusting, re-arranging furniture, and some of the decor. I have a big surprise I haven't shared with my family yet; however, since I know it's all finished and ready for viewing, I'll gather everyone together to see. Waving my hands above my head for attention, I yell, "Hey everybody, come over here,"

Daddy is the first one to come, "What's going on Baby-Girl?"

Very excitedly, I continue to get the attention of the rest of the family, "Come on, I have something I want to show you all." Everyone is standing in front of me waiting to hear what I have to say. "Well, I know none of you has been on a complete tour of the facility as yet"

Mother and Lamont respond almost in perfect sync, "Yes, we have,"

Clasping my hands together, with a huge grin on my face, "Nah, you haven't, you just think you did. There is another level downstairs you haven't seen."

Daddy has a puzzled look on his face and Lamont is looking at mother as if she must know more than he does; mother hunches her shoulders.

"No one in this family has seen it or even knows it exists. So, come follow me, it's my big surprise and one of my greatest accomplishments."

They follow me through the hallway to a door I told them was a storage closet. We go down two short flights and enter a carpeted hallway which has of-fices and dressing rooms on each side and another doorway that has two doors with glass panes. I open the door and hear each of them gasp. Charmin takes off running down one of the aisles.

"Mommy, mommy - oh wow - it's beautiful, it's beautiful. I'm going to be a star, a real star, wow."

Mother hugs me, Lamont can't close his mouth and daddy, well, daddy can't stop crying.

"Wow, Rae, this is awesome. A full theater, full stage, sound system, live or-chestra section, lights, the seating, everything; oh, my goodness, I'm speechless; this is wonderful. I am so proud to be your mother. This is astounding, amazing, just amazing."

Ms. Elaine can only say a few words, while patting her cheeks, "Aye, aye, aye; oh aye, aye, aye, oh look at what my baby did. Aye, aye, aye,"

Lamont and daddy slowly walk through the entire theater not missing a section. Daddy sits on the drums in the orchestra section, taking a deep breath; he continues to look around in astonishment. Lamont stands in the middle of the stage with Li'l-Ben and Charmin. I feel so proud and happy. I am filled with so much gratitude and accomplishment. I feel as if I am finally alive and I have just begun to be me, myself and who I am born to be. The looks on the faces of the people who mean the most to me give me total and complete satisfaction. Without one more word spoken, I can feel their approval. Nothing else matters.

After leaving the center, we go out to eat. Ms. Elaine enjoys the night; however, she snips about how much better her food is. She's probably right, but she deserves a good meal she doesn't have to cook. Besides, this is family night and she is my family.

Lamont asks the biggest question of the day, "Babe, you can't keep calling the youth center, The Center. Have you come up with a name yet?"

Mother agrees, "That's right, you never mentioned a name."

What they don't know is before the center was completed, I had a name selected. My intention to surprise them with the name I originally selected has been mentally demolished after I found out what grandmother did to my dad. However, ever since I decided to open this facility, I wanted the name to reflect family values and strong integrity. Realizing grandmother's actions forced me to change the original name, which would have been The Harper-Mason Youth Now Organizational Center.

After taking a swallow of my iced tea; I answer the question at hand. I've been carrying books and folders around all day in my over-sized bag. I reach into the bag and pull out a folder; I open it and give it to Lamont to read out loud.

He reads it to himself first. Then clears his throat, "The commissioner's office of commerce in the county of Fayette, City of Lexington, the state of Kentucky on this 7th day of May 2014 has henceforth established and acknowledges the structure standing at 5797 J. Mere Drive is hereafter known as The Thomas-Harper Youth Now Organizational Center & Theater."

You can hear a pin drop at this table; however, we may need more napkins; not a dry eye in sight.

Daddy clears his throat while wiping his face, "Well, that makes my gift fit right into the name. Give me a second, I must run to the car. Come with me Lamont, I'm going to need your help."

Li'l-Ben jumps to his feet and yells while running behind them, "Wait Pee-pa I want to help. I'm strong."

Daddy goes to the car and the three come back with a huge package that's almost bigger than they are. As daddy removes the cover, he reveals a hand-painted family portrait of him, Irene, Lamont, the twins, and me.

"I had this painted from different pictures I selected. I thought you could hang this in the lobby of the center."

It is absolutely breathtaking; no one would be able to tell that this painting didn't come from a sitting or from one single picture. It is so beautiful, and it definitely goes along with the name.

"Thank you, daddy, thank you so much. This will be hung in the entrance lobby, it's really beautiful."

Charmin touches the portrait, "Look at me Ben. Look Ben, we are painted."

Ben touches the portrait also, "Wow! Cool."

Everyone gives their positive approval concerning the portrait. We gather our things and leave the restaurant very satisfied with our day's work.

This night ends on a high I have never experienced before in my life. I lay in my husband's arms after daddy put his grandchildren to bed and he and mother leave. All is quiet and now all the love I wanted this morning is what I receive and even more, from the man I love.

CHAPTER TWELVE

And the Skelton got Life

The phone rings twice and I can hear Ms. Elaine picking it up. As I turn to look at her, I can see her face frowned. Oh, boy, do I know that look. It's been a while since I've seen that expression on her face.

Ms. Elaine holds her hand up towards me in a stop position, as she proceeds to empty her venom into the ears at the other end. With a mixing spoon in one hand being used almost as a weapon, and the other holding the phone. Her Latino accent is in full effect. This is most definitely one of those times.

"Okay, now you listen; number one; this is the last time you will call this number because after this call I am changing the number. Number two, nobody here wants you, because if they did, you would not be on the phone, you would be here. Number three, no self-respecting woman, would keep chasing a married man that doesn't want her unless she is insane. And if you are insane, let me give you some good advice: Either you check yourself into a hospital where you can get some help, or understand when animals go insane, they are killed and put out of their misery. Now you choose, but this is the last time I will hear your voice, and the last time you get to choose your fate; so good-bye."

Did I just hear my Ms. Elaine threaten a death sentence on that piece-of-smutty-unbearable-undesirable-underestimating-me-want-ing-to-be-me-ass-wipe? Oh, yeah, she's probably the one who taught mother that nice-nasty stuff, who in turn, with great expertise, taught me the art of handling oppositional annoyances.

With a smile on my face, I walk towards Ms. Elaine with my hand up in a high five position, "Ms. Elaine, give me some of that!"

We slap high five and laugh for a moment. Then I get serious about the call. A call I thought I wouldn't have to ever address again. I mean we are well over a year, why hasn't she stopped?

Ms. Elaine interrupts my thinking, "I'm calling the phone company now to change the number and I will call the few people; like the children's school and family members and give them the new number. Don't you worry about this; Rae, I'm going to fix this."

Unfortunately, I know changing the number will not settle this ongoing problem. It seems like I need to have a conversation with Ms. Robin. It's obvious she has some things on her mind; perhaps it's time I stop being afraid to hear what those things are. Enough is enough; can't keep running in this circle. Whatever she wants can no longer be ignored.

The truth is, I haven't asked Uncle Douglas about her in quite a while. Life has been wonderful, and she has not been a thought on my mind at all. Well, this is it; my minds made up to find Robin. It can't be as difficult as it seems. My first act is to call Uncle Douglas and find out what; if anything, he has found out about little-Ms.-pain-in-the-rear-end-itching-where-I-can't-reach-Bug-A-Boo-pest.

A million thoughts are running through my mind as I run to get my cell phone out of my purse. Dialing Uncle Douglas number, I head towards the family room for privacy.

The phone rings three times then I hear my uncle's voice sounding as if he just woke up.

"Hey, Rae; and to what do I owe the pleasure of this call?"

"Good morning Uncle Douglas. I'm good, how are you doing?"

I can hear him yarning, and then he answers, "I'm good, can't complain. What's going on? Are you alright?"

I take a deep breath, "Well no, I'm not alright. Uncle Douglas, I need to know where to find that woman. Do you have any information on her?"

He pauses for a moment; I can hear him flicking a lighter and then inhaling deeply before blowing out hard.

"Now, Rietta, I talked to that woman over eight months ago. She swore she wasn't going to be a problem anymore. Did something happen?"

Did I just hear him say he spoke to her over *eight* months ago? What the ... how the... Is he serious? There is no need in even trying to hide how mad I am.

"What did you say? Did you just tell me you spoke to her and you didn't bother to tell me anything at all about this? What the heck Uncle Douglas, what kind of shit is that?"

"Now hold up, baby-girl, I told mother and she felt it was best not to trouble you with this if the woman promised not to interfere with you and Lamont. Now, you haven't asked about her in a while so I figured she did what she said she would do and left you guys alone."

Whenever Uncle Douglas is explaining anything, he always lingers the word, now as if that word can calm the situation. Not this time, I'm really pissed-off.

"Please tell me what gives you and grandmother the right to decide whether or not I should talk to that woman? I asked you to find her for me and I expected that once you did, you would pass the information on to me, not talk to her yourself."

"*Now* hold on. First of all, you were not the first one who asked me to find her; mother did. And you know as well as I do, mother runs the show. So now if you have a problem, it's with her not me. Besides, as long as she doesn't break her word, it's all good. Isn't that what you wanted; her to not call and leave you and your family alone, right?"

Taking a moment to gather my thoughts, I realize Uncle Douglas is going to do exactly what grandmother tells him to do. That's all he can do. I do understand; but I can't help but feel somewhat betrayed. I wanted to handle that situation myself. And how did grandmother know about Robin first? You know what, never mind, I don't know why that is even a question in my mind. In a much calmer tone and very apologetic, I explain to him the suddenly awakened dog.

"She has been noticeably quiet for some time now but today all of a sudden, she calls. Ms. Elaine is changing the house number as we speak. I really do appreciate you Uncle Douglas; please forgive me for yelling at you. None of this is your fault. It's just that I want to speak to her myself."

For a few moments, Uncle Douglas is silent. I can hear him mumbling but I can't make out what he's saying. But this means he's thinking. I hear him slam the phone down and suddenly he yells, "Damn!"

I continue to hold on without saying a word. Finally, after he's finished with his private time he comes back to the phone.

"*Now* listen to me Rae; I know this is a problem and I know you would like to have this settled..."

I interrupt him, "No Uncle Douglas, I would not just *like* to have this settled. I want to settle this myself because it really *needs* to be taken by the root. There is a reason why this woman won't stop after all this time and I want to know why. Please allow me the opportunity to speak to her."

I can hear him mumbling again before answering me, "*Now* why won't you just let me handle this, why do you feel the need to speak to her? The only things she can tell you are things that will hurt your feelings. What is it you're looking for Rae?"

I am feeling somewhat anxious and angry at the same time; however, I know I have to handle my uncle very delicately or he won't give me any information.

"You know Lamont still doesn't remember what happened to him. And some of his short-term memory is gone. I think his memory of her is gone as well. Now I don't want her to pop up at his business or bump into him in the streets or somewhere and his memory of her comes back. Before the accident, Lamont and I were not doing so good Uncle Douglas. Now our life together is better than it has ever been, and I don't want to lose that. Please, please allow me the opportunity to deal with this woman myself. Please!"

"Wow, Rae; *now*, you listen to me and listen really well. If you insist on meeting this woman, I'll agree, as long as I go with you. Now that's the only way, I will agree. There is no room for any kind of negotiations on this part." He pauses for a moment, but I don't say a word, "*Now* is that clear, can you deal with this?"

Reluctantly, I agree. He's doing the right thing. I know deep down inside of me; well, maybe not so deep, but inside I want to put something to this trouble-some-trick-whore-daughter-not-realizing-who-she's-messing-with-brainless-broad's-ass. That's less likely to happen with Uncle Douglas there. But hey, I'll take what I can get.

We hang up with the understanding that Uncle Douglas will set up the meeting for me as soon as possible. Now all I must do is survive with my nerves intact until then. The funny thing is, I never gave thought to the fact that creepy-home-wrecking-dirty-down-rotten-decaying-shit-plaster, may have gone to Lamont's business. What if she did and he hasn't said anything. Perhaps he does remember, and he thinks I don't know about her. What if...

No, I have to stop this. No speculating, no playing ball in my own head. I can't ask Lamont, but I will ask enough questions to find out what I need and want to know from the whore's mouth when I see her.

With all the business of the community center and deciding when to have a grand opening, along with building a relationship with my dad; waiting a little while longer for this face-to-face should be a breeze. I said *should* be, however, it's almost agonizing, waiting for Uncle Douglas to call. I can't help thinking that Robin may not want to talk to me. Perhaps her only interest is in my husband.

A week and a half go by without any calls from Robin and no major problems in our lives. Daddy and mother are extremely close and happy. I am glad we can witness their happiness and be a part of it. Grandmother still has no idea daddy is on the scene nor does she suspect mother and daddy are together and always have been. Please tell me why do I do this to myself? I know there is absolutely nothing grandmother does not know.

Boy, I wonder how she felt when she got the memo that her biggest plan to destroy their lives didn't work. I feel grandmother has softened a lot over the years and she has become more flexible in some of the things she was so blindly passionate about. You know bigotry is an invisible blinder that prevents even the best of people the opportunity of experiencing true friendship and lasting relationships. There was a story I once heard concerning an old man who lived in a small southern town where bigotry was the way of common understanding. Even after the town became more interracial and open to racial change and acceptance; he refused to.

This old man separated himself from any and everybody who associated with any person of color. One evening the storm bells rang out, warning the citizens of an approaching hurricane. The schools were set up as fallout shelters and opened for anyone who decided not to stay at home to ride out the fast-approaching storm, which had the expectancy of becoming a category four hurricane.

About thirty minutes into the storm it was announced over the radio that the hurricane would in fact be a category four, and everyone was being urged to find shelter. Well, as life or karma would have it, the old man was trapped; mostly by his hatred which made him unable to join most of the other citizens who gathered at the school with people of all races.

The old man became the topic of the conversation, while a teenage young man listened on. He heard some of the neighbors of the old man say how they tried to get him to come with them, but he refused once they informed him that there were no separate quarters for blacks and whites. As the storm became fierce this young man left the safety of the school and his parents and went to that old man's home. Once he got in front of the house, he could see the windows had already given into the fierce winds.

Soaking wet; franticly that young man looked for the old man as the winds began to pick up almost blowing him off balance a few times. Nevertheless, he continued to search for the old man. When he began to think that perhaps the old man was blown away or buried too deeply underneath some of the gathering rubble; he heard a faint moan. He moved some of the furniture that had been tossed from the winds entering through the broken windows, desperately searching for the old man. Finally, he saw a hand, and then an arm under the turned over the sofa. Uncovering the old man who was badly hurt and bleeding; he helped him to his feet.

The young man tossed that old man across his shoulder and carried him to the safety of the school. Many of the people there assisted in bandaging up his wounds and attending to his care. When that old man became conscious, he looked around and found the brave young man that was determined to rescue him. In front of everyone in that school, he got up and walked over to that young man and stuck out his hand for him to shake it.

The young black man shook his hand as the old man thanked him and apologized to him for how foolishly he behaved towards him in times past. See, this old man, made life as hard as he could for this teenager's parents. Outbidding them on property he didn't even want; just didn't want the black family to have it. He would refuse to buy their seasonal crops or sell them seeds for planting.

Anyway, after this young man showed the old man that race is not a factor when it comes to the breath of God; that kindness and compassion come in all colors and from all types of people, that old man changed his ways. He then *gave* the land to Benjamin Sr.'s parents and paid to send the young man to law school, thus he became the father of my father and here I am today.

I don't believe grandmother is that bad; I just feel she was taught a way that is ugly and causes bitterness. I'm not sure how much she changed but like it or not, the reality is we are family and once she accepts that, we can all experience happiness *together.*

Not being able to wait any longer I decided to call Uncle Douglas. The phone rings and he picks up on the second ring.

He starts off his conversation as usual, "*Now*, look here baby girl, sometimes things don't work out the way we intend, and we have to come up with another plan." I remain silent, so he can finish fumbling over his words and get to whatever he has to say. "The problem is this; she doesn't want to meet with you. She's sounding as if she's afraid. *Now,* I don't know why she talks to me; other than the fact I'm a loveable guy and all, but don't worry I have a plan."

Afraid? Really? Uncle Douglas better not be trying to play nice with the enemy for the sake of getting some nookie. Whatever it is I don't like it and whether she wants to or not we will see each other face-to-face much sooner than later.

"Uncle Douglas I'm somewhat in awe at her fear, since it would appear that floozy-ass-wipe-piece-of-used-toilet-tissue-misrepresentation-of-a-real-woman, won't stop calling my home. It seems to me she wants my attention unless her true purpose is to get on my nerves. And if that's the case, let me be the first to say, she has succeeded. Now, I don't know what your plan is but let me tell you this..."

Just as my anger is taking over, he interrupts me, "Now listen up, baby girl I have your best interest at heart; so, listen to me. Little Miss-think-she-knows-it-all, who don't know nothing, I have her address and where she is currently employed. Now I figure we can take a little trip to her place of employment during her lunch break, which will be best since I happen to know where she eats most of the time. So now the ball is in your court; when do you want to do this?"

Okay, now I feel I should apologize to Uncle Douglas for doubting him but nah, he doesn't know what I was thinking. Eagerly, I answer, "How about tomorrow since it's already 1:30 and probably past her lunchtime?"

After pausing for a moment Uncle Douglas answers, "Now actually, she doesn't take lunch until 2:30, since she goes into work at 10:00. So, if you want to go now it's a great time."

Wow, Uncle Douglas really has done his work; I'm so proud of him and grateful. If I want to go, was his question; is he for real? Of course, I want to go; right now, I want to go. Without saying another word, I run for my bag and head for the door.

"Where am I meeting you; I'm headed for my car right now."

"I'll meet you downtown at that little sandwich shop on the corner of Washington and Reed. I should get there in about twenty minutes."

"Great, we should be pulling up about the same time."

All I can do is think about all the things I want to say to this got-on-my-last-nerve-got-an-ass-kicking-coming-to-her-hussy. My doggone heart is beating so fast and the palms of my hands are sweating. I wonder if I should call mother. Nah, I think I can handle this one.

No sooner than I toss the thought of calling Irene the phone rings and it's her. Damn, now I feel as if I shouldn't answer; she has this sixth sense thing about me and it's eerie. I bet if I answer she has some kind of notion she needed to call me. I'm not answering.

The voicemail picks up the call and it rings again, yep, it's Mother. I have to answer it, "Hello dear favorite, wonderful mother of mine."

Without even saying hello, "Where are you going?"

Clearing my throat, "Huh?"

"You heard me, where are you headed? Oh, and don't pull that innocent act like you're not up to something, because I know you are. So once again, where are you going?"

I remove the phone from my ear and look at it sticking out my tongue as if it means something other than a personal satisfying moment.

"I'm going to meet Uncle Douglas."

"That much I know already but where-are-you-meeting?"

Whining, like a small child, "Mother, how do you know that much?"

"Excuse me, I'm your mother and I have my ways."

Blowing my breath, "You should know you spook me out a lot and I don't think that's good for my developing-innocent-easily-influenced mind."

I hear her chuckle then back to her question, "So where are you meeting Douglas and when is Robin getting there?"

"Ma, how do you know any of this? You know I don't think it's fair you have spies and I don't know who they are."

I hear her chuckling again, "Sure, you know them, you can take a pick of everyone you know, and you would be right. It's all of them. Now, where are you headed, young lady?"

I mumble while giving up the information. Mother says she even closer than I am. I guess its best she's there; she will always have my best interest at heart. On her last note before hanging up she throws in her last statement, in a humorous yet serious manner.

"You do realize that your Uncle Douglas is my brother, right? And has been my brother for a very long time, as a matter of fact way before you were born. No matter what, there are rules to this family and one of them is never keep anything about my children from me. You think my mother has a sting; well the Queen-Bee has a daughter whose sting is just as deadly. Try to remember that, Douglas does."

We chatter all the way to our destination. As I pull up into a parking space, mother is standing outside of her car talking to Uncle Douglas. I park and walk over to my waiting family; I stand right next to Uncle Douglas and pinch him on the arm.

"Ouch, what was that for?"

Mother leans in for a kiss and hug. She laughs and answers Uncle Douglas, "Oh, she thinks you are my informant."

Uncle Douglas looks at me and says, "I thought you called her, I didn't. But your mother is the one who found Robin and gave me the information to give to you. Now, let's be clear, I cannot keep anything from Irene anyway, I would have told her if she didn't know, it's a rule. Besides, now, I just might be a little more concerned about Irene's bite than your grandmother's."

He looks at my mother and winks with a grin on his face. Now I'm really freaked out.

"Mother, how did you know, I mean, I really wanted to try and handle this without Lamont or anyone else finding out?"

Hugging me, Irene takes me by the arm and begins to walk slowly, "Rae, don't you know by now, that I know when something is bothering you. All I have to do is go to the right person and voila, I have all the information I need to work it out for or with you. Now let's go take care of this itty-bitty-little problem and get back to our lives once and for all."

I hug her and we head for the opening of the sandwich shop. As we enter, I spot Robin immediately as she stands in front of the counter having her sandwich made. We take a seat in the corner and wait for her to take a seat. Once she sits down, we join her at her table.

If a surprising look is worth money, this floozy would have gotten rich on the spot. I speak first, "Hello Robin, how are you? You do remember me, don't you? I'm Mrs. Lamont Harper you may call me Mrs. Harper. "

She slowly looks at mother and Uncle Douglas before shaking my extended hand. "Yes, of course, I remember you. How are you and to what do I owe this..." She pauses as she takes in the sight of all of us. "... surprise?"

I introduce Mother and Uncle Douglas; she shakes their hands as well and returns her gaze to me.

"So finally, we meet, so tell me, how can I help you?"

While trying to hold my composure and not be too snide I try to appease her pretense of ignorance. "Well, we did meet at the hospital, remember that moment when you leaned into my unconscious husband to remind him of your perfume." I chuckle and continue, "Well, I want to tell you that either it's not so much of his favorite or he doesn't remember your fragrance at all. Now there's a third possibility like perhaps it really doesn't matter to him." I look for a reaction to my trying-not-to-be-too-snide remark. "I want to know why you keep calling my home, what is it you want?"

Placing her sandwich in her mouth and taking a bite, she looks at me while chewing slowly and grinning.

"Umm this is so good. You should try it." Holding her sandwich out, "Would you like a bite?"

Then she passes the invitation of a bite to each of us, no one responds. I am somewhat annoyed, but I refuse to let her know it. I smile and pick up the half still in her plate. As if examining the sandwich, I turn it around and open it up.

"What kind of sandwich is it?"

I can tell she is ruffled but she is trying to hold her composure. Bet she can't last longer than I can; bet I get under her skin way before she does mine. I slowly move the half of sandwich closer to my lips as she answers, "It's pastrami and Swiss cheese, with mustard, mayo, lettuce, tomatoes, and banana peppers, please enjoy." Just as the sandwich touches my mouth she includes while chuckling, "Oh, it also has jalapeño peppers and spicy hot mustard; I enjoy hot and spicy."

I'm sure she thought I was not a fan of hot and spicy. If I were partial to my food being spicy, she will never know. Because nothing, I do mean nothing, is going to stop me from biting this half-witted-asshole sandwich. However, I happen to love peppers and spicy mustard, so in my mind, while taking a huge bite out of her lunch I imagine sticking my tongue out at her. Oh, and it's good.

I eat the entire half while she finishes her half without a word between us. Mother sits there with her arms folded across her chest and Uncle Douglas squirms in his seat as if he's restless.

After the last bite, she finally wipes her mouth and answers, "I call your house because I need to speak to Monty."

I look over to Uncle Douglas and ask him to please get me a sweet tea; mother seconds the request for herself. I don't respond to her until he returns, and I take a sip. Without reacting to the pet-name she uses in reference to my husband I launch deeper into my interrogation – nice and snippy – of course.

"Please tell me why you need to talk to my husband. Seeing he has not returned any of your calls and even better, obviously has not called you on his own accord?"

Robin wipes the front of her blouse to assure she has no crumbs on it. After she finishes her little purpose to pause, she looks me right in the eye, with clear sarcasm and boldness.

"Well Mrs. Lamont Harper, if it's an answer you want let me give you one. I happen to be very much in love with Monty, and I know he loves me. Now, I feel you are blocking us from being together and I also feel you are not up to a little competition. But if you are secure and think what I'm saying is untrue, then why not let Monty decide for himself."

Did this ... did this ... I mean what the heck did this mud-ridden-heifer-scandalous-gonna-get-her-ass-kicked-piece-of-dog-shit just say to me?

Mother slowly puts her hand under the table to hold my hands that are on my lap. She squeezes hard enough to help me remember I should not punch the hell out of this...person.

Uncle Douglas is looking at Robin as if she has gone crazy. His mouth is open wide, his eyebrows are frowned up and his head is leaned to the side. He turns to me and nods his head up and down, before saying, "Well, Rae, I do believe you need to handle this person and handle her quickly. Now, I'm a man and I want to punch her, so I'm going to go outside before I snatch her from across the table. The Mayor cannot be seen in such nonsense."

Uncle Douglas leaves the table but not without the last word. Pointing his finger at me then to mother and finally to Robin, "Now Rae, you are a Richardson-Mason make sure you conduct yourself as a true product of our family. Now, Irene, I know you are very classy so do what needs to be done. As for you Robin, you have either gone insane or just plain stupid. Don't really matter which one it is but I strongly suggest, rechanneling some, no most; probably would do best if all, that I-think-I-got-it-attitude fades away and you have a productive conversation with my niece."

Uncle Douglas leaves the restaurant. Robin sits in her seat with a cunning smirk on her face as she watches him leave. She pushes her chair out just enough to cross her legs. Clearing her throat, "Oh, he's so cute, adorable even. So, am I supposed to be frightened by his words of warning? Because if so, perhaps he's right, maybe I am insane, or, as Doug put it, just plain stupid. Either way, I want what I want, and I want to speak to my Monty. Let him tell me he no longer wants me."

I want to speak but I can't. I'm not sure what I was expecting but it's for sure I did not think I would be faced with someone with as much nerve and attitude as me. Why should I be surprised? Most men who cheat find women that are perfect replicates of what they think they don't want any more, oxymoronic behavior, almost self-errantly sadistic. So here I am, sitting across from a woman who believes she is my husband's choice between us. Here she sits giving me an attitude of the wife as if I am the mistress. How do I handle this with tact yet very abrasively?

Mother is squeezing my hand so tight as if holding them tight will help her hold on to her very lady-like demeanor. I take a very deep breath after blowing it out slowly; I look Robin in her eyes, "Wow Robin, it's very apparent you had a particularly good relationship with my husband. I know he's a charmer. I'm sure he treated you good and made good love to you. I'm sure he made you feel especially important trying his best not to make you feel like the slut-full-of-shit-low-life-wench-whore that you really are. Now, please don't take my calm approach to your insult and disrespect lightly. See, you never should have involved me. If Lamont, oh excuse me, my husband, wants you he'll call you; however, since he has not decided to do so, perhaps that's not what he wants. Therefore, the competition you so audaciously mentioned is neither necessary or merited since Monty has evidently made his choice."

Robin opens her mouth to speak and I hold my hand up to stop her, "Wait, I'm not quite finish; just one moment, please. Lamont should have given you just a tad bit of information about me and my family. You are a very little, in fact, a tiny problem. You are just a big enough pestilence to irritate me, you know like a small-slummy-wiggling-nasty-disease-filled-maggot. But it's apparent Lamont has already gotten rid of the garbage. Please hear me before you speak again so you can take the opportunity to choose your words with some measure of thought and care for yourself."

Fidgeting in her seat, I can see Miss-thang has just become a little uncomfortable, blowing her breath out hard enough for me to hear, she tilts her head to the side, with a smirk on her face; that still cannot hide her nervousness.

I continue, "You have no idea the ways I can get rid of noisome pestilences. So, I am asking you; very strongly asking you to cease and desist from calling my home. I am giving you the absolute best advice I can, by telling you I feel its best you forget about my husband. He is obviously no longer feeling you. Please stop."

As if she is fighting with her senses, her face changes expressions from pride to skepticism, yet she pushes her envelope with her next statement, "Oh, look at you, your fangs are showing; cute even." She smiles showing her teeth. "See I have some too. For the record, I am not afraid of you or your family. I want my Monty, and I won't stop until I hear him tell me to go away."

Mother lets go of my one hand. Putting her finger up with her head turned and eyes closed, "Whoa, okay I have had enough. Look whoever you are; what's the matter with you? It's as if you are purposely pushing for an out of control confrontation. Now, if that's what you are looking for, it's not going to happen; not here, not today. You are a grown woman, and the games you're playing are dangerous. Do whatever you want, but hear me clearly, we, The Richardson-Mason-Thomas-Harper-Family do not work well with enemies. Now we can walk away from this table understanding you and my son-in-law had an affair, which is over now. Or we can walk away feeling you are placing yourself in the position of an enemy. And please trust me if you make yourself an enemy, you will be treated like that maggot that needs to be gotten rid of. Now maybe you don't understand that, okay, I got it. But my suggestion to you is that you go home or back to work and take the time you need to digest everything you have heard at this table."

Visibly upset and shaken by mother's words; Robin's breathing has gotten faster, and she fumbles with her handbag. With her lips squeezed together, she smacks her teeth. She opens her mouth to speak, "Perhaps you should have come alone so we could have had a nice conversation, but I guess you needed your minute army to..."

I cut her words off by interrupting her sentence, "See now I am sure I am dealing with a crazy-air-headed-idiot-trying-to-make-me-become-everything-I-have-tried-not-to-be-dumb-ass. So, I'm going to leave without giving you any more warning, I am done."

Mother and I get up to leave before we go, Mother turns to Robin, and says, "Oh, you-silly-little-minded-penny-wench, you should be very happy Rae didn't come alone. We were not here to protect her; it was for your protection. However, from the looks of it, you will learn the hard way. Have a good rest of the day."

We walk out the door without looking back.

Once outside I see Uncle Douglas is gone. I know he has to pretend to do Mayor stuff. Mother and I talk about Robin for only a moment leaving each other with the notion we may have to turn into grandmother to deal with this problem. I truly hope not. I truly hope not.

CHAPTER THIRTEEN

Love, Commitment, Trust & Remembering

The breeze from Lamont's breath blowing in my ear, wakes me from my sleep. I slowly turn over to see his wonderful smile.

"Good morning my lovely lady; did you rest well?"

I look over at the alarm clock and see it's three in the morning. With a smile on my face, I turn all the way over on my back and put my arms around his neck.

"Well, wonderful-dear-sweet-husband-of-mine; yes, I was resting very well. To what do I owe this extremely early morning wake up?"

I figured Lamont wants early morning loving, which I am always ready to give him.

"It's going to be a great day, can't you tell?"

"Oh really, so tell me how I can tell, when it's still so dark outside?"

Lamont puts one leg across me straddling my body. With his hands on each side of my head, he leans in and kisses me gently on the lips.

"I know it's going to be a great day because I woke up fifteen minutes ago, feeling as if I could not live without you. My heart is for you and you only. I love no one but you Rietta, the mother of my children and the woman who stuck by me although I was not a good husband. It's a great day because you are still my wife."

What is he talking about? Did he remember how things were? I dare not ask. I dare not, but the tears flood down the sides of my face.

Lamont lifts me in his arms and holds me tight and he cries with me. Without another word, we cry together. Taking a seat on the edge of the bed, my husband takes my hand in his.

"I was so horrible to you. I was selfish, abusive, and evil to you Rae. I-I-I remember who and what I was. I remember all the things I did to you without cause. You remained a good wife through all I did. I am so, so, sorry. I don't know what to say."

I wrap my arms around him and hold on to him with all my might. I kiss the tears flowing freely down his face.

"Lamont, the past is the past and I forgive you. All that matters is our here and now. We have a wonderful life and I love you more and more each day."

Wait a minute, he remembers! Oh, my goodness he remembers! Does he, remember what I did to him? Suddenly my joy and happiness turn into fright. I hug my husband, holding him as close as I can waiting for the big boom.

Sorrow is trying to creep into my happy moment as I remain shaken, yet happy Lamont has his memory. I wonder how much he remembers; I wonder if he remembers all I said and did while he laid bleeding and half lifeless on the foyer. I wonder if he remembers Robin. *Oh God, please, please help me.* I don't know how much I should say. Perhaps I should say nothing and let him continue to do the talking.

My invading thoughts are quieted as this wonderful hunk of a man removes the covers off my body. Looking at me in such a loving way, he reaches for my hand.

"Rietta, you and my children mean more to me than anyone in this world. I've been a cheat, a liar and mean. I don't know how to make it all up to you, but I want to spend the remainder of my life trying to love you more than any man can love a woman."

His words penetrate my very soul; and it suddenly does not matter how much he remembers. Suddenly all that matters is our love for one another.

Lamont stands up and reaches for a small box laying on his night table. He falls on his knees; gently taking hold of both my hands, he looks me in the eyes. There is a feeling of calm that's moving completely through me almost like an awakening, making me feel as if this moment is the epitome of my existence. I realize right here and now, I was born to love this man, and I was born for him to love.

Kissing each of my hands as his tears wet them, he continues, "Rea, I want to ask you a question. We have been married for 12 years; we have two beautiful children, a wonderful family, and friends. I must admit, I was acting foolish, selfish, and was being a total jerk. So now that our life is where it should be, I need to know if you will marry me - again?"

He opens the box, exposing the most gorgeous ring. It's a clear exquisite diamond, encircled by three rows of smaller diamonds. The three rows of smaller diamonds cover the entire band. He slips my other rings off my finger, replacing them with the ring in his hand as I gasp in total awe. Holding my left hand up to gaze at this perfect ring I cover my mouth with the other. I'm speechless; never in my wildest dreams did I expect this.

Lamont reaches for my chin, turning my face back toward his, "Hey, my lady, you didn't answer me. Will you marry me again?"

Shoot, is he crazy? Of course, I will, after all the hell and trouble I've been through. After finally seeing the proof of loving him unconditionally, after spending twelve hours in labor having his children, after...jolting myself from my silly thoughts I realize my husband is still waiting to hear my answer.

I lean in to kiss him and kiss him I do, with more passion than even I thought I had. I kiss him long as I run my fingers through his short hair. Finally, I look into his eyes and say, "Sweetheart, you can most definitely remain my husband and I will be honored to be your wife yet again. I cannot see completion in my life without you. Yes Lamont, yes, yes and yes!"

We embrace and my husband makes love to me until the sun comes up, making me feel just as special as he did our very first time. The unanswered questions fade away with each kiss as Lamont confirms his devotion to me.

Ah, he is right this is a great day, and I can hardly wait to tell my parents we are having a wedding. Mother will love helping me plan it. Not only is this a great day, but it's a great life. Daddy will be a part of this wedding and that will be the happiest day of my entire life.

CHAPTER FOURTEEN

*Prepping
for Secrets*

Grandmother announces the family vacation this year will be spent on-board a luxury liner headed for the Philippine Islands. She also announces she has some especially important information she'd like to share with the entire family. Wonder what that can be? I mean, it's not like this family isn't packed with enough secrets.

I guess, looking on the bright side, sharing all the things we all have kept bottled up on the inside can only be liberating for the secret-keepers and eye-opening for everyone else.

Without having the scalla-wagging-trying-to-break-up-my-happy-home-chick calling and harassing us, I have been able to relax. Well as it turns out, she's not the only noisome pestilence I seem to have been given a break from. Mr. Long-legged-smacking-that-damn-gum-annoying-probably-needing-a-per-manent-vacation-detective hasn't been around in a couple of months. So, for now, all is quiet on the Kentucky front.

It will be quite interesting to find out what grandmother has to tell us. Lam-ont and I played a game last night. Each of us wrote a list with ideas of what we think she has that is so important to tell us. After about fifteen minutes we gave up. Each of us had an empty sheet of paper. Trying to figure out grandmother is not an easy task. Wonder if mother knows? Nah, if she did, I would know. Oh well, guess we must wait until she tells us.

Guess I was thinking so hard of mother she picked me up in the air. I giggle as her face pops up on my ringing phone.

"Hi, my most favorite mother in the entire world."

I can hear her snicker before she responds, "Favorite huh; well I am technically your only mother; however, I still consider that a compliment."

We both laugh out loud. I break into the fun, "Have you begun packing?"

"Of course, we only have a week before we leave. Besides, I am trying to find a way to sneak your father on board. I don't want to ruin the way we plan to tell the family we are together and always have been."

The fact that no one knows about my parents being together is almost amazing. I cannot figure out how in the world they kept this from grandmother and Uncle Douglas.

"If I had my way, I would walk on that ship with my arm tucked under daddy's arm, and with my head held high, nodding as I walk past all the opened mouths and surprised looks. Of course, I would have a few bottles of smelling sauce for grandmother; she will need it after she passes out."

We both laugh. I mean the thought of it all makes me laugh hard. However, as usual, Mother has a more peaceful way of handling all the sloppy messes, and untidy thing-a-ma-jigs.

"Now Rae, you know we have been living in secret for an exceptionally long time. I want to reintroduce him into the family, not shove him down everybody's throat. So, we talked about it and he's coming on the trip and we will live openly from that point on. I promise."

"I know you're right. As long as you promise daddy will no longer have to be in anybody's shadow after this trip; I can live with the sneaking-him-on-board thingy."

Mother assures me that after the family trip, daddy is forever taking his place in our family, whether grandmother accepts it or not. Mother reminds me that the Big-Cheese has information of her own to share.

"Well, I know mother also has something she wants to share with the family and I also know this trip will be good for us all. Did you know your sisters will be there?"

I pause. That's shocking. "No, I didn't. But I think that's a great idea. It's about time we all get together and fix what can be fixed in this family. I never hear from Danna, but Kristy sends me emails every now and then." I hear silence, "Mother, are you there?"

"Yes, and I am incredibly happy to hear that. And yes, I hear from them both quite often."

Interrupting, "Wait, I didn't know that. You never mention them to me. So, you are incredibly good at keeping secrets, I see. And keeping them from me, me, your ride and die, your baby girl, your favorite, your..."

Interrupting me, mother jokingly replies, "Okay you, that's enough. You do realize you are not my only daughter, right? Besides, you never told me you and Kristy were in contact with each other either. So, don't you try that Rietta-smooth-slick-naïve-oh-someone-knows-more-than-me-crap; it doesn't work on me."

"Oh really, it doesn't huh?"

"No, it doesn't Mrs. Rietta Richardson-Mason-Thomas-Harper, it does not. I only pretend it does sometimes; just to appease you." I hear her laughing, speaking in a shy-girlish tone, "Don't worry; you are still the closest daughter I have; however, I do have a life with your sisters, and I do keep their secrets just as I do yours."

Well, I guess that's only fair, Irene is a wonderful mother and a great person. I wouldn't expect anything else from her, except to do what is right by everyone she loves.

"Well tell me, mother, how are my sisters doing?"

"They are just fine, and they have a few updates of their own to share with the family."

Wow, all I can say is this is going to be some trip. So far, I think almost everyone has something to tell except Nylah and Mr. Charles. Perhaps I should wait before I relax with that notion, because in this family, along with family-associates, anything is possible.

Lamont walks in our bedroom where I'm sitting on the bed. I hang up from mother to pay my husband some attention. With a big smile on his face, he leans down towards me and kisses my lips.

"Hi sweetie. I see you've started packing. There has got to be ten bags downstairs."

Laughing, "No, it's not, Lamont but I did start packing. Most of the bags down there are empty. I just needed to get our luggage in one place so I can figure out whose clothes go where. And how was your day?"

"My day was good. I decided tomorrow will be my last day before our vacation. I have a few things I need to do before we leave."

"Oh, really, anything I can help you with?"

Leaning close to me to kiss my lips again, "Nope, I got it."

Turning on his heels he walks into the bathroom. I wonder what he has to do. I thought I took care of everything. Because of my inquiring personality, I must ask.

"Lamont..." I hear the water running in the shower, so I get up and go into the bathroom. I stick my head in the shower where my wonderfully made husband is, "Hey babe, if you have something you need to do, I can help you if you like."

While he continues to lather his body, he turns his back to me, "Nope, I got it. You have your hands full enough. I got it, thanks for asking."

He has it. Thanks for asking. What? Oh no, I cannot, I will not sleep knowing he didn't tell me what he has to do. In my very seductive and innocent voice, "Babe, so what is it you have to do?"

Totally ignoring my question Lamont turns towards me and says, "Rae, pass me the shampoo please."

He turns his back towards me so he cannot see my face. I know he knows me better than this and I know he knows this is killing me not knowing.

"Lamont, you want the shampoo?"

"Yes sweetheart, I do."

"So, babe, what you got going on?"

"Rae, I know you cannot help it. I know you have a need to know everything going on around you. But I'm afraid I have my own stuff and all I need from you right now is the shampoo. I love you, sweetie."

What? What did he say? I don't have to know everything, just some things; and right now, I don't need to know what he's up to.

Interrupting my thoughts, "Hey sweetie, the shampoo – please."

I don't say another word. I simply walk out of the bathroom and let him get his own shampoo. I slam the door on my way out. Lamont laughs so loud I can hear him through the running water and shut door. I know he's being a butthole on purpose. Well, everyone else has a secret, I guess him having one is fine. But that does not mean I have to let him know I'm not really upset.

Lamont finally comes out of the shower with a big grin on his face. I'm lying on the bed with the remote in one hand and a glass of wine in the other. As soon as I take a sip of my wine and place the glass on my night table, Lamont leaps on top of me.

"Now you listen to me Mrs. Harper, I don't want no-nonsense out of you."

I smile and poke out my lips, repeating what he just said in a question, in my best imitation of Cuban-singer Ricky Ricardo voice, "Okay, you don't want no-nonsense? Are you sure? Because if you want nonsense; I'm very good at that."

With one eye closed as if trying to see something in my face, Lamont moves closer to me, "Just what do you mean by that, my dear?"

Licking my lips and squirming under his naked body; in a very sarcastic tone, "Well honey, you know I try to be the best wife I can be and for the most part I do very well following your instructions, right?"

He eases up off me and sits on the side of the bed, as if he's waiting for something; he holds his hand out, "And..."

Now, in a Lucile Ball comedic way, without taking a breath, I quip, "I'm just saying, you said you don't want any nonsense out of me and you made the statement and you had the two negatives in one sentence which anyone knows the second negative in a sentence cancels out the first one and you are actually saying you want me to give you nonsense. All I was saying is I am very good at that."

My sweet husband looks at me with the most loving smile on his face, without another word he takes me in his arms and kisses me with a fiery passion. Once he finished kissing me, he says, "One of the reasons I love you so much is that smart-ass mouth and witty personality of yours. I cannot believe, I almost blew it, no one can make me feel so loved and safe."

That's my husband saying all the right things...whoa; did he just say he almost blew it? I cannot respond to that statement. I have to pretend I didn't hear it. He must remember, he has to remember, to make such a statement. How much he remembers is the real question.

As if he knows my thoughts, Lamont wraps his arms around me and loves me in a way only he can, for the rest of the night. In his arms I cannot feel anything unsafe, I cannot feel anything wrong, all I feel is love and comfort. At this point, I don't even care he has things to do that I don't know about.

Although the night seems to slip away fast, the morning is just as wonderful.

Birds chirping, children laughing, coffee percolating, and a loving husband's arms wrapped around me, is what I wake to. And I am incredibly happy. Not to forget to mention how excited I am about our family trip. I feel like a kid a week before Christmas; butterflies and all.

Today I will spend most of the day helping Ms. Elaine pack the twin's clothes. I know she also has to pack her things. This trip is for her to enjoy also not just work. There will be enough of us taking turns watching the children.

Ms. Elaine says I overpack, so she needs to watch over me while I pack. I guess the truth is she's helping me, not the other way around.

The wonderful voice of my woken husband brings my thoughts back to our bed.

"Good morning Sweetie." I turn in his arms to face him, "Good morning you, I don't need to ask you if you rest well since you were snoring."

With a look of surprise, pointing at himself, "Snoring, who me?"

Propping up on one arm, while his other arm remains on my stomach, "I can promise you without a single doubt, I did not hear any snoring going on because if I did, I would have put an end to such racket. Therefore, I must say, in all honesty, there was no snoring going on in this room."

I smile at him, "Oh, really, so please tell me what that noise was I heard coming from your open mouth?"

Opening his eyes wide, as if he's surprised, he hunches his shoulders, "See, there it is."

Sure, I'll continue to play this cute game, "There what is?"

"Proof,"

Now I have to laugh, "Proof? Proof of what my dear husband?"

"Proof you were dreaming because I do not sleep with my mouth open."

He can hardly keep a straight face.

"Lamont, sweetie, baby, let me explain something to you. When you are very tired, your mouth opens; on its own and this loud, lions-roar comes from deep-down inside of your throat. From what I have been told it's called snoring. I mean I'm not aware of any other name it has been called. Besides, I did put it on you, last night."

"Oh, you did huh? I thought I put it on you last night, that's why I was so tired and singing in my sleep. That was my Tarzan yell not snoring."

We laugh. Lamont kisses me with an open mouth. Yuck! After he gets his fill of kisses, he runs towards the bathroom, "Well since you had to listen to my wonderful singing voice while I slept, I figure dealing with my morning breath should be a breeze."

I grab a pillow and throw it at him just as he turns the bathroom corner. I'm grateful, so grateful and so deeply in love. I pull back the sheet, which was covering my naked body and get out of the bed, ready to start my day. With a huge smile on my face, I join Lamont in the shower.

Although my wonderful husband is trying to get me to stay in the shower a bit longer, I protest using the fact that we need to organize packing. Therefore, I leave him in the shower holding his private in his hands looking like he has been deprived of good, no, great morning loving.

From the sounds of it, I can hear Ms. Elaine in Ben's room. As I get closer to the door, I can hear him questioning her. Ben takes his time as if he wants to be sure she understands his questions.

"Ma-ma-Lane, tell me again where are we going, and how long are we going to be in the ocean? Then please tell me why, why I can't take my toys with me."

In her delicate tone, which produces only a slight very understandable Latino accent, "Benjamin, the only reason why you're calling me Ma-ma-Lane is because you want to have your way."

I peep into the room and as always, Ms. Elaine is on point; she's already got them dressed. Ben is holding her with both arms by the waist, looking up at her with those big beautiful eyes.

"Uh-uh, I love you, you know I love you. You are my Ma-ma-Lane. All I want to do is bring a couple of my action figures and one remote control car. That's all, I promise." He releases his hold just long enough to put up a scout's honor sign.

She pauses for a moment. I know she will never fall for that childish manipulation, no way. It never worked for me and I know these kids are not as charismatic as I was.

Without waiting for her to respond he continues his attack on her heartstrings, "You know you're my favorite, I love you more than everyone."

What, where did he learn that kind of con from? He's good, he may be running neck to neck with me, and I'm a pro. I must say 90% of the time I got my way with Ms. Elaine. After me, I know she knows the con game and there is no way she will give in to that nonsense, no way.

Slowly she places the folded clothes into the suitcase. With one hand she rubs the top of that spoiled son of mine head. Hold it; I need to add a few words; that spoiled-con-artist-most-beautiful-manipulating-clever-lovable-son of mine; that is.

There is no way she will fall for this weak stuff. She's still rubbing his head, "Well Ben, you know you and your sister are my favorite over everybody,"

What, she told me I was her favorite over everybody! And she continues to destroy my childhood, "You can take two action figures and one car, not the remote control it may cause some disturbance. Will that make you happy?"

Will that make him happy? Of course, you gave him everything he asked for. Nodding his head up and down in agreement, he wraps his arms around her again and squeezes. "I love you Ma-ma-Lane; thank you. You're the best."

I can't help it; I have to laugh. I grab my mouth and run down the stairs, so I won't spoil their moment. I'm sure the little princess is in her room putting aside all the things she wants to bring on the trip. After what I just witnessed, there's no doubt she will get her way too. *Ma-ma-Lane,* really? Now why didn't I think of that?

My ego can't take any more eavesdropping on my incredible manipulative little pride of joy. I guess I can start packing Lamont's and my things. One week away does not seem like I have enough time to get everything packed; especially since I have an entire week to change my mind about what to bring, over and over again.

Considering the fact that grandmother has something she wants to share with the family is like waiting for the plot to a very intense movie, or better yet waiting for the climactic moment after great foreplay. Either way, this trip should be just what the therapist orders for this family, along with a prescription for a lifetime refill on happiness.

Whoa, I almost forgot Uncle Trouble, I mean Douglas; he may have a few secrets of his own to tell. It shouldn't be too bad. For a while now, Uncle Douglas and his goons have been exceptionally well behaved. It's been years since Uncle Douglas became the mayor, he has done a great job. Although he has used his position and power, it has been beneficial for the most part.

It's funny how the bad reputations outlive all the good a person has done. I am so guilty of continuing Uncle Douglas' bad rap even when he's on point with the good things we all in this family call on him to do.

Most of his bad reputation is because of his attempts to protect this family. I remember about fifteen years ago, grandmother called Uncle Douglas to handle a situation with my sister, Danna. This is a secret only mother knows I know about. Well, I guess that's because she's the one who told me.

Apparently, Danna had a stalker; someone who just could not take no for an answer. At that time, I didn't know who the person was or how socially important he was but from what Mother tells me...Danna is living in Texas and a relationship she's in becomes violent. Grandmother calls Uncle Douglas from a Texas hospital where she and mother rushed to earlier, "Douglas, get here immediately we have a family crisis."

In the way that Uncle Douglas has always conducted himself when it comes to grandmother; he drops whatever he's doing and jumps on a shuttle-plane and arrives in a matter of two hours after the call.

Danna is lying on a hospital bed with fifty stitches in her face from a box-cutter, another fifty or more from being stabbed, a concussion, and a broken arm. Her left eye is completely shut, and she is going in and out of consciousness. After her attacker raped her, he stabbed her just missing her heart. According to the surgeon, three inches to the left and she would be dead.

I suppose no one told this stalker that no one, I do mean no one messes with The Queen-bee's family and gets away with it. See, grandmother issues out her own wrath on her family as she sees fit; however, no one else had better even think it's due process for them.

Danna gives grandmother all the personal information of her attacker. Solomon Prichard, a resident of Dallas. He is the heir of a very prominent realtor, developer, and construction company. Apparently, their contracts are for the extraordinarily rich and powerful. I don't know if that power is powerful enough to stand up to The Richardson-Mason Queen. Nevertheless, we shall see.

In turn, grandmother gives all the information that Danna gave her, to Uncle Douglas. Oh, please don't think for one second, he is alone. Oh no, his goons; Melvin and Tyrone are right by his side ready to do whatever grandmother and/or Uncle Douglas sees fit.

Uncle Douglas rubs Danna on the forehead, and tells her: "Now, listen here baby-girl we are going to find this person and don't you worry about anything but getting better. You hear me?"

As the good-good, pain medicine dripping through the I.V. into her arm, takes control of her faculties, Danna slightly nods her head.

Mother is darn near-hysterical, grandmother is so furious she is crying. They comfort each other as much as they can. With dignity only grandmother can display while giving an order to destroy someone's life.

Mother continues to tell me in detail, "Douglas, take heed to me and understand me clearly. This is my granddaughter laying here and the only one who distributes out retribution on my family is me. Look at her lying there," Grandmother points towards Danna as if Uncle Douglas needs to have her pointed out to him.

"Regardless of where she resides or the path, she has selected for herself, she is still and always will be a Richardson-Mason, and this is non-acceptable, and it will not be tolerated. Am I making myself clear Douglas?"

Uncle Douglas shakes his head up and down for yes. Grandmother continues, "My heart is damaged Douglas, my head is hurting Douglas, my feelings are bruised too, Douglas. Have I expressed how injured I am right now?"

Once again, Uncle Douglas shakes his head in agreement. Grandmother is not yet finished. "Well then, that ought to tell you what is essential. I should not be hurting more than this Solomon person and Danna should not be hurting more than he does either."

With a shaky voice and a fierce look in her eyes, grandmother issues her final words on this subject before embracing mother and allowing herself to cry aloud. In total honesty, I know grandmother could not fake her internal pain; h However, I know breaking down in front of Uncle Douglas and his friends only help to fuel the fire heading Solomon's way.

"I don't want the information of it from your lips Douglas, do you understand me? My preference is to read about it or discover it via the news. That means make it newsworthy, do you comprehend Douglas?"

Mother says that was the day she found out how sensitive grandmother can be about her family. Also, how her anger is not to be taken lightly. It's an exceedingly rare moment when grandmother cries and is caught in a position where she feels helpless. Looking at her granddaughter lying on that hospital bed makes her feel just that, and it's not a feeling she is going to live with.

Mother and grandmother stay in Texas, mostly at the hospital until Danna is released. Grandmother tries to convince Danna to come back to Kentucky to live; however, she is now independent, living on her own the way she chooses. Owning her own dance company is another factor that causes her to refuse the offer.

The Dallas police arrested Solomon, but he never even had the handcuffs on his wrist. His attorney comes to the police station and signs the necessary papers and he walks free; declaring Danna was delusional and infatuated with him. He even said he thinks her real boyfriend did this to her and this was a ploy for them to extort money from him.

Of course, the police didn't believe this crazy story; however, he does have the power and his family has the golden goose, money. Therefore, they did what any other intimidated police detectives would do; let him walk, and then called grandmother to tell her.

Although Danna won't move back to Kentucky, she will: however, come to stay while she heals and until this matter is solved; one way or the other. Perhaps the legal way would be a better solution for the idiot who did this. I don't know if the Dallas police can outdo Uncle Douglas in detective work. Knowing my family, the police may have the information first, but Uncle Douglas has it now and there is no way he will allow the police to have a crack at Solomon. Even if it means paying someone off.

I enjoy Danna while she is here with the family. We mend broken fences and get to bond as sisters should. The twins meet her and fall in love with their Auntie Danna. It's hard keeping my dad out the picture, but we manage it.

The news doesn't take long, not long at all. Just three weeks after his arrest, a special report came on the news, announcing the Millionaire Tycoon, Solomon Prichard remains were found lying twenty stories down from one of the penthouse high-rises he constructed and owns. A very touching and informative suicide note was found in his luxurious home; stating how broken up he was over his addiction to cocaine; which caused him to hurt the only woman he truly loves. Realizing he has lost her forever; he can no longer bear to live with himself.

Eavesdropping on mother and Uncle Douglas; I hear all the gory details grandmother refuses to listen to. She feels there is no need in her knowing the details as long as she knows the results.

Apparently, Tyrone and Melvin kidnapped Solomon, they kept him in a secluded place for three weeks; most of the time torturing him. They had him at gunpoint making him call his friends and family telling them how sorry he was for what he did to Danna. I'm sure he shed real tears; not from the sorrow of his deeds but from fear of what he was facing; however, they probably were more for him than anything he had done to my sister. Hhm, wonder who appears to be delusional now.

I'm sure the detectives don't believe this story any more than they believed the one Solomon originally told.

Although the incident was a bad one, it is always good to mend broken relationships. Danna and I became sisters during her stay and our relationship is a good one.

CHAPTER FIFTEEN

A Family that Vacations Together...

*Y*elling from the front door, "Let's get it moving, the car is pulling up now and I am leaving!"

The sound of running feet and loud screaming; like only Charmin can do, "No mommy, don't leave your little princess. Leave the guys, they are not ready."

Ms. Elaine, as usual, is on point and waiting by the door for all of us.

Ah, it has to be in the genes, girl power rules. Neither Lamont nor Ben answers to my empty threats.

Ms. Elaine takes a look at her wristwatch and grunts like only she can. Tapping the watch-face, "Rietta, you may want to yell out the warning again; it looks like the men in this family don't believe in being on time, ever!"

After yelling once more, all three of us ready-always-on-time-very-beautiful-women-who-enjoys-showing-off; we fold our arms while tapping our right feet waiting for the always-late-very-much-loved; did I say always-late-good-looking-men, to make their approach towards the door.

Finally, hearing the pitter-patter of Ben's running feet racing down the stairs; close behind him is Lamont, we can now leave.

I call mother to see if we are picking her and my dad up or meeting them at the airport for our flight to Florida. As I listen to the phone ringing, I feel the anxiety of a child waking up on Christmas morning. Mother finally answers the phone, "Hello, my dear child, have you guys left the house yet, or are you still waiting for Ben and Lamont?"

Taking a deep breath, I smile,

"You already know how it works in this family. Good morning dear mother and of course your right. However, we are in the car now. I just want to know if we are riding to the airport together or what?"

There's silence over the phone before she answers, "No, I think it's best if we meet you guys at the ship in Miami." Just before I can pose the question to her listening ears, she interrupts me, "As difficult as this may be and trust me I know you well. However, I need you to trust me and allow me the opportunity to play the mother's role; just for today and let me have it my way."

What? Did she throw a line at me I have no come back for? Well, having no come back has never stopped me from pretending I know what's best for her and it sure isn't going to give me pause now. Just as I fix the words in my head; mother speaks her final words into this conversation, "It's not up for negotiation, so please bow out gracefully; no one will know but you and I and I won't tell. Simply pretend you and I discussed this weeks ago and it's no surprise to you. This way you keep the upper hand on the rest of the family. Besides, as of right now you are the only one who knows I'm not meeting at the airport."

Ooh, this is truly my mother and she is so good at what she does with that wit of hers. So good 'til, not even I am a match for her. Oh well, I will do what is extremely difficult for me to do; mind my business until I'm face to face with my parents.

"Well okay; but daddy is coming, right?"

"Yes, we want to make sure we can get on board without anyone seeing us. So, truth is we took an earlier flight so we can get there before the rest of the family."

Taking out a moment to allow her logics to sink into my brain; I realize she's right. There is no sense in creating an uncomfortable situation until its necessary.

"Well, my dear mother, as usual, your ability to be tactful is logical and I totally understand. The children will be full of questions; however, I'm sure once

I explain this is an extension of our family secret concerning their G-Pa, they will be fine."

In an afterthought, "What can I say, but I am so happy you understand. I was afraid that militant persona you have would clash once I told you. Looks like someone is flourishing into a - well, me."

"I guess having a fit at this moment, about the fact you didn't tell me sooner; after, I have been so understanding would just push my ability to be mature right out the window huh? I will bite the bullet and swallow my aching desire to be difficult and just tell you how much I love and adore you."

I can hear mother snickering and daddy laughing on the other end. I guess I'm on speaker. What else can I do besides join in on the laughing?

Mother composes herself for a brief moment to finish our conversation,

"See how wonderful it feels to consider what's more important; to be able to weigh what really matters; to swallow your compulsion to be confrontational? I'm so proud of you and we will see you shortly."

I can hear both my parents laughing before Mother hang up the phone. And they wonder where I get that personality from.

The entire ride to the airport Ben and Charmin are full of questions. It's easier to get Charmin to stop with the twenty and five questions than Ben. Simply acknowledging the fact she is speaking usually does the trick even if you never answer the question. Ben will not stop until he feels his news-hungry-appetite has been satisfied; and not with any ole answer. No, it must make sense, or the questioning will continue much longer than most people have patience.

"Where are my I-Mee and G-Pa? Why didn't they meet us at the house, are we going to pick them up?"

Before I can answer the question, he zooms in for another,

"I don't understand why they didn't spend the night. Huh, why didn't they spend the night mother?"

Without turning around to face Ben, I try to get away with a vague answer,

"Now Ben, you know your I-Mee and G-Pa will be at the ship waiting for us. They made plans to surprise the rest of the family."

"Oh okay. What plans?" My very determined-to-get-a-proper-answer-son asks.

"Your grandparents, will be at the ship Ben, don't worry, okay."

I hear the seat belt unlatch. Before I can protest his head is over the seat right in my face: "I'm not worried; I know they will be there. I'm only wondering why they didn't spend the night and ride with us. If you don't know, you can say that. Did you speak to her this morning?"

As I try hard not to laugh in the face of this very precocious-so-innocent-still naïve-cute son of mine; I reply with caution.

"As a matter of fact, Ben, I did, and I-Mee simply said they will meet us at the ship. Is that okay with you?"

Easing his way back into his seat, he straps his seat belt back on. I glance back to look at him and he has the oddest look on his face; as if he's in deep thoughts. His glance moves from me to his father to the window. Finally, he takes a deep breath as if he's settling down.

As I turn around to get comfortable in my seat, Ben proves he is cut from the very same cloth as the Mason-Richardson's. "Well mother, perhaps I-Mee and G-Pa didn't want to tell you any of their business this time. You know you are always asking a hundred questions. I think maybe they wanted to be alone for a little while. I'll find out what happened when I see them; I know they will tell me."

Why that little sniffling-spoiled-can be-overbearing-sweet-very-innocent-ly-cute-brat; the nerve of him. Oh, I'm doing all I can to not laugh. I glance over to Lamont and he is in tears laughing as hard as he can. Ms. Elaine isn't doing a good job at holding in her laughter either.

I compose myself and take a deep breath while clearing my throat.

"You're probably right Ben; I ask way too many questions and they will meet us later and I am sure one of the first things on their agenda is to share with you why they didn't spend the night."

Motherhood does amazing things for one's self-made-highly-over-rated-and- probably-clichéd-notwithstanding-somewhat-unnecessary-ego. Oh well touché my dear son, touché. Dear little Ben got that, and I'm sure judging from what I just witnessed he will have plenty more winning conversions with me.

Ben settles down with whatever answers he is clinching to, in order to make himself happy. I guess that's the most important thing, his happiness.

Although Charmin is sitting quiet, I'm sure, she not only heard the conversation but has her own take on it. At her appointed time, no doubt, she will give her input. Ah, the sounds of mothering are so sweet at the birth and yet so challenging while growing up, but I wouldn't change a thing.

Lamont is quite entertained by his wonderful children. He seems to bathe in their self-awareness and growth. Like the proud papa he is, he sits there with a smirk of pleasure on his face. Ah, I love this man and I am so glad he is alive and well. Okay, and above all, I am so glad he is happy.

This trip is not only needed for the relaxation and family unity, no, not in the least. This is more about leaving the pains of clashing-destructive-pesky-wanna-be-the-wife-Robins behind. Oh, and all the other stuff attached to that tramp. Including but not limited to my secret that has the power to destroy my happiness.

I can't pretend I don't consider my position every day and weigh my options. The argument in my mind is whether I should confess to something no one has any idea happened. Then I argue back since no one knows, no one needs to know. My heart remains heavy on this topic. All I know is, I love my life and my family and the secrets I keep are for them just as much as for me.

Forgiveness is hard to come by. Especially when living in and around such a demand for a flawlessly painted picture of the family. Family they are, however, forgiving the offense is easier than forgiving getting caught and having to openly admit the flaws. Giving up anger and finding the weaknesses within ourselves; no not just the weaknesses but the necessity of the failures that will eventually help to build character, are almost obsolete. Perhaps this is the very reason why I should tell. Told secrets can serve as the glue to a falling apart structure. So then again, why bother? Since right now nothing is falling apart.

What the heck? There is that argument again in my mind, within me, saying not to tell it. By now I know that's the stronger voice, the voice I will listen to over my beaten conscience.

Finally, we arrive at the airport. Grandmother is waiting with patience, which she has lacked all her life. Mr. Charles is at her side as usual. What is pleasantly unusual is he's not in his uniform. He looks ready for a vacation and fun.

Perhaps I should not be surprised since this trip is for all the family and Mr. Charles is indeed a part of this family.

Charmin spots grandmother and takes off running to her waiting arms; Ben follows her lead. "Good morning, grandmother,"

Without waiting for Ben to give his greeting, Charmin continues her conversation, "Did you know I-Mee was not riding the plane with us? And she didn't spend the night with us last night."

As if she is deliberately tuning out the snarling look from Ben, she continues her news-woman headline.

"Did you speak to her this morning Gramps; do you know why she is not coming with us and meeting us at the ship instead?"

First of all, no one and I do mean no one calls grandmother, gramps. Secondly, Miss-all-in-the-mix hasn't given up one breath to allow grandmother an opportunity to speak one word.

Taking a deep breath; I bite my lip, hoping her excitement won't give her a river mouth and she spills the beans about daddy. We make sure to remind the children every day not to ever mention daddy to grandmother. This morning we did not remind them.

With a surprised look on her face, grandmother manages to force a smile. The little children may not know this, but I can see the corners of her lips twitching and her eyes piercing right in my direction.

I want to throw up my hands and yell, "I have nothing to do with this, on either side of this monstrosity." Well, it's not really a monstrosity but knowing grandmother, she will make it sound as such. Only because something is occurring in this family she doesn't know about. The fact that the-little-precocious-very-adorable-yet-sneaky-too-smart-for-her-own-good-grandchild, oh oops, great-grandchild has a scoop she knows nothing about, does not make it better, not one bit.

"Good morning my dear child; now tell grandmother how is it that you have so much on that pretty little mind so early in the morning? You should have nothing on your mind except how much of a great time we all going to have. I'm sure your I-Mee will explain her decisions when we all see her. Now give your; gramps a big hello kiss."

Charmin kisses and kisses her repeatedly, making sure she kisses every part of grandmother's face.

Wow, what? I can't believe it. She referred to herself as gramps and her facial expression changed from a snarling snare to a soft gentle smile. We haven't gotten on the ship yet and already this trip is causing some amazing changes.

Ben finally gets the opportunity to kiss her and greet her in his most impressionable manner. "Hello Grandmother; I'm so glad to see you."

Her smile appears to grow, "Well, I can promise you, not as glad as I am to see you. Are you ready to have a wonderful time?"

"Yes, I am. I am also excited to hear what I-Mee has to say. Aren't you... *gramps?*"

As grandmother plants a kiss and smiles at the generation of children that have no fear of her, only pure love; I see such a softness that is so rarely present.

I can almost go through the floor; I mean right through it and keep falling as long as I can. My stomach is vibrating from holding in the burst of laughter punching inside trying to get out.

Lamont eases up behind me and wraps his strong arms around my waist and whispers, "Although I know you never miss a thing; I still have to ask just to make sure we both witnessed the same thing. I can accept I may still be suffering from some small delusions from the *accident.* So, my dear beautiful, sweet, and almost darn near-perfect wife, did you just hear all that?"

Turning to face my dear husband; with a snicker that is trying to explode; ignoring the mention of his accident. "Why my dear-wonderful-generous, and closer to perfection than I; yes, I did. Yes, we both witnessed what could be a miracle in the life and times of grandmother."

On second thought, however, very carefully, in a whisper only Lamont can hear, "I mean Gramps!"

We both chuckle and look around to make sure we are having a private moment and lo and behold Ms. Elaine is staring right in our faces chuckling with us. This only made it funnier and harder to compose ourselves. Lamont, in his very smart way, steers us away from the gathering so we can laugh without controversy.

We bend over laughing so hard until we both have streams of tears flowing from our eyes. Each look at one another, results in another burst of laughter. We take time to walk to one of the airport bars and get a much-needed drink before the flight.

The flight is on time and the children enjoy their grandmother as they take turns pointing to the clouds and calling out their shapes. So far, there are hats, dogs, houses, and angles in the clouds. Ben declares he sees grandmother.

I enjoy the short flight in the arms of my husband as we travel further away from Kentucky and from any and everything that may cause us grief.

Once the plane lands; with eagle eyes; I immediately began my search for my mother. There have to be hundreds of people at this airport, perhaps even thousands. I don't know what color she has on or where we will meet.

I'm going to call her. Before I can reach for my phone Lamont grabs my hand. "Now, I've been married to you for over twelve years, and I think I know you very well. Step away from the phone and leave Irene alone. She will show up when she is ready." Holding his hand up, shaking it as if he's Italian, "Capisce, il mio amore?"

His accent stinks but I get the drift. I end my call before it connects . From the looks of it, no one else is even thinking about her whereabouts. The children are holding grandmother's and Mr. Charles' hands and singing songs as we stroll through the airport.

Ms. Elaine and Nylah are walking together having their own private conversation. Close behind them is Uncle Douglas; no doubt closely watching the switching hips of Nylah. As of yet all of his advances have fallen on deaf ears, and I've never seen her with anyone.

I'm not an Uncle Douglas fan but they may be good catches for each other. She may be the balancing beam he needs, and he can be the open door she needs (if you know what I mean).

I haven't spotted my sisters yet. It will be good seeing them; it has been much too long. This trip should help bring some unity and hopefully love into the family. Well, at least that's what I'm hoping for.

As we top the escalator, a man dressed in a very bright colored uniform is holding a sign with the infamous name written in bold letters; Mason-Richardson. As Mr. Charles leads the way, we all follow. Once outside, the driver opens the doors to a sharp limousine Hummer. Inside Danna and Kristy are sitting, sipping on glasses of champagne.

After our greetings and hugs, they hand each of us a glass of champagne and the children sparkling cider. We toast to a happy trip and eternal family unity. I wanted to say love, but unity is good.

The chatter in the limo is filled with questions for Danna and Kristy. They both look good and from the sound of it, happy. Danna now lives in Colorado Springs where she moved a few months after the death of Solomon. His family kept the pressure on the sheriff's department since they refused to believe the suicide story. She now owns and operates a center for troubled youth along with a dance studio. Kristy lives in Alaska with Nathan; her military husband and their two children.

Although I knew I had a niece and a nephew, this will be my first time meeting them. The rip in this family has been much too deeply cut for way too long.

"You're my Auntie Kristy, right?"

Kristy, smiles and nods while answering, "Yes, sweetie, I am. And I am very happy to finally meet you."

"I'm very glad to meet you too."

Charmin reaches out and holds her hand. "Hi, Auntie Kristy, I'm Charmin."

This is Ben's cue to join in on the conversation. "I'm the oldest."

Charmin looks at Ben with a frown on her face, "Ben, we are the same age, remember we are twins."

With a winner's smug look, he replies, "I know we are twins, but I was born first so I am the oldest."

Charmin takes a few moments to think about what Ben just said. Then, as if she had a brainstorm, "You're right. Ben, you are the oldest."

Just like that, the brief conflict is over.

We chuckle and try not to pay much attention to the private tug-of-war the children are having. They enter their own world of made-up villains and heroes.

Kristy pulls out her picture albums and we all take turns looking and passing them around the limo.

At the end of sharing her family photos; she hands me the albums, "I put these together for you to keep. This is Irene and Nathan Jr."

Now counting the surprise, I got this morning from Irene, I would say that is surprise number two, or should it be counted as two surprises, therefore making this actually three altogether. This is going to be some trip.

It sounds refreshing; however, somewhat odd watching the twins get acquainted with their aunties. Charmin can't quite digest the fact that I have sisters equivalent to the relationship between her and Benjamin. Her questions are unyielding and continuous.

Ben can't hold his peace any longer, concerning the name, "Irene is my I-Mees' name too. We just call her I-Mee because she is mommy's mommy. Did you know that Auntie Kristy?"

With a big smile on her face, she replies: "Yes Ben, I knew that. As a matter of fact, I named her after your I-Mee."

There's that puzzled look again; I'm sure by the time this trip is over Ben and Charmin will have a better understanding of their family. The old ones as well as the new ones should as well.

It appears Charmin has a few more questions of her own.

"Auntie Danna,"

Charmin looks Danna in the eye and waits for a response before continuing.

It looks as if Danna is enjoying the question and answer session, "Yes Sweet-ums, how can Auntie help you?"

Tilting her head up as if thinking: "Well, I was wondering if you are mommy's sister, does that mean my I-Mee is your mommy too?"

Benjamin whips his head towards Charmin and then he looks at me with the most disturbing look on his face. As if he just ate something very sour, "No, my I-Mee is not Auntie Danna's mother; my I-Mee is mommy's mother. Gramps can be her mother. Right mommy? Right Gramps?"

Lamont jumps in right on time, "Ben do you know family is extremely important? So many little children wish they had aunties and uncles. You are so lucky to have Uncle Douglas who is your I-Mee's brother and Auntie Danna and Auntie Kristy who are your mommy's sisters; oh, and now, two new cousins. You are a part of a huge family."

Benjamin and Charmin are looking a little confused. I can guess the idea of sharing their I-Mee with anyone is too much to think about. Grandmother interjects, putting the period at the end of the sentence.

"Benjamin, your father is correct; you and Charmin are part of a huge family and I am the matriarch. Do you know what that means?"

Charmin is shaking her head no, "I don't know Gramps." He turns to Ben. Do you know Bi-Bi?"

Ben follows suit shaking his head no.

Grandmother explains in a way the twins can understand and an answer they can live with, "The word matriarch means I am the head of the family, which makes me everybody's mommy."

Ben grabs grandmother by the neck and plants a kiss on her lips: "Oh, I understand now. "Do you understand Charmin?"

Jumping around in her seat, "Yep, I understand. I-Mee is our I-Mee only."

Children can make the atmosphere so uncomfortable. Lamont interjects again, "Yes, she is your I-Mee, but it would be very nice of you to share her with your cousins. I think they would love to have an I-Mee and since you two have the only one there is, perhaps you can share her."

Grandmother interjects again, "You know all the love and attention you both get from all of us who love you?" They both shake their heads yes. "Well, now you have two cousins, two aunties and a new uncle to give you more love. Now you have more people you have to love as well. You also have cousins you can teach how to play all the games you know. Now, won't that be a lot of fun?"

The car is totally silent; a pin could drop and be heard. Everyone is waiting for an answer from these precocious twins, who no doubt think they run the world. Wonder where they got that idea from.

Lamont reaffirms the necessity of an answer, "So, what do you think, you can share I-Mee, right?"

Charmin is the first to agree, "I don't mind sharing daddy, I can share. Well, I think since Re-Re has I-Mee's name she needs to have I-Mee too."

Ben doesn't look as if he is ready to give in so easily. With his forehead frowned, "Are they going to call I-Mee, I-Mee?"

Before Kristy finally speaks; I can hold my breath hoping this conversation with little people doesn't cause conflict.

Surprisingly, Kristy appears to be unmoved by the children's ownership of our mother, "Yes, Ben they are waiting at the ship to meet all of you along with their daddy. Perhaps they will have their own name for your I-Mee. But if they don't, perhaps it will be good if your I-Mee only had one name to worry about answering to. What you think about that?"

As we approach the piers, Ben finally relaxes his face and gives in to child-logic. Shaking his head yes, "I suppose that will be good. I know I-Mee will like that."

Charmin may have gotten more excited than we want her to, and she dispatches a no-no conversation, "They're with their daddy? My mommy got a daddy too and he..."

I quickly interrupt hoping I ended her announcement on time, "Sweetie, remember I told you everyone has a daddy and today we are going to meet your new uncle who is your cousins' daddy. Isn't that great?"

I dare not look towards grandmother, I know she heard that, and I know she is intuitive enough not to be tricked on any level. However, she does not say a word, not one word concerning what my dear daughter just blurted out.

Thank God; finally, the loading docks, this twenty-minute ride seems endless. We all pile out of the Hummer-limo and stretch, while the driver removes our luggage from the car following behind us. Oh, I forgot to mention there is a car following behind us, filled with our luggage. Well, there was no room in the Hummer.

Ship horns are blowing, people are rushing, bags are swinging, and the children are looking up, turning around in circles; as if amazed. Oh, I'm looking for my mother, of course.

Mr. Charles is acting like he is on vacation and does not touch a bag. I love Mr. Charles; he has always been a good, decent man. He may in fact truly be the only person grandmother has never disrespected. Well, not in front of me and I have never heard of any such behavior towards him. I have witnessed him checking her attitude on an occasion or two; perhaps three or four. Well, whatever it was; one thing I can remember is, she never responded negatively. She pretty much listens to him...imagine that!

How in the world am I supposed to find Irene in all this chaos? I better make sure the twins don't get so happy and run off. Just as I turn to yell their names, here is my wonderful husband, holding a child in each arm. With a smile on his face while holding them towards me,

"Looking for these?"

I should have known I had nothing to worry about. Trying to hide my concern and small-tad-bit of enviousness, "Of course not, I knew you would have them."

Giving me that look of, knowing better, "Oh really; you did huh. I guess that means I'm like every other person who does not know the real you, huh?"

I try hard to bounce back, "What in the world are you talking about Mr. Harper?"

Lamont still has that look of whatever on his face. "There are only two things on your mind right now. One thing is, knowing the children are safe, the other is finding Irene. Both of these things are concerns more pressing on your brain, than casual thoughts. So, my lady," Leaning in close kissing me, and then laughing, "Play that head game with someone other than your husband."

Okay, I'm quiet, very quiet. He knows me as well as I do him; he got that one.

Lamont puts the children down and walks them over to Ms. Elaine. After handing them over to her he comes back to me. "Well, now that the children are safe, let's get everyone to their cabins and then I can help you find your precious mother."

Bursting out laughing I have to admit he got that power over me. Irene is grown and I'm sure at this point, it's more nosiness than concern on my part. Ooh, I do not want to miss the introduction of my daddy.

Smiling, and hugging my dear hubby, I shake my head yes, "Okay, that sounds good."

I look around and grandmother and Mr. Charles are gone. I guess she's tired from the plane and car ride. I can imagine Mr. Charles vacation may be limited to grandmother's whimsical needs, or desires. She shouldn't need too much out here except a place to relax and eat.

As a matter-of-fact, everyone is gone except Ms. Elaine and the children. I thought we would meet the new additions to the family now. Well, perhaps during dinner.

Lamont reaches into his pocket and pulls out our cabin information, "Okay, let's get to our rooms."

Winking his eye at me, Lamont whispers in my ear, "Before we go Irene-hunting, your husband needs some of that good-good loving you got.

After we get Ms. Elaine and the children settled, I am going to do some hunting of my own in those clothes you're wearing." Licking his lips as if he had something good to eat, "And by the way, did I tell you how beautiful you look and smell. Oh yeah, I noticed that new perfume you're wearing; and I like, it; with your sexy self!"

With raised eyebrows and a grin on my face, I gaze into his eyes. His ability to be sensitive and respondent to my women-hood is just one of the reasons I love him so much. Oh-my-goodness this man makes me quiver. After kissing my cheek, he continues his planning on my body.

"I have the only weapon needed on this hunt, and you are my prey; consider yourself already caught. All you have to do is surrender, I got the rest."

The look in my husband's eyes is so sexy and sexually hungry. Irene can wait. This man of mine doesn't have to wait; I am his, as long as he wants and needs me. Shoot if he keeps this seduction going, we may not make it to the big family dinner tonight. I can feel tingles all over and up inside; whoa.

We follow Lamont closely, trying not to get lost in the pushing and shoving crowd of people. I'm excited and expecting us all to have a great time.

CHAPTER SIXTEEN

The Good Ship of Truths

Rubbing my eyes to see the clock, I realize after our three-hour sexual episode, we slept for another two. Surprisingly, no one interrupted us before, during or after. As a matter of fact, not even the children. Not even Irene, hey where is Irene?

I reach over and kiss my still sleeping husband while rubbing his shoulder. Slowly he opens his eyes, with a huge smile on his face. He stretches and reaches for me to come closer. I do.

"Hey there beautiful, how's my favorite girl doing?"

Hugging him tightly, I close my eyes and take a deep breath. Almost two and a half years ago, I could not see this moment. As a matter of fact, I can hardly remember how much I felt lonely and rejected by him. Now, this man, this man that holds me tightly in his arms loves me and wants me more than I have ever been wanted in my life by anyone.

The ringing phone snatches me away from my private thoughts. I wonder for a moment if I should even look to see who's calling. Another kiss from my Dear Lamont, "Go ahead and answer it, after all, we are on a family vacation and I'm sure everyone's wondering when we are going to make an entrance."

Looking at the phone to see who's calling; I anxiously rush to press the talk button without responding to Lamont.

"Well, well, well mother dear; about time I hear from you. And might I ask where you and my daddy have been?"

Clearing her throat and snickering, "Well, I see you still haven't gotten the chain of command right. I'm the mother and you are the daughter; grown perhaps but nonetheless the daughter."

Laughing out loud, I respond, "Now you know there's no point in pretending, I ask the questions and usually you answer them; except for today. So, Ma, what's going on, where are you guys at?"

Lamont looks at me and lip syncs while checking my grammar, "Where you guys at?"

I wave my hand at him and smile. "We are getting ready to come to the family dinner; are you both ready yet?"

"No, not yet we're just waking up, but we will be taking a shower and getting dressed as soon as I hang up the phone. What time did you and daddy get here?"

"I'm sure we were the first people to arrive here. We took an early flight so we would not run into any of the family. I think we did well; we are all aboard and all is well, so far."

"I'm excited and yet a tiny bit nervous. Are you nervous, is daddy nervous?"

The moment's hesitation before she answers seems too long.

"Ma!"

"Yes."

She said yes, does that mean yes, she hears me, or yes, they are nervous.

I look at Lamont and he's laughing; I point my finger at him and cover the phone, so Mother does not hear me. "Don't laugh at me; I'm not being pushy, just curious."

He stops laughing long enough to put up his scout's honor sign and cross his heart, "It sounds a little pushy to me. Leave your parents alone. If they are not nervous, you sure will make them nervous. Besides, we are family, and all is well, and nothing will ruin this family trip. So, leave Irene alone and let them get dressed so we can do the same."

With my lips squeezed tight I manage to take a deep breath and ball up my fist at my dear husband. Once my attention is back to the phone conversation, I can hear mother laughing, "Well, well this must be one of the pleasures of having such a wonderful son-in-law."

I remove the phone from my ear and look at it, as if she can see me, I stick out my tongue. Now Lamont is holding his stomach and bends over with laughter. I see what's going on. I have my husband and my mother ganging up on me. Fine, I have a father:, "May I please speak to my daddy?"

I can hear mother laughing before I hear daddy's voice over the phone, "Hello, my name is Rae-muffin, how are you? Daddy, I know you hear these two acting up and ganging up on me, right."

After he composes himself, "Yes, baby I hear them but don't worry I have your back. Let's get dressed and let's get this introduction started. I can hardly wait to see the look on dear old granny's face."

We all laugh since we both have the speaker up on our phones. "Okay daddy, just call us so we can come to your cabin and go to dinner together. You know, like a big happy family."

"Sounds good baby girl. We should be ready in about an hour."

We both hang up. As I sit here with my lips poked out and mother holding on the phone; I suppose they are concerned, and Lamont is right; my questions will only make them more nervous.

Lamont turns on the shower and escorts me to the bathroom. With the gentleness only he can give me; he washes my body. With each rub of the soap-soaked towel, he kisses my neck. Trust me, he is maneuvering well since this shower is no bigger than a linen closet, a very small linen closet.

With each kiss, I forget all about the secrets we are keeping. I rather bathe in my man's love and passion, as he bestows it to me once again under the warm running water.

Lamont calls Irene and she gives him the cabin number, its way across on the other side of the ship. Irene is determined not to let the cat out the bag before time. We walk quietly to the other side of the ship; right before we get to the door, Lamont turns to me and holds me close, "Look babe, I know it will be hard for you to hold your peace and allow your parents to do their announcement on their own; however, I urge you to allow them the opportunity to say whatever they need to say and respond in their own words."

Oh, my goodness, he always knows. I had a speech altogether in my mind on how I was going to say this and that. I know he's right and so does he; so, he continues, "I understand you were directly hurt from the decisions made by your grandmother and uncle. Today is not just for you, it is also about the pain and suffering of your parents, they suffered a lot. So, let them handle this one, okay."

I can't say anything, for some reason in my gut I feel a knot as if I just had been kicked. As un-understood and unwelcomed tears fill my eyes, I can't shake the feeling of standing on the edge of a cleft. Before I can come to grips with this flood of emotions, Lamont holds me tight.

"Come on babe, it's all good. You know Irene and your dad. They love you and will never do anything that will cause you to be disappointed or hurt. The wonderful thing is, they love each other, and they are living their lives together with no more secrets, no more hiding after today. We have so much to be happy about and grateful for. Now fix that face and let's enjoy this vacation and our family."

I hold on to him as tight as I can. Using my bad Spanish accent, "Okay Poppy you got it." Holding my fingers up like a scout. "I promise I will behave and be good and be polite and be nice to everyone and I will do my best to do my duty as the daughter and let my parents be the parents, okay Poppy?"

Holding my chin upward towards him; in his W.C. Fields interpretation; that he still and probably never will be good at, "Well then My-Little-Chick-a-Dee let's get to knocking on this here door and get this party started before I change my mind and take you back to our cabin for more snack-time."

Just as he wanted, I smile and chuckle as he knocks on the door. I know he's right; mother and daddy are due all the Al Greene's "Love and Happiness" they can stand, and I must act right. They also deserve the space to say whatever, however, they want to say.

After a few moments, the door opens. As I look up to the man standing there with his arms stretched out; I gasp for breath while trying to maintain my composure and hug my daddy tight.

"Hi, daddy!"

"Hi Baby-girl, how's my Rae-muffin?"

While still holding me in his arms he reaches his hand out to Lamont, they embrace while I'm squeezed in the middle. "Hey son, how's it going?"

Lamont answers: "I'm good Pops. You two look great, with the perfect color out-fits on."

I release my embrace and take a good look at my lovely parents and they are dressed as a couple. Mother has on a long flowing summer dress. It fits at the top to her waist; the bottom is sheer loose layers. The base color is a pastel lime green with soft colors of yellow, and my favorite, orange. Daddy is wearing a lime green dinner jacket with an open color pastel orange shirt and lime green pants. They look great.

I quickly begin to snap pictures of them. Then we take a few together. Mother takes a few of Lamont and I. Lamont is wearing the same outfit as daddy and me. Yeah, we planned it. After a few pictures, good conversation and a couple of glasses of wine, we decide it's time to leave and head to the dining room.

We check and double-check each other just to make sure we are perfect in our appearance. We discussed not having negative and nasty attitudes. We decide to hold our heads up and walk into that dining room with pride and class. Mother said we should act as if we all have been together for years and the only ones surprised are those already sitting at the table. I totally agree.

As a matter of fact, we will walk into that dining room acting as if this is an everyday occurrence. Yep, that's the plan; to act as if this is the way it has always been, and everyone knows about it already. In my heart I am rejoicing so much, I feel as if I will explode. Mother and I are in the center with daddy holding on to her free arm and Lamont holding onto mine.

Once in front of the doors leading into the main dining room, we pause. With smiles on our faces, we take one last breath before entering through the door. As we stand there for a moment, we smile at one another; almost chuckling. Boy, oh boy, I can't wait to see the looks on the faces on the other side of this door.

We enter and the room becomes silent, it's damn near deafening silence. Mouths are as wide as some of the eyes staring at us; however, grandmother doesn't drop a sweat. She smiles, stands up and slowly walks over to us. My heart is pounding so hard I feel faint. I look over at mother and her smiling face has now turned into a frightened look. But she holds her composure and grips onto daddy's arm so tight his sleeve wrinkles under her grip.

Then the unbelievable, the unthinkable and, never thought of, the astounding, incredible and, almost totally ridiculous, not to mention totally unthought-of happens. As I prepare my mind to wrap around the inevitable attack on my father, grandmother reaches out her hands towards my dad grabbing him while pulling him into her waiting arms. She hugs him and kisses his cheek as if he was her long-lost son. Mother covers her mouth as the tears flow freely down her face and me; well, I am happier than I have ever been in my entire life. The table clears as each and every one take turns hugging and welcoming my dad.

Even Uncle Douglas shakes his hand; not a miser-mediocre-I-really-ly-don't-want- to-do-this-because-you're-not-family-shake; but a really glad to see you, and you are welcome here shake.

After the welcoming ceremony ends, we all take our seats. Benjamin and Charmin sit on their grandfather's lap, each taking a leg. As usual, Ben asks the first question, "Grandmother, do you know my mommy's father? And do you know his name is Benjamin and that's where my name came from?" Without waiting for an answer, he continues: "I'm named after him Gramps, did you know, huh? Oh, and Granny I wanted to tell you all about my G-Pop, but I couldn't because they told me I had to keep the secret. So, Granny don't be mad at me." The way he waves his arms around the whole table to dramatically include everyone is hilarious.

Charmin jumps into the conversation, "Me too grandmother, I wanted to tell everybody."

Ben continues, "That's right Gramps don't be mad at the children, we only did what we were told to do, okay?"

Why that little weasel. And he is calling my grandmother; gramps and granny and she is not saying a word. She looks as if she's going to pass out from laughing so hard. I have never heard my grandmother laugh out loud and she is being loud. Grandmother finally composes herself, but she must wait until the rest of the table is composed because everyone is hysterically laughing. I'm not so sure what part of what's happening has them all laughing. Whether it's Ben's explanation or grandmother's laughter; either way they both are very funny and obviously feeling really good.

With tears in her eyes, grandmother answers, "Yes, Ben I know your mommy's father and yes, you are indeed named after him and I am so happy you have him in your life."

Ben replies, "I'm so happy too grandmother; I'm happy to have my own grandfather."

Charmin is bouncing on daddy's lap. Suddenly she stops her bouncing and wraps her arms around his neck and kisses his cheek and as loud as she can, she blurts out, "I always wanted a granddaddy and I'm glad you're my granddaddy, please don't leave us; ever. Did you hear what grandmother said? She said she's happy. Grandmother is not always happy, so I think you made her happy."

Daddy buries his head in her arms and weeps. Mother is rubbing his back and weeping right along with him. I look at my husband and he's crying; I take a look around the table and there's not a dry eye here. Ah, this cannot be a better family vacation, all my family is here, and it seems as if we are all happy for each other.

Now, I know there are things we are going to find out on this trip, but nothing can be as surprising as my dad being alive and with my mother...I think.

I meet my brother-in-law, Nathan Sr. and niece, Irene and nephew, Nathan Jr. for the first time. Benjamin and Charmin have already made the best of friends with them since meeting them earlier this morning. The children have changed seats and are seated next to each other. Leaving the ownership to grandmother and my parents at rest.

Danna taps on her glass while clearing her throat; giving a signal she has something she would like to say. As she stands up, she takes her time looking around the table before speaking.

Once she is ready and has everyone's attention, she begins: "It's so good to see everyone; I must say it has been much too long since we came together as a family. There is a saying that 'time heals old wounds'; I can vouch it does. There is another one that goes like this: 'Absence makes the heart grow fonder'. Again, it's true because I have missed you all so much. And I can tell by the wonderful greeting, you feel the same way. Let me first say,"

Holding her glass up for a toast, looking in my direction, "I am so happy for you Rietta and you, mother. I know how it feels to love and need the special people you care about to share in your life. That brings me to my secret. I feel it's better to show than to tell."

Danna quickly moves from the table and walks over to a table on the other side of the room. As everyone appears to be holding their breaths; well, I know

I am, we watch every move Danna makes. She reaches out her hand towards a person sitting alone. They take hands and begin the walk back to our table. Not one word, not a sound, nothing, nothing at all is uttered as Danna reaches the table with her guest on her arm. With her face lit up and a smile that appears to reach from one side of her face all the way to the other; she introduces her mate.

"Well everyone this is Curtis, my life-partner and husband."

Oh yes, I know grandmother is going to burst a blood-vessel, right here and now. Whoa, I just love this family and all their secrets. As we all wait for grandmother to make the first move, my father gets up and walks over to Curtis, the other black man in the family and shakes his hand while pulling him close and say: "Hello Curtis, I'm Benjamin," Reaching for my mother, she rushes over to his side, "This is my beautiful wife, Irene and, this is my daughter, Rietta and my son-in-law, Lamont, we are so happy to meet you." We rush over to them and extend our hands.

Grandmother follows suit as well as everyone else. Damn, I mean shit, what the heck, wow, this is amazing. Grandmother truly looks as if she is okay with all the surprises that are springing up in this family. I wonder what's next; I know there's a next, somewhere at this table.

I almost want to stand up and yell; n-n-n-n-n-next! Oh, this is the kind of stuff you can only hope to read about but who in the heck lives it? We spend most of dinner getting to know the newest additions to the family. Curtis is very nice, and grandmother is being very nice to him and to my dad. She is acting as if nothing is out of the ordinary.

Nathan is fitting in and appears to be having a good time as well. As for the children, it's apparent no matter what the situation is, children are resilient; they just bounce into a happy place no matter what. The endless platters of food are amazing. Seafood, steak, poultry along with endless veggies and pasta. And the wines are exquisite. There are so many varieties of juices and desserts for the children.

We laugh, apologize without bringing up entire old stories, and share lots of pictures. The table is totally undivided, and love fills this room. It only becomes silent once Mr. Charles says the grace and we eat more than any of us should. Each and every one of us makes a toast, giving a reason to refill our glasses. Uncle Douglas and Nylah are seated next to each other having their own conversation.

Suddenly, grandmother stands up and taps her glass. I guess this is her moment to make a speech. We all stop talking and eating and give her our undivided attention.

She starts by addressing my dad. She nods her head in his direction, "The first thing I need to attend to is the matter of Benjamin. I want to say please forgive me for being a judgmental self-centered, busy-body racist old meddling woman. I have done you and my family a great injustice. I realize my bigotry and ignorance has robbed my daughter of true love and my granddaughter of her father."

Turning her attention to my mother and me, then back to daddy, "All I can yearn for is your forgiveness and the forgiveness of Irene, and Rietta. I have befallen as a reckless woman. And I know no explanation, and no words, not even my apology; can give you back what I have stolen from you. I hope you can find it in your heart to please accept my sincere apology, please."

With tears falling freely from her eyes, she walks over to my dad with her arms outstretched, beckoning him to come close to her. All eyes are on my dad. He slowly stands while looking at Grandmother, then he turns his head facing Mother. She shakes her head in an agreeing yes manner. Daddy kisses her and then walks towards grandmother with his arms reaching out towards her.

This is amazing, simply amazing, watching this moment. Here I am, with my father and my grandmother hugging and everyone is showing love towards each other like family is supposed to. One after the other we join in.

After a few minutes of kissing and hugging all the newest members of the family, grandmother takes control of the room again by tapping her glass. She continues her speech.

"I would like to welcome Curtis into our family; also, Nathan; my new son and my great-grandchildren; Nathan Jr. and Irene. It is so excellent to connect with you all. I am so eternally appreciative to be here to see my complete family come jointly once again. As the matriarch, I may have forced some harsh judgments and almost certainly made those decisions being very closed-minded. I cannot give those moments in time back to any of you but what I can do is make up for them from this moment forth."

She takes her time making eye-contact with each of us waiting for an answer. One by one we all nod in agreement to let the past stay in the past and work on our now and the future. This vacation is more than I ever expected. I could not have imagined any of this happening. We have so much to be thankful for and so much to learn from and about each other. Just as I think all the surprises are out of the bags, grandmother taps her glass yet again. "There is one more thing I need to say to this family. After this, we should be able to continue this vacation, enjoying every bit of it."

Grandmother turns to Mr. Charles who has been a faithful chauffeur, confidant, manager of all grandmother's affairs and her friend. She reaches her hand out and he takes it in his hand and stands next to her. This is getting weird; grandmother is smiling while looking into Mr. Charles eyes. Whoa, what the... is he gazing into her eyes as well? I turn to mother trying to find something in her eyes that will erase the thoughts dancing in my head. But before she can; grandmother commences: "You all know Charles. We actually grew up together in the very house I call home. There is no single person in this world, I trust more than him. For the past eight years, we have been engaged with each other and we are proposing to end the tiptoeing around and live publicly as we select. Now that's that. Now, let's continue to eat our dinner and enjoy the rest of our vacation."

She sits, and then the next great thing happens; Mr. Charles remains standing and speaks. Turning to grandmother, he takes her hand, "I am not one for many words; however, at this time I feel I must speak." Looking at each of us, then fixing his gaze and attention on grandmother, "I have loved you for many years Catherine and we have enjoyed each other immensely, there is no way I can continue this relationship without you being my wife. Now, I know your greatest concern is your family's wealth, I am willing and ready to sign a prenuptial, as long as I can share the rest of our lives as your legal husband."

While every mouth is wide opened in surprise; grandmother stands back up as an afterthought, "We do love each other and frankly I am no longer worried about social concerns. I have always done what I was taught to do. That is true to the unwritten rules and unethical laws my forefathers instituted for this family. I must finally admit, I have not always been happy with those choices and I have not always been content." Turning to Mr. Charles, "Sweetheart, yes, yes, I will marry you and legally and openly live as your wife."

Total silence! No one says a word! No one moves! We are stiff like statues. Then Mr. Charles turns to my dad and reaches out his hand, and my dad, yes my dad gives him a small gold box.

He leans in and kisses my grandmother on the forehead and then on the lips. I mean a real kiss. I didn't think she even knew how to kiss. Wait a minute that means they do the thing-thing. Oh, my goodness my grandmother and Mr. Charles are getting busy; nasty-grown-folk-busy.

He opens the box and there is the most beautiful ring. There is one big diamond encircled by smaller diamonds shaped like a triangle. It is beautiful. Grandmother stands to face Mr. Charles as he places the ring on her finger. Mr. Charles holds grandmother close and says: "I guess we are having a double wedding right here on this ship."

I have no idea how my dad and Mr. Charles pulled this off; however, it is quite apparent, Mr. Charles knew my dad was present in our lives. Lamont takes my hand and walks me to the nearest corner. With my joyfully tearful eyes, I gaze into his sky blues as he tells me: "This is something you yearned for all your life and today you have found the peace and joy you need and want. I love you honey, and I am so glad you are my wife. Take a look around the room, you have more than money can ever buy; you have a family; oh yeah, and all their secrets. I am so happy we survived our hard times and I'm thankful you held on through them."

We hug and laugh. I close my eyes and thank the good Lord above for this trip. I can't wait to get my man into the bed tonight. I'm going to rock his world. I sure hope there are no more secrets; we have had enough of them. Well; except for mine, and I'm not ready for that to be told as yet. Judging from Lamont's statement, I feel he remembers more than he is letting on. But that is one shell I refuse to work at cracking. Shoot, it will open soon enough on its own.

Therefore, the rest of this trip will be great. After this overnight stay in The Bahamas, we will be heading to Puerto Rico, where we will dock for three days. After that, we are headed to Jamaica for four days and three nights, after that the ship will turn towards home headed for a two day stay in The Cayman Islands, our final stop before heading back to Miami is Cancun, Mexico where we will dock for three days.

By the time we return home, we will need a vacation to rest from our vacation. The men take a night without the women and it allows us females to talk girl talk; while allowing us to share some of the personal things we may have missed out in each other's life. Grandmother's secret may be the biggest surprise, after my dad and Kristy's husband Curtis, I don't know but all the sharing is great. The four children are tuckered out and tucked into bed in Ms. Elaine's cabin fast asleep. To our surprise Nylah, Mr. Charles niece finally breaks her silence and joins in on the conversation: "I have a secret I would like to share with the family."

For some reason, as we sit on the deck in our own private space, with mother, Danna, Kristy, Ms. Elaine, Nylah; every eye looks towards grandmother, although Nylah is speaking. Grandmother takes her time looking at each of us before she speaks, "Look, all of you are my daughters in some way. So, do me a favor and stop treating me like the warden. I know it's what I demanded for years; however, tonight we are equal…"

She pauses as if thinking, "Well, perhaps not exactly equal. But it's almost equal. The point is, we are all grown and we are letting our hair down; so none of that looking at me for my approval; well at least not while we're on this ship."

Grandmother refills her glass of gin and juice and then raises it in the air for a toast. Then she says the unbelievable, "So, fuck rheostat, and the order of it! For the rest of this trip, we throw it all overboard." She reaches her glass out towards each of us to tap in agreement, and we do indeed agree. Then after we all take a gulping gulp of courage and comfort, grandmother looks at Nylah, "Go on child, tell them the secret!"

Nylah's shy disposition has loosened some, probably since we have been throwing back drinks most of the evening; however, she still keeps silent except for laughter.

Mother raises her glass, we all follow suit, "Well then, I guess we need to toast to that as well."

We all laugh and take another drink.

Grandmother adds: "Can hardly wait until we dock back in Miami; then I'm back on my post; probably somewhat different since I can now do whatever Charles and I want to do out in the open."

We all gaps then burst out in laughter. Mother takes another gulp of her gin and juice, then pats her chest before saying: "Why mother, I dare not ask you what those things may be. However, since I think you are in the mood to tell, please do so after another drink. On that note, Nylah has a secret to share."

As soon as Nylah can compose herself from laughing at grandmother, she raises her glass to toast, "Well, I guess the best way to tell my secret is in a toast..."

Before she can say another word, grandmother interrupts yet again. This time she is peeping over her raised glass like a small child trying to hide, "All you want to share is about you and Douglas, right?" We all laugh, not so much at Nylah's secret but at the fact she thought we didn't know. With her eyes stretched wide open, Nylah gasps, "What, you know? You all know?"

Kristy is laughing so hard she can hardly sit in her seat since she is bending over so far. "Girl please, how long you've been in this family? Don't you know there is nothing that goes on grandmother doesn't know about? Once grandmother knows about it, my mother knows about it and then Rietta."

After she sips on her drink she continues: "The reason why Danna and I don't know is because we have been away for way too long. But that's changing right now; from now on we are all up in each other's business."

Nylah holds up her hand as if in class, "Well, I did want to be the one to say it. You all could have let me get it out. But what-the-heck, as long as it's out. Obviously, it must be cool, or we would have heard the disapproval before now. Besides, I knew about Uncle Charles and Aunt Catherine."

As if we are a chorus, we say at the same time: "What?"

Danna raises her glass for the next toast. I'm not sure if she can get it out before bursting a blood vessel from laughing so hard. "A toast to secrets no longer being secrets. Oh, and boy am I so happy there are other secrets juicier than mine. Whoa, I am happy, that the biggest secret is grandmother's. Now let's drink and be merry."

Kristy turns to Ms. Elaine and asks: "Ms. Elaine, got any secrets you want to share?" In an extraordinarily strong accent: "I'm too busy to have secrets, but maybe I'll find a secret on this ship before we dock back home and if I do, I will make sure I leave it right here on this ship. I'm not taking anything back home with me, too much trouble. All I need is fun."

She raises her glass and strangely pokes out her chest then taps beneath her breasts, "To, whatever we do on this ship stays on this ship. Let me tell you I saw a man looking at my tatas and I will find him tomorrow and let him know he doesn't have to just look. I'll give him permission to touch."

Mother screams out in laughter: "Oh, my goodness, Ms. Elaine got some freak in her. You better go Ms. Elaine."

We drink more than we should and laugh more than we ever did with and at each other. Before the night is over the men have to come and escort us back to our perspective cabins.

We spend the next day at sea; enjoying our children and sharing all the activities the ship has to offer. From fake surfing to swimming, from wall climbing to mambo dance classes. We eat some of everything and as much of it we can. By nightfall, the children pass out from fatigue and the grown-ups continue to bond.

All of the men in the family are doing great. Daddy and Uncle Douglas are becoming friends. I don't know if I could be so forgiving. Daddy is a good man and he has the enigmatic ability to put all the bad behind and look forward to better days. I admire him, I really do. Lamont, Curtis, and Nathan are almost inseparable. They act as if they have known each other for years.

The children are also getting along well. Ben feels he needs to be in charge since he is the oldest male child. Charmin couldn't care less about the chains of command. As long as she's having fun; she cannot recognize Ben's controlling nature. N.J. and Irene are easy-going; they cling onto their older cousins and follow them wherever they want to go. Daddy and mother are having such a great time loving each other openly and sharing the past few years of secrecy with us all. Uncle Douglas surprises us all; including grandmother when he takes Nylah by the hand and leads her to the center of the dining room.

Uncle Douglas nods at the bandleader and they began to softly play, Vanessa Williams', "Save the Best for Last." They slow dance for a moment while we all watch. I can't help but feel like I'm waiting for something. As the song plays out to a soft violin solo; Uncle Douglas slowly bends one knee. The lights begin to change color to a dim slow flashing red and blue. He holds Nylah by her left hand and holds the other out. A server comes to him with a red heart-shaped small pillow with a beautiful silver box covered with what looks like diamonds. Uncle Douglas removes the box from the pillow. Looking into Nylah's eyes, "Hey, beautiful."

Nylah is covering her mouth with her free hand. The tears flowing from her eyes are visible from where I am sitting. Her body is shaking. All she can do is nod her head. Uncle Douglas continues.

"I have loved you for three years and I am very sure I will love you for the next three hundred. I dream of you almost every night. Even when you're lying right next to me. Sometimes, I reach out to touch you just to make sure I'm not still dreaming. We have enjoyed every stolen moment every open moment and all I want to do is spend the rest of my life loving you openly and freely where our families and friends can see. I've already asked Charles if I can ask you to please be my wife, my partner for life. Please let me be the man who gives you uncon- ditional love and happiness. Please be the woman I will grow old with the one who loves me beyond all my flaws. Nylah, will you do me the honor of being my lovely wife?"

He opens that gorgeous diamond-covered box and takes out a ring with a blue diamond.

Nylah is standing with her mouth uncovered and open. Without doing what every other respectable woman would do; check out the size of the ring. She kneels in front of Uncle Douglas. Now on her knees, she wraps her arms around his neck, kissing him with passion for longer than the proposal.

Uncle Douglas finally gets the ring on her finger and wipes her tears of joy with his hands.

"Oh Doug, yes I will be your wife. Yes, yes, yes."

Grandmother is the first to greet the newly engaged couple and we all follow suit. I'm not sure which is more surprising; the proposal or the fact she accepted. I see how loving the right person can change one's character. I understand the change in Uncle Douglas now. Oh, by the way; they have been dating for over three years. Imagine that, three years and I didn't know. Oh Rietta, you're losing your touch, or just too busy with your own stuff.

Danna and I talk a little in private about her choice of a black mate. While we walk to the restroom area, I decide to ask, "So, Danna, where did you meet Curtis?"

She smiles while holding her head to the side. I can tell she's thinking; I hope I'm not being pushy. Danna stops walking and looks at me, she holds her arms out to me for me to embrace her. We embrace and she says: "I want to share this with you, I really do. Mostly because I think you won't judge me, and I hope I'm right."

I smile, "Danna, I will not judge you. But I do have another question that's more important than any other question I can ask."

"Okay, go on."

"Are you happy, is Curtis happy?"

Danna takes a deep breath and blows it out hard, as if trying to contain herself. She shakes her head yes while almost screaming: "Yes, I have never been so happy and in love with my life. I know some people say we shouldn't, but the way we make each other feel, is incredible and wonderful, and great, and oh, I cannot find the right words to describe how awesome and good we are for each other. The color of a person's skin should never be an issue. I loved Curtis the moment I laid eyes on him."

"You sound like you love him. Your face lights up while you're talking about him. How long have you been together?"

"We met about six months after I moved to Colorado. He was the administrator of a Center for Abused Women, believe it or not. We talked and he played a huge part in my personal healing process; you know, after the whole Solomon situation."

Although I cannot identify the measure of pain Danna went through, I saw enough of her physical wounds to know she was in pain. We talked enough at that time for me to know she was not in good mental shape. I dare not judge her choice of relationship.

"Danna, as long as Curtis makes you happy; live your life with him. What about his family, how do they feel about you and him?"

Now Danna's face changes to a sad look, "He lost both his parents when he was ten in a car accident. He's the only child, but he has an aunt and two uncles that absolutely respect and love him. Curtis was in a very emotionally abusive relationship for two years before we met. That's what prompts him to work in the arena of abused youths. He studied and found out there are so many different stigmatisms directly related to the emotional challenges, youths go through. Now we own our own place for youths. Hopefully, we can help them make better decisions."

I hug my sister as tight as I can. "I'm happy for you and so proud of you. We must stay close from now on, so promise me now we will."

I hold out my pinky to her to make a pinky swear. She does the same and we swear to stay as close as possible.

Lamont, Curtis, and Nathan are bonding and spending time together. Kristy is hanging around mother and grandmother as much as daddy and Mr. Charles can make room for. I must admit those two men are enjoying their freedom to be acknowledged. It is apparent that spending as much private time with their women is one way to proclaim that acknowledgement.

I am not mad at them, go daddy and Mr. Charles. I wonder if I will have to start calling him gramps. Oh, too funny!

As for Ms. Elaine, I do believe she contacted that man she was talking about since there are large spaces of the time none of us can find her. When she does pop back up all she says is: "Everybody's got their secrets, and there is nothing wrong with me having mine. I'll let you in on them when I'm good and ready, or maybe never." Then in that strong accent and her by-the-way attitude, "Besides some of the things you guys tell, I may never tell, who knows. I'm not trying to bring him home, just having some vacation fun."

We all almost passed out when she pulls condoms out her beach bag. It turns out her boo works on the ship as a chef. While holding up the long string of condoms she laughingly yells out: "Safe sex is the best sex, no matter how old you are."

CHAPTER SEVENTEEN

Are All the Cat's Out the Bag???

Tonight, we will all get together for our last family dinner on this ship, but we will be meeting for Thanksgiving. Grandmother, of course, will be hostess at the family mansion. Tomorrow we will dock in Miami and head back home. I have a new family with new relationships and old family with better relationships; I guess I can't ask for more. It's been many years since Kristy and Danna were at the mansion; they both seem to be excited to return and share the experience with their families.

This day is spent with all of us together doing everything. That includes laser tag and messing up my hair by the pool in a water fight. I declare the men in this family are as bad, probably in some cases, worse than the children.

Grandmother, mother, Ms. Elaine, Nylah, Danna, Kristy, and I are reluctantly sitting pool-side; since our protest was defeated. We figure the suggestion to spend the entire day as one unit should not mean getting sunburned, wrinkled skinned, or frizzy hair. Apparently, we didn't take into consideration that the children would reject every single suggestion we made and have some ideas of their own.

I don't care what anyone thinks, I believe the men in this family have something to do with the whole pool thing. These children have ventured all over this ship, engaged in every activity they had time to do in a day. The pool is going to make them want to nap.

We women, on the other hand, did everything we could to stay away from the pool. That's because we know the men in this family have a knack for pranks.

Being this close to water can only ignite their inner child, causing them to do the unthinkable to unsuspecting women, who just went to the salon and got new hairdos.

The first accidental splash came from the most innocent and youngest male child, N.J. Now pardon me if I am incorrect, I mean I can understand how accidents happen. However, N.J. wet grandmother when he was trying to throw water on his dad, who was nowhere near his tiny hands.

Now I don't know if the women are thinking about the conversation mother and I had with them the moment I knew we were going to the pool. We both told them the men were up to something because they sent Ben to be the spokes-man. Ben had that little smirk on his face along with that "I'm so innocent" look. I know my child, that innocent look is camouflage.

After the mistaken splash, I look at mother and she looks at me. We slowly get up and ask if anyone wants a drink. Everyone holds up their glasses for refills. Mother and I slowly walk to the nearby bar to get drinks. As we stand there together, we can see everything our wonderfully-made-men are doing. Although they are acting like nothing is going on while they horse-play with the children, we see it's really a huddle for planning. Even daddy is planning. They are so busy planning on the group of the females still sitting at the pool; they don't see us looking at them.

Grandmother is laughing, out loud laughing. I mean we can hear her laugh-ing, out loud; she's doing a lot of that since we boarded. My sisters are simply enjoying every word grandmother is saying and Ms. Elaine and Nylah are bot-tom-upping their glasses. I wave for Ms. Elaine to help with carrying the glasses.

Once she gets to us, she asks: "What's going on? I know something is going on. I can tell from the looks on your faces. So, what's up?"

Mother leans close to Ms. Elaine so no one but us can hear her. "Okay, listen up. I know you have no way of knowing this, but the men are up to something and they think we don't see them." Ms. Elaine attempts to turn around to look at the men and mother grabs her arm, "Oh, no, don't look until I tell you to. That was no accident that little N.J. threw water on mother. That was to see her reac-tion. I cannot believe mother is oblivious to what they are up to."

Ms. Elaine leans in closer to whisper, "Okay, you guys know this family so what's next? I mean, what are they going to do?"

Mother takes a sip from one of the seven glasses the bartender filled and sat on a tray for us to carry back to the waiting women. Mother shakes her head up and down, "Yep, they are going to wet every one of those, totally-un-aware-good-looking-sun-bathing-beauties, who all just got new hair-dos. They know we don't want to get wet." Mother looks down at her outfit and takes a spin to show it off, "Look at me, look at us, we all went shopping to get sexy and gorgeous, for the boys...I mean men."

We three laugh; mother continues, "I can't wait to see how mother responds after she's dumped in the pool; because that is exactly what they are going to do. As for me, I think I will stay right here for a minute and bring the drinks after it's all over."

Ms. Elaine is laughing and looking at mother strangely. Finally, she asks, "What if they want all of us at one time and decide to wait until we go back to the side of the pool?"

I am simply taking in the scene in the pool and poolside. I see the men huddling and whispering. Every now and then Lamont glances at me and nods his head. I can tell they won't wait for us, "No, they will get the women by the pool and try something else later. But they are not going to risk getting any of us, for the sake of us three. No, the prize is sitting right there totally unaware of the plot."

Ms. Elaine snickers a little and then says: "She can't see it coming, she's in love. Grandmother's character is much softer and much more pleasant than it used to be. That kind of tenderness comes when a person falls in love."

Mother and I just stare at grandmother and then at each other. Ms. Elaine continues, "Look at her, look at the smile on her face and look at her eyes gleaming. Yep, she is in love."

Silence, that's all there is, total silence. I guess Ms. Elaine is right. I also guess that cliché is more than idle words, about seeing from the outside. All this time we did not see the love grandmother and Mr. Charles has for each other. I also guess we were so stuck in her past we couldn't see her present.

Look at her; she is glowing, and I've never heard her laugh out loud in front of strangers before. I have never seen her play a game or let herself go and enjoy life. She has always been so stuck-up and stiff-necked-and absolutely controlling.

I look at mother who now has a smile on her face and tears of absolute joy streaming down her face.

"Mother, what's wrong?"

She wipes her face and smiles, "Nothing is wrong, sweetie. I've always known something happened in mother's life that made her so bitter and overly strict. I also realize something, and someone has made her feel safe enough to love and be loved. Hearing her share her private feelings and seeing her openly soft, is an incredible experience. I'm so happy for her. I'm so happy for me; to be witnessing her change.

She has been such a hard stone, doing her best to keep her family together. Although sometimes her choices were brutal and very wrong; she did what she thought was best. I am so happy for her and Mr. Charles."

I reach over to hug my mother and Ms. Elaine joins in. while we are having our own private moment, Ms. Elaine says: "Well, I guess you need to find another name for Mr. Charles since it looks like he will be your daddy soon."

We burst out laughing and mother adds a spin to the tale, "Wow, you are right. But I will not call him daddy; I'll leave that for mother."

We fall out with laughter. We each take a glass from the tray and bottoms-up. We stay at the bar waiting for the inevitable to happen. We don't wait long. I know it's not too long because we still have four of the eight glasses filled. As we begin to work on the four remaining glasses, the battle begins.

Mr. Charles comes behind grandmother and leans down to say something to her; when he does, Daddy grabs her by the legs and Mr. Charles got her by the waist...in the pool, she goes. Before anyone has time to respond Nathan grabs Kristy and in, she goes, Uncle Douglas is right next to them with Nylah in hand.

Danna escapes by a hair, running towards us. The battle of the sexes is on and popping. Lamont runs to the bar and grabs Ms. Elaine. She is kicking and screaming all the way to the pool; she even throws in some little Spanish cuss words. The men don't stop until all of our sisterhood is in the pool, screaming and holding their soaking-wet-new-hairdos. Ah, it's hysterical, especially from the side-line, with more drinks than we should drink.

Mother holds up a drink in her hand towards everyone in the pool, "That looks like so much fun. Please go on enjoy yourselves."

Daddy points at mother, "Don't worry, by the time the night is over, you may wish you were in the pool."

Mother stops laughing and looks strangely at me. Whispering, "What do you think he means by that?"

I answer with a second thought, "I don't know ma but that sounds like a threat. What you think they have in mind?"

Before she can answer, Uncle Douglas joins in on the unknown threat, "Oh yeah, no pool, that's fine, but the both of you will be got before the night is over."

Mr. Charles: sweet innocent Mr. Charles, "Yep, you two just stay over there and simply worry what's coming next."

Now the unexpected; my dad! "Poor, poor babies, have no idea you are standing on the wrong side of the fence. Poor things but you gotta learn."

Mother and I, then takes a gulp of the last drink left, Mother smiles, "What do you suppose they mean by all that?"

We look at each for an answer, we know we cannot give to one another. I take a deep breath, "I don't know but I am feeling somewhat threatened and perhaps a tad bit concerned. I mean I'd rather have my hair wet with water than perhaps food or powder or something. It's just no telling with these guys."

Hunching our shoulders and shaking her head from side to side. Without another word, we finish our drinks. Mother yells at the men, "Timber!"

Everyone else laughs. I think for a moment and consider us jumping in on our own, "Look Mother, if we jump in ourselves, the men will still get us because they have been cheated out of the opportunity to get us, which is what they want."

Mother smiles and agrees, "My dear child, you are so right. So, let's go to our poolside seats and wait for the conquering kings to get us." As an afterthought she says: "Mother looks like she is really enjoying herself. She isn't complaining about her hair or anything."

I think for a very brief moment, and nod my head no. We order another round of drinks for all our soaking-wet-sisters and head back to our pool-side-lounge-chairs. We sit and hold up our drinks gently tapping each other's glass in a toast. And we wait for the men to make their move. But they don't budge. They just stare at us with silly grins plastered to their faces. As if they are the cats after swallowing the canaries. Danna slowly joins us at the poolside.

Mother leans in to whisper to us, "I don't think this is what we had in mind. They are not moving."

I respond, "Yeah, I think they are plotting something else. Do you think they have something else in mind? I mean look at them, acting as if they aren't even interested in getting us in the pool."

Before Mother can answer, daddy gets out of the pool and walks towards us. Mother says, "Okay, here comes your father. I guess I'm going in the pool next."

However, daddy leans down and kisses mother on the cheek. He then whispers something I cannot hear in her ear. Mother looks up at daddy strangely and then laughs out loud before saying, "Oh, come on, you can't be serious."

Daddy nods his head up and down, "Yes, I am serious. It's either our way or something you won't be expecting. So, it's your choice."

Mother is laughing so hard; she makes me laugh and I have no idea what they are talking about. I look over at everyone else and everyone is laughing. Now I feel as is if I'm the only one in the dark. Now I feel as if I am standing alone. I look at Mother with my stern look. It fazes her not. She and daddy just keep laughing. All of a sudden, while I'm looking at mother and laughing, I am swooped up in the air by my ever so wonderful-sneaky-turn-coat-husband and thrown into the pool. Totally not ready! Once I get my composure and get the water out my eyes, I look up at mother and see her and daddy laughing and toasting drinks.

I yell, "Mother, how could you?"

Mother replies: "I love you; however, all is fair in love and war. We still girls; I'm just the dry one, with my new hairdo; that's all."

We all laugh, and daddy gently carries mother into the pool. I did say he carries her, not threw her. Oh, those two. We enjoy the rest of the day, simply doing all the things we thought we were too sophisticated to do, and it's refreshing. Danna gets dumped again as soon as mother leaves her side. All the rest of us soaking wet gals get her.

Tonight, we will have our final family dinner on this ship before heading into our separate directions. This family vacation has been the medicine we needed in order to heal. Grandmother is so wise.

We all rest before dinner. We ladies do our best with our hair and join each other in the fabulous dining area. As we walk in, the dining room is decorated in white and gold trimmings all around the ceiling. There are gold and white suspended balls hanging from the ceiling. A live band is playing soft jazz music. Soft lights are circling the room.

The men have left our side and disappeared as we ladies huddle together wondering what they are up to now. Grandmother speaks first, "Where are they going?"

Mother answers, "Whatever it is, they are in on something together."

We slowly find our way to the middle of the dining room table that has been elaborately decorated. There are cards in front of each set with our names on them. We each sit in our assigned places. The children even have nameplates. Since this is our final night, we all are dressed in evening gowns and our men in black tuxedos.

No one is talking, we just sit in anticipation. Finally, after a few moments, the ship's captain appears and announces, "Good evening to all my fine guest and passengers. I am Captain Yahoshua Meems, it has been a great pleasure of mine to host these past two weeks of fun, happiness, and bliss with each of you. I truly hope you have enjoyed your experience on our cruise ship, The Queen Diamond.

One of the things that never seems to fail is, no matter how long I've been in the position of cruise captain, I am always pleasantly surprised and extremely happy for each guest experience."

As we remain seated, we glance at each other. I am still wondering where our men are. The captain continues his speech.

"This is our final night for this trip. Again, I hope you have enjoyed yourselves."

He pauses and looks around the room, before continuing. "Tonight, we are celebrating a very unusual yet exceptional occasion."

As he pauses, we all take the opportunity to clap. Then the captain continues, "Each and every guest on this ship is important and very special and I want to say thank you for cruising with us here on The Queen Diamond."

Once again, the captain takes a look around the ship as if looking for someone or something. He takes the mic from his face and motions to one of the shipmates to come to him. After whispering in his ear, he turns his attention back to the audience.

"I haven't gotten any complaints on this cruise, most times I don't. I think that is a great thing. Therefore, I can conclude you all have enjoyed the amenities and the activities afforded to you on this fine cruise."

The captain is interrupted by the shipmate returning to whisper in his ear. The captain shakes his head and smiles, then continues speaking once again. "However, here we are at our finale and last night and this is going to be a fantastic night for us all to enjoy and never ever forget. Without any further delay, I introduce to you the chaplain of our cruise ship. Chaplain Christopher Brown."

The captain hands over the mic to the chaplain and disappears from sight. We all are looking at each other, still waiting on our men to return. The chaplain clears his throat before speaking, "Good evening ladies and gentlemen, it is truly an honor for me to be standing here before you on this joyous occasion and glorious night. I know most of you are in suspense and are probably anxious to know what's going on. Well, allow me to explain, there is a couple of very lucky gentleman on this ship that have found their life-long mates and want us all to share in their ceremony of matrimony."

Grandmother, clears her throat and takes a look around the table, "Oh, my goodness, they didn't."

Mother responds, "I think they did."

Ms. Elaine chimes in, "This is wonderful; I am so excited."

I, on the other hand, am totally confused. "Who did what?"

Grandmother wiggles in her chair staring at the chaplain. "Rae, where are the men? Have you seen them at all since we sat down?"

I shake my head slowly, still bewildered.

Mother starts giggling, "Just wait for it Rae, just wait for it."

I want to ask to wait for what, but at this moment I feel somewhat lost and feeling just a tad bit silly that I have not reached the conclusion grandmother, mother and Ms. Elaine reached. Now, to add insult to injury of my ego, Nylah gets it before I do, "Wow, yes, oh yes, I think they did do it."

She is wiggling in her seat like a hot jumping bean. Mother has both her hands on her face, one on each cheek and grandmother is smiling so big, I'm sure her face hurts. Then if that's not good enough I see Charmin and Li'l-Irene heading in our direction with baskets full of roses. The baskets are practically running over with red, blue, orange, white and yellow roses. The girls have the same roses in their hair. Then here comes Li'l-Ben and N.J. dressed in tuxedos with white roses in their pockets. Like a speeding train, well, perhaps, my train was not so speeding since it took me so long to get what was going on, I realize there is a wedding happening. I wonder whose.

As Mr. Charles steps from behind a white and gold curtain, the band plays soft jazz. Right behind Mr. Charles comes my dad, then my handsome husband and Uncle Douglas. Each of them stands right beside the chaplain on his right side facing the audience.

I gasp, and yes, I finally get it.

My two sisters, Danna and Kristy and Ms. Elaine stand up and Danna reaches for grandmother's hand, Kristy reaches for mother's and Ms. Elaine mine and Nylah's. We stand and they escort us to the stage where our waiting husbands and soon-to-be husbands are standing.

Grandmother stands right next to Mr. Charles, mother next to daddy, Nylah next to Uncle Douglas and I, Lamont. The chaplain begins by saying: "This is what a family is made of. Changes that produce growth. Not just numerical growth, but growth in understanding, growth in peace and most of all growth in love. As we gather here today, let us celebrate true love and happiness with these four couples that are standing before us. As they promise to love, cherish and commit the rest of their lives to make each other happy."

With that said, he prompts the exchanging of rings. With no surprise, Ms. Elaine and my sisters pull out rings for the men they had secretly hidden for them. And we promise to continue to grow together as a family better than we were before. In a moment we are reunited and united as husbands and wives.

CHAPTER EIGHTEEN

Back to Reality

Three weeks back, and all is well. The family is planning to get together at the mansion for Thanksgiving. In the meantime, we will all enjoy conversing with one another via phone, e-mails, and social media.

The children are very happy to have met their cousins, aunties, and uncle. They quickly adapted to calling Curtis, Uncle, and Mr. Charles is Grandpapa. Explaining how Mr. Charles is no longer Mr. Charles but grandpapa is complicated to me. So, I do what I think is best, I turn that portion of business over to my sweet-wonderful-dear-totally-understanding-one-of-a-kind-mother. Let me just say; I truly wish her the best with that task.

Now that we are home, I know the twins will not forget the promise of an explanation concerning their new uncle and grandpapa.

The phone is ringing, and I hope that is my contractor telling me he has completed the small fill-ins that remain at the center. Our opening is due in just a few short weeks. Although I'm extremely excited, I must admit I am equally just as nervous.

I answer the phone; without recognizing the number, "Hello."

The voice on the other end is one I recognize as the one I want to hear from, the contractor. Yeah!

"Hello Mrs. Harper; how are you doing today?"

"I'm great Mr. Marshall. How are you?" I am holding my breath since his tone does not betray the reason for his call.

"I'm good. Thanks for asking. How was the family vacation?"

I know Mr. Marshall is being very cordial and sincere; however, I am about to explode if he doesn't get on with the reason for this call. But I will play nice and pretend to be patient.

"The vacation went extremely well. We honestly had a great time becoming reacquainted with family and enjoying new family members."

I need to jump right in now and ask him about the center. I feel like I played cordial long enough. Okay, brief but long enough to get the formalities out the way. Right?

"So, Mr. Marshall, tell me, how's everything going at the center? Were you able to get those few little problems fixed?" ...and I hold my breath

After a few moments of silence, "Now Mrs. Harper, you know I know how much you want to open in a couple of weeks, right?"

Slowly I answer, "Yes."

Slowly, he takes his time before continuing his conversation as I continue to chew my nails.

"Well, I would go down the list of things that had to be fixed."

Oh, my goodness he is taunting me purposely. However, I will pretend to be patient; silently praying he does not go through the list.

"Mrs. Harper, Mrs. Harper, are you there?"

I take a deep breath before answering, "Yes Mr. Marshall, I'm here. So, can you tell me just where we are standing with my schedule opening?"

"Well, of course, we are on schedule; everything is completed, and you are all good to go."

My heart suddenly stops doing involuntary flips and my nails are secretly thanking me for releasing them from the sentence of total destruction. I take a deep breath before responding to the great news. "Thank you so much Mr. Marshall. I knew you would not let me down."

I can hear him snicker a little before he responds.

"No problem. I know your opening will be great. If there is anything I can do for you, please do not hesitate to give me a call."

Anxiously, I bid him farewell so I can call Lamont and my parents to share the great news.

I call Lamont's cell. As the phone continues to ring, I hold my breath, waiting for him to answer; however, the call goes unanswered. I call mother and daddy.

Mother answers on the second ring, "Hello, dear-wonderful-mother of mine. How is your morning going so far?"

With as much enthusiasm as the happiest women in the world can muster, she answers, "Sweetie all is so good. Your father and I are having brunch on the patio. How are you this awesome day?"

"Yes, it is, an awesome day mother. Is daddy sitting next to you?"

She laughs for a moment, "No, actually I'm sitting on his lap. Do you need to speak to him?"

"I need to speak to you both. Put me on the speaker."

The voice of my dad brings even a bigger smile to my face.

"Hi Muffin; what's up?"

"Hi daddy, I have some good news and I want to share it with my two most favorite people in the world."

Daddy cannot help but to jokingly challenge my remark.

"The most favorite?"

"Okay well, the most favorite next to Ben and Charmin, and of course the father of my two pride and joys; after them, you both are the most."

We all laugh before I continue with my great news.

"Mr. Marshall called and he said all is a go for the opening of the center."

Just as most of the time; both my parents answer at the exact same time, saying the exact same thing. "Sweetie that's so wonderful."

Daddy asks: "What will the opening date be?"

"Well, I was thinking since the family will be getting together during Thanksgiving time, we can do the opening around that time while everyone is here in town. What do you guys think?"

Again, they answer as if they have rehearsed their timing, "Sounds good."

"Well, okay, I have to call my dear husband now. You two enjoy the rest of the day and I shall speak to you later. Love you."

Mother asks, "You called us first?"

I explain that I called Lamont first, but he didn't answer. Mother and daddy say their so-longs and I love yuzu and hang up. I attempt to call my dear husband again, without an answer. He hasn't done this in quite some time.

Hhm, that's strange. Usually if he leaves the office he calls me. Oh well, perhaps he's in a meeting or something. I leave a message on his cell phone and decide to call the office to speak to Terrence, his assistant.

"Hello Terrence, how are you?"

"Well hello Mrs. Harper, I'm good how are you doing?"

"I'm good Terrence. Is my dear husband around?"

He immediately answers, "Oh no, Mrs. Harper, he went out to run an errand."

I think to myself, an errand. However, I simply tell Terrence to let him know I called.

I wonder what errand he had to run, instead of his assistant doing the running. Isn't that why assistants are hired? I try his cell once more, and yet again no answer.

For some reason, my heart is palpitating, I suddenly feel light-headed from the nervousness that is quickly invading my being. Where can Lamont be and why isn't he answering his phone? The questions are coming quicker than I can think.

I try Lamont's cell once more before all the blood feels like it's draining from my face due to thinking the worse. The worse is a thought consisting of his memory returning and him hating me. I haven't had to think about the secrets I've been keeping in so long, I foolishly dismissed them from all my thinking. Now I cannot reach Lamont and all I can think about is lies and memory.

Calling mother and daddy will only make them worry when perhaps there isn't anything to worry about. Maybe, I'm just being a silly wife and need to calm down and understand he may be in the middle of an important meeting and cannot answer his phone. He will call as soon as he's done; I know he will.

There are other things I need to be doing. The twins are off to school and I can go by the center to take a look for myself at all the work Mr. Marshall has completed.

I get myself together trying not to think too much about the what-ifs. I head for the garage, get in my car, turn on the radio. My girl Mary J. is playing, and I begin to sing out loud trying to drown out my own imaginations loud voice of doom. As I open the garage door to leave, there right in front of the garage door stands the slender well-dressed Robin.

My mind can't think fast enough to call her all the names I previously fixed to her existence. All I can do is one of two things. Step on the gas and run her nasty-home-wrecking-stubborn-curmudgeon-intolerable-rejected ass over or, hear what she has to say, which will answer all the questions I never had the opportunity to ask.

Logic overtakes anger and I turn off the car and get out. I quickly walk to the front of the car where she stands.

"Hello Robin, how can I help you?"

She looks as if she'd been crying. There is absolutely nothing inside of me that cares an inkling of the why's or what's; however, I do my best to be as cordial as I can, considering she is at my home, standing in my yard, in front of my garage.

Robin looks at me and shakes her head from side to side; in a no fashion before she speaks. "What is it you have, that I don't? Why does he stay with you, when I love him so much; can you tell me why?"

The first thought in my mind is to punch her in her face but, no, instead I hear her clearly say he chose me not her. I don't answer; I simply look at this pitiful-sorry-low-grade-miserable-female-dog, as she continues to whimper.

"I know my Monty-Poo loves me. It's you who is keeping him from me. It's your manipulating ways."

Did this heifer just call my husband by a pet name again? She is sick, I know she is sick. Yet I refuse to say one word, and she continues.

Wiping her eyes as the tears fall, she begins to slowly walk towards me. I notice her shaking uncontrollably. I don't know what it is but suddenly I feel as if I need to be somewhat cautious.

"You and those children you claim are his is the reason why he won't leave you. He doesn't love you; he loves me. I'm telling you this only once. Leave my man alone, do you hear me, leave him alone so we can be happy again."

This is when I notice the bat she has hiding behind her back. This woman is crazy. I begin to move back towards my car, putting some distance between us as

I use the car as a medium. I still say nothing; she continues to talk while moving in my direction.

"Don't make me kill you and your mixed-mistakes called children."

Okay, that's it. I can only take but so much and she has crossed the line saying anything about hurting my children. She has mistaken my silence for weakness. Now I'm going to have to let loose some whip-ass on this thing-a-ma-gig. I'm not sure why she came, other than to get her feelings more hurt than what they are and getting the shit beat out of her to go along with those destroyed feelings.

"Robin, this is the only warning I will give you. Please leave my property and leave right now."

Well, I guess she is not afraid of me, and obviously, my warning means absolutely nothing to this psycho-idiot-bitch because she raises her bat and begins to beat on my car.

I reach for the driver's side door trying to reach for my gun. My thought is not to kill her. Oh, I feel it would serve her right for coming here but for some reason, all I want her to do is leave. I feel sorry for her. Whatever she is feeling somewhere along the way Lamont had something to do with it.

Unlike most women, I refuse to think this woman is delusional all on her own accord. Although I never confirmed it, I know my husband had an affair with her and he is just as much to blame as she is for how she is feeling.

I can't reach the gun because she starts coming towards me too fast. I move quickly, pushing the lock before shutting the door so she can't get in the car.

As I look at Robin becoming more and more unraveled, I understand they had more than a sexual relationship. Right here I wonder, where Lamont would be if whatever happened to him had not happened. Perhaps he promised her he would be with her. Perhaps the accident changed his mind. There is one thing for sure; he was not being a good husband to me, as a matter of fact, he was not being my husband period. He was cold and very distant, mean and intentionally spiteful and argumentative. I knew he was going to end our marriage. No matter how much I begged and pleaded, he refused to be moved emotionally by me or his children.

Now here, right here; standing in my garage, is the woman of his past desires, beating my car with a bat that she clearly wants to beat me with. Now, I feel some empathy for her; however, I know my pity for her is not what she wants. I know it will not surface her anger or soothe her pain. She wants to hurt me.

I try to bring a conscious thought to her, "Robin, I did not know about you at all until the day you showed up at the hospital and continued calling and sending packages to my home. I am Lamont's wife, the mother of his children. I do not know what he told you or what the relationship between you two was. All I know is, we are in love and happy and hurting me or his family will not make him want you."

The look in her eyes shows me nothing but hatred, now frowning her face so much 'til it's distorted and ugly. I can see no trace of the confident, cocky, pretty woman that walked into the hospital room to see Lamont.

Finally, she offers me a small bit of information that may help me to under-stand the twisted mental state she now lives in.

"He promised me he would leave you; he said he loved me, and he wanted to spend the rest of his life in my arms. He said I made him feel alive and that you were nothing more than his trap, his gloom. He called you a robotic frame of a woman."

Oh god, how could he, how could he feel this way about another woman. Am I robotic; have I been robotic? My heart is filling up with grief and I want to cry, I want to scream. Deep inside I want to be so angry at Lamont; but no, I know she is trying to hurt me. Even if he said all these things, he is living at home with me, his wife, and children. This is all that matters to me, nothing that she is saying will affect my home and marriage. What's in the past is in the past. Besides, I'm not the one at her home looking for my husband.

She continues her relentless mental-emotional attack, "I warned him; I told him I would not stand for him to leave me. I warned him. I could have killed him the first time, but I didn't. Now, look at what he made me do."

She looks as if she is insane, punching herself in the head and slamming the bat over and over again into my car. She continues, "You need to know the truth. Monty loves me. The only reason he is still with you is that he does not remem-ber what we had."

She laughs like an insane woman. Slowly she continues to walk around the car to come after me. I stay a safe distance from her by walking around the car ahead of her.

"But he will remember this time. I keep telling him I'm sorry for what I did. I keep begging him to forgive me and come home with me to our place; the home we built together. But no! He wants to play daddy and hubby over here!" She viciously slams her bat on the ground. "So, I know what I need to do."

This woman is totally crazy and I'm completely afraid, not just for me but for my children and husband. I'm trying to think how to get away from this woman and call for help. My cell phone is locked in the car. *'Where's Lamont? Oh God please, wherever he is, let him be okay, please.'*

Robin's screaming brings my attention back on her. "Stop running, you stupid bitch! Stop running! I'm going to bash your stupid head in, then I'm going to wait for your bratty kids and bash their heads in. Then Monty and I can be married and have our own family. I will be Mrs. Harper! *ME! ME!* Not you!" Her insane rants did not slow her pace as she continues to chase me around the car. "Be still! Be still!"

Suddenly she runs to the back of my car and I run to the front; still trying to keep the distance from her swinging bat. Without hesitation, Robin swings the bat. After a few hits, the back windshield yields to the force of the hits and shatters. The glass flies all over the back seat, back hood and garage floor.

I scream to the top of my lungs hoping Ms. Elaine will hear the commotion. And she does, just as Robin jumps on top of the car in an attempt to get to me. As she climbs to the roof of the car swinging her bat, I move from the temporary safety of the car; trying to avoid her wild swings.

Ms. Elaine yells, "Hey, you crazy bitch, one more move and you will never use that hand again."

Robin acts as if she doesn't hear the only warning Ms. Elaine gives. Just as Robin jumps off the car and begins her chase in my direction, I hear a shot.

I see the bat fall along with Robin. I gasp, holding my breath. Ms. Elaine rushes over to Robin and kicks the bat away from her reach. Even now, while the blood is gushing from the wound to her shoulder, she shows no remorse of her actions.

"You shot me, you shot me. I'm going to kill the whole family. You'll see, I'm going to get you all."

Without another word, Ms. Elaine grabs me by the hand and we both run into the house to call the police, locking the door behind us. Once we are in the house, I think we both feel a sense of relief; however, it is a false sense of security. I can hear Robin banging on the door leading to the garage.

Ms. Elaine looks at me and says: "Now you look at me Rae and understand this one thing; if that crazy bitch breaks down the door, I will shoot her to stop her for good. I will not shoot to hurt her the next time. Now, you go call Lamont and your parents. I'm calling the police."

While waiting for mother and daddy to answer the phone, I feel the tears welling up. I couldn't cry before this and as soon as I hear daddy's voice, I burst out crying. I try to explain but daddy doesn't wait. I hear him calling to mother and saying: "Let's go, Rietta needs us."

They keep me on speakerphone while they drive. There is not much I can say past the crying.

I tell mother I can't reach Lamont and she uses daddy's phone to call him, but again, he doesn't answer. My mind begins to play tricks on me. Maybe Robin did something to him; maybe he's bleeding to death laying in an alley somewhere. She already admitted it was her who hurt him before.

Before I can even try to make sense of all this mess, I can hear the police sirens. I tell mother the police are almost here. To my surprise, I turn to look up and I see grandmother standing behind me. She extends her arms to me; I fall into her waiting arms and cry my heart out. Grandmother takes the phone and speaks to mother and daddy,

"Irene, I am here, how far away are you and Ben?"

Mother answers, "About another fifteen minutes."

Grandmother responds, "Okay, be safe, but hurry. Douglas and Charles are outside waiting on the police."

There is no point in asking how she knew anything was going on. Besides, I'm pretty sure, when Ms. Elaine called the police; they called Uncle Douglas while Ms. Elaine was still requesting assistance.

Uncle Douglas finally appears in the doorway, visibly upset.

"Now listen here, I don't know where she went, but I can't find her anywhere. Rae, was she driving?"

I lift my head from grandmother's bosom hunching my shoulders, "I-I don't know, I don't know. I didn't see a car, but she could have driven, I just don't know Uncle Douglas, I just don't know."

I hear my voice becoming more and more hysterical, "That woman was trying to kill me. I can't reach Lamont. I've been calling him, and I can't reach him. I think that woman may have done something to him."

Uncle Douglas tries to keep the calm; however, that's not going to happen with the three of us very high-strung women. Ms. Elaine has resorted to speaking Spanish. All I can understand are the cuss words. While she paces the kitchen, she bangs her fist on the countertops as she walks past them.

Grandmother is breathing fast; almost huffing but not saying a word. Not one word; that's not a good thing. Mr. Charles puts his arm around grandmother's waist and tells her: "Calm down Catherine, everything is going to be alright."

As the police pull up in front of the house, Uncle Douglas meets them at the door. Ms. Elaine is still carrying her pistol in one hand. The police enter the house and ask Ms. Elaine to put her weapon away.

She complies while still cursing loudly in Spanish. Chief Dillon knows the family quite well. He's done work for Uncle Douglas; whatever work that may be at any given time.

"Hello Mrs. Mason, how can I help you and your family?"

Grandmother looks at him and speaks in her true Richardson-Mason manner. She tilts her head up and clears her throat. Without releasing or relaxing her arms that are around me; she uses his first name.

"Listen, Mathew, the woman's name is Robin Petrez, she is 34, and her birthday is May 29th. Her address is 2497 Penfield Court, her cell phone number is, 555-6262 she is formally an employee of my grandson-in-law, she drives a 2018 red on red Dodge Charger; her personalized license plate reads, 4HR-LUV."

I lift my head so I can look into the eyes of my grandmother. How can she know so much about this woman? I then turn to look at Uncle Douglas. He is looking just as surprised as I am. Grandmother continues giving more information about a woman whose name I barely know.

"Ms. Petrez is parentless; however, she will more than likely be at her sister's house, which is located at 619 Crescent Blvd. on the west side of town. Her sister's name is Camille, she's a very sweet child; so be careful not to involve her too much into this mess. All I want is this Robin person."

Grandmother waits for Chief Dillon to finish taking notes before she speaks again. Once he lifts his head, she does not wait for him to speak or ask any questions.

"You now have all the information you need to find this person; My family and I expect she will be in custody within two to three hours. Please call my husband, Mr. Charles Bennet."

Grandmother turns her attention towards Mr. Charles and then Uncle Douglas, "Douglas, call Judge Hargrove and have him sign any warrants you may need. Go along with Mathew to pick them up and find this woman. Do I make myself clear?"

Without a word both men almost run for the door. As they approach the door to leave, they step aside for mother and daddy to enter. I run for their waiting arms. With my emotions still in an uproar, Ms. Elaine explains everything that occurred.

At this point, no one has heard from Lamont. I am so afraid for my husband. What if she got to him before she came over here? Where can he be, where? The next half hour seems like two, the next two; five, still no word from Lamont. We continue to call his cell. I pray all this is cleared up before the twins get home. I don't want them to come home to so much commotion; it will scare them. However, as usual, Ms. Elaine is way ahead of me. I see her get her bag and car keys.

"Rae, I'm going to get the little ones and we are going to the ice-cream shop then to the movies. Perhaps the park, I don't know, but you call when we should come back, okay."

I nod my head yes, mother verbally responds, "Yes ma'am, that will be great. Thank you, Ms. Elaine."

In her usual way, Ms. Elaine tries to add a clam to the atmosphere, "Look, I don't know what you are thanking me for. Those are my babies, just like you and Rae so what happens to one of us, happens to us all. We are family and that's all to it." On her way to the door, she fusses out-loud. "Damn, that crazy woman, I should have killed that idiot. Should have shot her in the poo-poo then she never can use it again. She loco, what she thinks, she can come here with her shit." Out the door she goes, still fussing all the way to her car.

Mother fixes everyone a stiff drink and continues to call Lamont. I suggest she speaks directly to Terrence; so, mother calls him.

After asking Terrence how long Lamont has been gone and if he knew where he was headed; we still had nothing. Mother explains to him it's of the utmost importance, and we have reason to believe Lamont's in danger. Terrence tells mother, Lamont told him he had to meet with a Mr. Holmes, concerning a surprise he was setting up for the center's opening.

Daddy then asks if there was a number for this Mr. Holmes. Terrence looks in the call log and finds a number. Daddy calls.

"Hello, may I speak to Mr. Holmes?"

Daddy pauses, we all are looking at daddy waiting for his response.

"Hello, Mr. Holmes? Yes, my name is Benjamin Thomas; I understand you had an appointment with my son-in-law, Lamont Harper? Yes, yes, I understand, yes. That's fine. I simply need to know if he attended that appointment and if so, what time did he leave?" The pauses in his conversation are driving me crazy. "Okay, yes sir, thank you very much. I appreciate your assistance. Yes sir, thanks again."

Daddy barely hangs up the phone before, Mother asks, "What did he say, Ben?"

"He said Lamont made the appointment which was at noon. They had a lunch to talk about booking a band for the opening of the center."

Okay, so we know he was fine at noon. Noon, that crazy woman was here at noon so Lamont can't be her victim. Before I can ask the obvious questions, daddy continues.

"According to Mr. Holmes, Lamont was looking for his phone to note his next meeting with him, but he couldn't find it. He also stated Lamont was somewhat perplexed since he said he had the phone earlier and had no idea where it was."

So that's why he didn't answer. Daddy then concludes, "Mr. Holmes said Lamont told him he was going to purchase a new phone once they were finished finalizing the contract, if he didn't find the phone in his car."

I want to breathe a sigh of relief, I really do, but I can't seem to settle down, I can't seem to get rid of these nervous butterflies in my stomach.

Daddy reaches for me to come to him, and I do, I bury my head in his chest. He kisses my head and holds my face between his comforting strong hands. Kissing my lips, he wipes the tears away.

"Now, you listen Rae-muffin, stop that worrying, Lamont is a smart man. It may take a little time to have all his information from that phone transferred to the new one. Mr. Holmes said he will call us back in a few minutes to see if Lamont made it to his office to get the corrected contract from his secretary. It's now 2:30, time is on our side."

Daddy's' phone rings. It's Mr. Holmes, confirming Lamont made it to his office and picked up the contract from the secretary. He stated Lamont jokingly told his secretary he was running to get a new phone because he needed to check in with is wifie-poo before she gets worried.

Ah, we are all sighing a sigh of cautioned relief. Nonetheless, it's a relief we didn't have a few moments ago.

Mother fixes another round of scotch and grandmother speaks for the first time since the police and Uncle Douglas left.

"Irene, I require you to know I love you and have continually done what I believed was appropriate. I know I've stood a meddlesome old inconsiderate malicious and inflexible woman; however, loving you was what I believed I was doing. Now I consider not just from the inside but the outside as well and I understand my family principles were lacking in so many ways."

Mother looks strangely at grandmother and walks closer to her, "Mother, we've moved beyond all of our past and have forgiven each other for everything. Look around at us. We are a strong family because of you and who you are, and we were built to be strong because of who and what you were and are now. You've already made amends and you have been totally forgiven. Look at us, we have never been such a loving understanding family. However, once again because of your decisions we are together and strong. This family is what it is because of you! So, stop that. We all love you."

Grandmother is visibly emotionally stricken. The tears fall from her eyes and her bottom lips are quivering. She reaches her hand for her husband.

"If it were not for Charles, I would have died alone, as a rancorous old woman. He has been such a powerful influence and a marvelous companion." She looks at daddy. "I don't know how you found the resilience in your heart to forgive me. And now look the very thing that triggered me to spurn you, I now love. I've been a dreadful individual." She takes a moment to wipe her face and sniffle. Clearing her throat, she continues, "I realize as strong as I assumed I was, I have been anemic, now I understand terror and fear are only momentary means of control; it's love that makes relationships eternal. Thank you all for loving me past my own fears."

Grandmother releases all of her inhibitions in a flood of tears. She cries as if she's been holding those tears her entire life. Mr. Charles holds his wife tight while kissing her. We hug and daddy adds the finishing touch to grandmother.

"Mother, I forgive you not just a little but completely. I could not love my family like I do if I can't forgive the matriarch, the woman who is responsible for their existence. Who knows, perhaps we would never have loved so strongly or so totally if it were not for the obstacles. I look at you and I see someone who was deprived of a truth, yet God loves you enough to allow you to have and experience what so many die without. So please no more of this. What is past remains in the past, I never want my grandchildren, no, our grandchildren, to hear of such tales. Not when they have so much love around them. The past stays in the past and never should be spoken of."

As we all cry together, I hear the door slam. Then the voice that makes all this nonsense so much better.

"Hey what is going on? Terrence told me to come straight home. What's wrong?"

Without knowing exactly what's going on, he joins in the group hug. I attempt to break the circle to hug him alone. The tears I cry are not for all the commotion I've just endured. No, it's for the relief I feel in my heart, knowing my husband is alive and well.

We all take refuge in the family room where we tell Lamont everything that has transpired concerning Robin. Robin is a subject Lamont and I never discussed.

With tears flowing down his cheeks, Lamont stands in the center of the room, clears his throat. With his head bowed; as if ashamed, he begins to pace the floor. I want to hold him and tell him it's all okay but in my heart, I know he needs to bring clarity to the mess that has invaded our lives.

And he does. Looking me straight in my eyes he begins, "I need to first say how sorry I am to my wife for all the hell I have put you through. I remember; I remember everything I did to you. I remember how badly I treated you for no cause. I remember Robin and all the things I shared with her and the lies I told. I remember. I remember the betrayal, the conniving and most of all; I remember the hurt I saw in your eyes each morning I came home after being gone all night. The shame I feel is now deserving. In my own, yet deceitful mind, I thought I could end it without telling the truth. After I got out of the hospital, I felt I had a second chance and I was more than happy to seize the opportunity to pave over my lies once again."

I hold my hands to my mouth and try to control my breathing. I think if I take in a breath too deeply it will hurt more. So, I slowly pant and listen as he continues.

"I look at the life we have, and I cannot believe I was so stupid and thought-less of my family, my wife, and my children. I could not ask for a better woman; I could not create a better life. I started remembering small things after about six months. Once I went back to work, most of my memories begin to flood in. some days I would sit and cry thinking of all the things I put you through. Then Robin came to see me and everything, I mean everything came back to my memory."

Like a little child begging for something they really want; Lamont falls to his knees, with his hands cupped together as if praying and begs for forgiveness. None of which he has to do. See, I forgave him a long time ago and the choices Robin made today are hers and hers alone.

I get up from my seat and join my husband on the floor. I wrap my arms around him and hold him as if this is the last time I will ever hold him. Mother and daddy are holding onto each other and grandmother is smiling while Mr. Charles holds her, although tears are rolling down her face. I move back from Lamont just enough to look in his face, and I ask: "Do you remember what happened to you and what I did when I found you laying in the vestibule?" I look over at mother; the only one I told the story to. At this point, since we are all telling truths, I may as well get this over with.

Lamont shakes his head and responded, "Yes, I remember. Robin became angry because I told her it was over, and I chose to stay with my family. She hit me in the back of the head with a bat when I turned to leave. I remember seeing her grab the knife. I was too dazed and hurt to fight her. I saw the knife when she raised it above her head, I felt her stabbing me. I think she went to the bathroom and I crawled out the door into the garage. I made it to my car; it took me all of the night to drive myself home. I thought I was dying, and I needed to see you and my children once more. After I made it home, I collapsed; the next thing I knew, I was in the hospital."

I cry. I cry because I'm not sure if he remembers and doesn't want to say or if he truly has no memory of what I did. In my soul, I need to release myself of this luggage I'm hiding; however, the shame I feel is overwhelming. I look over to mother and she nods her head up and down. I know this is my moment of truth. As I clinch Lamont's arm, I begin my tale of truth.

"I came down to get the newspaper and I saw you lying on the floor bleeding. You were semi-conscience and mumbling. I could not make out everything you were saying but I understood the name you kept calling over and over again, Robin, Robin. At the time I thought you were calling her for help; as if you needed her to be here for you."

My heart is pounding as fast as my aching head. Yet I need to get this out.

"I tried to help you, but you continued to repeat her name. I had no idea you were telling me she did this to you. Like a jealous woman, all I could feel was rage and pain. Hearing you call another woman was more than I could bear. Before I knew it, I was pounding you in the chest with my fist and yelling for you to die. Once you were unconscious, I sat and waited for you to stop breathing. But a half-hour later you were still breathing. I was going to let you die. My blind rage wanted you dead."

Uncontrollably I cry; the sounds escaping from my lips are of agony. Both of us cry. Lamont attempts to hold me, but no, not yet. I need to finish. I push him slightly away so I can see his face as I finish.

"I heard Ben and Charmin running down the stairs; that's when my senses came back to me. The very thought of them not having you is what shook me. I called out to Ms. Elaine to get the children. I grabbed the phone to call for help but not before I whispered my hatred of your life in your ear. You may not remember this, but I said..."

Just as I open my mouth to repeat the words, I whispered in his ears that day, he spoke them along with me, word for word.

"I hate you and I want you to die. If the children were not here, I would kill you myself. I will sit right here by your side watching you die slow and painfully."

I collapse in Lamont's arms as he holds me even tighter than before. In my ear he says: "Please forgive me for making you feel such pain and anguish. Please forgive me for what I have done to your beautiful heart. And thank you for forgiving me and loving me after all that."

Without another word spoken, we hug and kiss. Not a kiss of sexual passion but a kiss that signifies our newest beginning. Lamont holds me tight and with unspoken words, he promises to never let me go.

There is not a dry eye in the house. Finally, the silence is broken. Lamont looks around the room and makes what sounds more like an announcement, "There were so many lies I told and lived by. In my self-imposed delusions, I was blinded. I couldn't see that everything I ever needed; I already have. The deceit I webbed for my family, only betrayed me, almost to my own death. I couldn't remember what happened to me while I continued to bathe in my lies. It wasn't until I was able to accept the truth about myself, was I able to piece all the broken pieces together. See the truth is, lies have no memory, no memory of truth; but in my truths, I can remember how wonderful of a life I already have."

The doorbell rings before we can get up from the floor. Daddy opens the door and Uncle Douglas walks in. He begins to inform us that Chief Dillon and he were not able to find Robin as yet.

With his arms around grandmother, Mr. Charles says: "Cat, I think everyone should pack a bag and come to the mansion until all this is cleared up."

Grandmother shakes her head yes. Mr. Charles then does something I never witnessed him doing before; give out orders.

"Lamont, get you and Rae's things together, Ms. Elaine, get yours and the children's things. I've already informed Ms. Rachael to expect everyone."

Turning his attention to daddy, "Ben, I feel it would be better if we all were together. So why don't you and Irene go get somethings together and meet us at the mansion."

Daddy hasn't been back to the mansion since the day grandmother put him out; however, without any hesitation, my hero exuberates the epitome of being a real hero and simply nods his head yes.

With the clapping of Mr. Charles' hands, we very quickly follow all his instructions. Grandmother's facial expression is soft; almost childlike as she reaches for Mr. Charles hand and kisses it. Right in front of us all, she shows her womanhood, her love, and her gentle submissiveness to a man she must truly love. All I can say to myself is, wow!

CHAPTER NINETEEN

The Conclusion to All that Matters

The past week has been incredible. Although Robin has not yet been found, we all have given her truly little to no thought. Each day is filled with some new astounding revelation about my wonderful family.

Guess what? Grandmother and Mr. Charles sleep in the same room, the same bed; while all of us are here, in the open! I mean she is not hiding at all. I suppose that's what married couples do. Oh, and Mr. Charles has a wardrobe other than a chauffeur's uniform. Oh, wait and he only drives because he doesn't trust someone else to do it. According to grandmother she tried to get another driver years ago, but he wouldn't hear of it.

Kristy and Danna decide to come now because they feel we all should be together. Funny, how trouble pulls a real family together. All the mis-haps-confusions-hatred-pain-uncomfortable-moments-embarrassing-situa-tions-and-things we thought we could never forgive; we find our love is greater than it all.

Thanksgiving is still a month away, yet I feel a holiday celebration in the air already. My sisters will arrive Thursday, the day after tomorrow. There is some-thing about the air of an October breeze.

Fortune is a funny thing. It's apparent to me that what we have in abundance is taken for granted and unable to be missed or even appreciated to its fullest value. We complain about what we don't have and hopelessly descend into, "the dog with a bone syndrome". We put everything priceless on the line, like love, family relationships, commitment, our happiness, and peace. We try to get more of the things we already have; without realizing we already have enough.

I take in deep breaths as I gaze into the eyes of my family members. My dad, my mother, my sisters, my grandmother, Mr. Charles, Ms. Elaine and Ms. Rochelle, Nylah, Uncle Douglas, my children and finally; my husband, all my family. We have everything any family can ask for. We really could not ask for more. Still, it is tragedy that brings us together.

The more I think about it, I can see how Lamont's relationship with this, un-dignified-ridiculous-unethical-malicious-irrational-idiot, has a good intended end. And that end will be assisted by this ass-whooping my sisters and I will provide. I cannot help but think, if it were not for the affair, we all would still be living lies we can't keep up with.

Mother always says, "lies have no memory because, after a while, you forget the first lie and have to continue to make up lies to cover all the ones that came after it and that first one too." Secrets are the same as lying. If we live hiding our true selves, then we live a lie by creating a persona for others to see when we are something different.

This wonderful revelation does not alleviate my total dislike, okay - hatred, for Robin. Only because she should have never continued her pursuit of my husband and most definitely not come to my home. Uh, trying to kill me!

Li'l-Ben enters the room pulling me quickly from my private thoughts. Screaming as if he just got beat-up, "Mommy, mommy..."

Quickly, I glanced over him to make sure he isn't bleeding, and nothing is broken. With all that checked, Ben still sounds and acts as if he is in desperate need of my attention. Although I am standing right in front of him, he is jumping up and down, waving his arms above his head and continuing to call me.

"Mommy, mommy, it hurts, it hurts!"

He is yelling so loud, it brings his dear sister running, "What's the matter, Ben?" Looking at me she asks: "Mommy, what's wrong with Ben?"

I usher Ben over to the couch and sit him down, I sit right next to him. Who by the way, is still acting as if I'm not right here in the same room with him.

"Ben honey, what's the problem, where are you hurting? You have to tell me, sweetie."

Now the tears are flowing down his cheeks and he is uncontrollably crying and screaming. Before I can call out for Lamont, I see him, along with daddy coming to see what's going on. Lamont asks; while he attempts to go through the same steps I did by checking for any visible wounds. "What's going Rae, what's wrong with Ben?"

"I don't know, he hasn't stopped crying and calling me long enough to answer."

Daddy also gives him the once-over. Just as daddy calls for mother, everything goes silent as Ben collapses in Lamont's arms. I gasp and scream for mother and grandmother. Both of them run into the room with Kristy and Danna right behind them.

No one says another word, we all head for the door to go to the car. Once outside, I see Mr. Charles pulling up to the door. We all jump in on top of each other and he drives like a mad man trying to escape from the police.

Lamont checks to make sure Ben is breathing. I'm almost hysterical as mother tries to calm me. Charmin is sitting on Kristie's lap with her head buried in her chest as if she doesn't want to look at Ben.

Grandmother is in the front with Mr. Charles; however, she continues to look back to see if Ben is conscience. After she does this a couple of times, she turns to Mr. Charles and says: "Charles, please hurry, the baby hasn't opened his eyes yet. Can you go faster?"

In a very understanding tone, he replies: "I'm going as fast as I can, honey. I want all of us to make it to the hospital in one piece and without causing anyone else harm. We are almost there Catherine; we should be pulling up to the emergency room doors in about three minutes."

Just as Mr. Charles said, we pull in front of the emergency room almost immediately after he said it. Grandmother called ahead for Ben's pediatrician to meet us there. Once we open the doors of the car, the nurses are standing in waiting with a gurney for Ben. One of the nurses begins to ask questions.

"How old is he, how long has he been unconscious, when was the last time he ate, what did he eat, does he have any visible wounds, does he have any allergies or is he allergic to any foods and/or medicine?"

Lamont answers all the questions. I look around for Dr. Franklyn, and I begin to panic because I do not see him. Frantically I ask: "Where is Dr. Franklyn, he is supposed to meet us here?"

The same nurse who asked all the questions is checking Ben's vitals. Without stopping she answers me. "He is here in the hospital Mrs. Harper; he should be here in a moment."

I ask: "Does he know we are here?"

While she removes all Ben's clothes, she answers, "Yes ma-am he does, he will be here in just a moment."

Before I can ask another question, Dr. Franklyn walks into the room. He immediately looks at Ben and checks his chart, then his vitals again. He orders lab work and oxygen for Ben. I feel faint, I feel as if I am reliving an old nightmare. I cover my face and cry. What is wrong with my child?

Mother tries to console me, but she is finding it difficult keeping herself together. It seems more like, every man/woman for themselves; except Charmin; who is still in Kristie's arms. The nurse places the oxygen mask over Ben's face and begins to draw blood from the I.V. in his arm. One valve, two valves, she took four valves of blood. Then she stuck a catheter in my poor baby to get urine. Daddy and Lamont are crying as much as we women. Mr. Charles and grandmother are trying to console each other but it's working about as well as the rest of us.

All of a sudden Charmin yells out: "Mommy, I told Ben not to take the candy from the strange lady. I told him, now my brother is sick. I told him Mommy, I told him."

We all gasp and look at each other. Mr. Charles speaks first while the rest of us try to gain composure. Taking Charmin from Kristie's arms, Mr. Charles holds her tight and asks: "What strange lady are you talking about, sweetie?"

With her arms wrapped around Mr. Charles neck and her head lying on his shoulder she begins to cry. "I didn't take any Pa-Pa Charles, and I told Ben not to either, but he wouldn't listen to me. I told him; I did."

I jump in the conversation, "What strange lady, Sweetie, do you know her name?"

I can see her tighten her grip around Mr. Charles neck as her crying be-comes more intense. Mr. Charles puts his hand up in a stop motion to me, then moves away from all of us and talks to Charmin alone.

I look at Lamont and I cannot help but think the worst. I know everyone is thinking the same thing, I know they are. Finally, Mr. Charles returns with Charmin still holding tight to his neck.

"Charmin said a lady dressed in a purple sweat suit wearing a black hat, came to the fence of the playground outback. The woman offered them candy saying she is the other Mrs. Harper. She said the woman told her to make sure she tells her mother she was here."

I explode! Fuck this Miss Congeniality bullshit! I turn to Lamont, screaming in pure agony. From the very pit of my stomach and with all my might I scream: "This is your fault, your fault. Now that woman of yours has hurt my son. You are the reason for all this bullshit, you are. It's your mess, yours, yours, not mine, not my children's; it's yours!"

With all my strength I punch Lamont as he stands still absorbing every hit. With all the pain, from all the hurt, I punch him. Finally, once all my strength is gone, I collapse in his arms, out of breath and out of answers.

Lamont repeats the same thing over and over in my ear, "I'm so sorry, Babe, I'm so sorry. You have every right to blame me, I am the reason for everything that's happening. I promise you I will fix this; I promise I will."

Daddy jumps up and runs to tell the doctor Ben may have been poisoned.

Everyone else is silent. I'm out of breath and Lamont, literally picks me up in his arms and carry me to a waiting room for families. My heart is in my throat; my mind can only go to the worst possibility. I cling to my husband. I know he created this situation. Yet, I know he is hurting as well.

With no doubt, I know he is truly, truly sorry. After all, the same pain I feel, I can see in his eyes. The same hate I feel, I can feel that energy coming from him as well.

The entire family wait for the doctor to come back in and tell us something, anything.

Mr. Charles does his usual and asks everyone if they need anything. He pats the hand of grandmother he'd been holding for the past hour. He stands up and asks: "I'm going to get some coffee for us all from the cafeteria down-stairs. Would anyone like for me to bring them back something other than coffee?"

Without saying exactly what we wanted, we all simply nodded and said yes. Mr. Charles kisses grandmother's hand and says: "Catherine-Honey, I'll be right back, I know what to get for you."

Nylah and Uncle Douglas went with him.

As we all sit in this tiny room together, I'm starting to feel as if the walls are closing in on me. I look at each member of my family and try to guess what they are thinking. I know Lamont's thoughts are about ending this. I wonder what he means by that.

Mother finally breaks the silence.

"I swear, I will find this crazy-stupid-bitch, and when I do, she will wish she had jumped in front of a moving train."

Daddy re-enters the room just in time to hear Mother's statement. He speaks, "Shush Irene and don't you worry, if I find this woman, I am going to choke her to death."

Grandmother bangs her hand down on the arm of the chair she sits in. With each word, she raises slowly out of the chair. With her face frowned and her eyes moving around the room. She stops to gaze in each of us eyes; one by one, saying: "All of you be quiet! I am the matriarch of this family and I am going to deal with this woman myself. This I promise! I will not rest until the last breath is gone from her body and her heart beats its last beat."

Every mouth is open in disbelief. Grandmother is fuming, I don't ever re-member seeing her so angry or hearing her speak openly in such a murderous tone. And she is not finish, "I don't know what makes her think she can get away with this. Nobody messes with this family. Not with my grandchildren, not with my family. I mean no one will ever think this is acceptable, or an act they can get away with. Oh, she has ended her life! She has hammered in the nails to her own cardboard coffin. She is done; this-miserable-stinking-low-gutter-insignifi-cant-dysfunctional-fucking-with-my-grandchild-dead-piece-of-shitty-sewage is dead!"

A pin can be heard if dropped.

Grandmother is visibly shaking. Her hands won't be still, and she cannot stop crying. Mother and daddy go to her; they each take a side next to her and helps her to sit back in her chair while trying to comfort her.

In the middle of this, I think how great my dad is. He is so very special and such a wonderful soul, so many wasted years. None of that stuff matters now. We are family now and that is the conclusion of it all.

I don't think any of us can be comforted at this point; however, that does not stop us from trying. Hugging and speaking soft words are far from all of our minds. We are fueling each other's anger by the angry words we speak. As long as we don't know Ben's condition, I can't see this changing.

Charmin is still clinging to Kristie's neck whimpering. Danna is pacing the floor and answering her phone each time Curtis calls - which is exactly every five minutes.

Danna comes over to where Lamont and I are sitting. "I want every bit of information you have on this woman. I need it right now."

I relay to her everything I heard grandmother say, which is much more than I knew before. Danna then gets up and makes a call. I cannot hear everything she is saying, however, I do hear her repeat all the information to the person on the other line.

After her call is completed, she comes back over to Lamont and me.

"Look, sis, don't worry. This situation will be taken care of before the night is out. This I promise you. I'm so sorry we missed so much time together but all of that is going to change. I planned to wait until all this mess was cleared up, but I think I need to let you know now. Curtis and I are moving back here to Kentucky. We already found a place. It was going to be our surprise to the family, but I think you need to know this now. I refuse to miss any more time away from my family."

I release Lamont's hand for the first time since we entered into this waiting room and hug my sister. We hug and cry together. Danna releases her hold on me and grabs my hand, walking me over to Kristie.

As she wipes the tears from her eyes, she reaches for Kristie to stand up. Kristie hands Charmin to her daddy as we three sisters group hug and cry together. This cry is not just about Ben; no, not at all. Without one word spoken, we clearly understand we are forming a brand-new bond, even greater than the one formed on the ship.

Finally, Danna speaks directly to Kristie.

"I already told Rae, Curtis and I are moving back here."

They must have spoken about this between themselves because Kristie responds: "Good, because I'm not sure how long I was going to be able to keep that secret. I guess I may as well tell Rae, we're moving back also. Nathan already found a place not too far from the mansion. And he put together a proposal for you for a Public Relations Manager position at your center."

My goodness. In the middle of all this, I find happiness. See this is what a functional family can do. I jump up and down like a kid in a candy store. Hugging and kissing my sisters, I tell everyone in the room the great news.

Mother runs over to us to join in the hugging, and then daddy, grandmother - with her prissy-proper-self - runs faster than I ever saw her move. Just as we begin to chatter about all the moving arrangements, the doctor walks into the room. We break our hold on each other to give the doctor all of our attention.

Suddenly, all the knots are back in my stomach, as Dr. Franklyn turns all his attention towards Lamont and me.

"Mr. and Mrs. Harper; um, I'm glad you got Ben here so fast, it may have very well saved his life. It appears he was indeed poisoned. Thank goodness your baby was able to let you know about the candy and your father was able to translate that information to me and my staff. This allowed us not to waste time on running unnecessary tests. It truly saved his life; the poison would have killed him."

Holding my stomach, I ask, "Can we see him, please?"

Nodding his head, he replies: "We just finished pumping his stomach and giving him something to relieve the pain and relax. Give the nurses a few minutes to settle him in his room and they will come and get you. He's going to be a bit groggy, so try to let him rest. The little fella has been through a lot of pain. Whoever did this, meant for it to hurt; there are so many poisons that would not have caused so much pain. However, good thing it did, or you may not have known until it was too late."

Group hug again. This time happily.

CHAPTER TWENTY

More Secrets?

*I*t's been three weeks since the poisoning of my Ben. No one speaks or asks about Robin. Kristie and Nathan are scheduled to move three miles from the mansion tomorrow. Danna and Curtis are already here.

Somebody is pressing on the front doorbell like they have lost their mind. I run, beating Ms. Elaine to the door. She is waving the large wooden spoon in her hand. I'm sure the Spanish words coming from her mouth are curse words.

As I get close to the door, I see the frame of a man. Oh no, it can't be. I reach for the knob and open the door. Yep, it is, Mr. Congeniality himself, Detective Mayfield.

I quickly promise myself I will try to be cordial.

He takes a break from chewing on the gum in his mouth to reach out his hand. I hesitantly, but indeed, shake it. I said I was going to be cordial and I am trying; he just better murder that gum quieter.

"May I come in Mizz Harper?"

I should ask him if he spoke to my grandmother. Shucks, I did say I would play nice. "Sure, come on in." I open the door wider so he can come inside but I don't offer him the opportunity to sit or move beyond the foyer. "How may I help you Detective Mayfield?"

There it goes, with each word he says, he's smacking on that gum. It's as if his words are attached to the gum; damn. Breathe Rietta, breathe.

"Mizz Harper, it's been a few weeks since the poisoning of ya son, Benjamin. I hope he is doing well nah."

I nod my head yes as he reaches into his jacket inner pocket and pulls out his pad of information. Reading and flipping pages, he continues to freaking smack outrageously on that, gotta-be-out-of-flavor-stale-like-cardboard-dry-like-dirt-full-of-mononucleosis-I-hope-he-swallows-and-chokes-on-it, gum.

"Um, can ya tell me about this Robin Petrez person?"

I look at him as if he lost his mind. I thought for sure he was not the detective on this case. I act like I know what I am talking about and answer him.

"Excuse me Detective but I was not aware you were working on this particular case."

He looks at me over the top of his glasses, while continuing his assassination of whatever is in his mouth. Clearing his throat, let me add, all of this takes him way too much time to do.

"Well, Mizz Harper, I think I found a connection between your husband's accident and your son's poisoning."

My stomach suddenly begins to bubble like I have to use the bathroom; however, I know if I abruptly end this conversation, I will have to deal with this man again. I answer him the best way I can.

"Oh no Detective Mayfield, you have it all wrong."

Taking a break from the gum, "Oh really, I do?"

"Yes. My son Ben was accidentally poisoned from a substance in my grandmother's garage. He thought the bright label made it good to eat. As for Ms. Petrez, I don't know what to tell you."

With his face frowned, he looks in his pad once again. Slowly flipping through pages and humming as he flips. Finally, he looks up at me, "Well, according to my records she came here to ya home, swinging a bat and doing a substantial amount of damage to one of ya vehicles. Would this be correct?"

"Yes, it is correct; however, my insurance company paid for the damages and the police could not find her. So, at this time I don't know what I can tell you."

I can feel my skin beginning to itch like something is crawling on me. I know this is pure aggravation from having to deal with this man. Oh, my goodness, he is running his tongue through that disgusting gum in his mouth as if he's going to blow bubbles. I lied to him about Ben's poisoning because I did not want him to know Robin was involved. You know, covering your own behind and not giving motives.

Ugh, the compulsion to slam this door right in his face is almost more than I can resist. Blowing out the deep breath I took in, sounding very aggravated; I try to end this conversation. I reach for the door while I speak.

"Well, Detective, if that will be all; I have a few things that require my attention."

He is totally ignoring the fact I have the door open for him to leave. Instead, he continues to ask all the questions I refuse to answer.

"If I may, please allow me to ask you this. Were you aware that Ms. Petrez was found dead about a week ago?"

My legs almost give out from under me. I gasp and ask in total surprise, "Wha-wha-what, she's dead? When and how did this happen?"

"Again Mizz Harper, I was hoping ya can tell me something about it."

"Unfortunately, I can't. I don't know anything about her death. Please, Detective Mayfield, I have things to do. Perhaps we can talk another time."

Still smacking, he looks at me and says: "Okay, Mizz Harper, I will be in touch. Have a nice day."

Before he can leave off the front steps, I decide to use my influence to prohibit him from coming back unexpectedly.

"Um, excuse me Detective, please do me a favor and try to remember what my grandmother told you concerning your unannounced visits."

He holds his finger up in an attempt to speak. I begin to close the door, once more giving him a warning...nicely.

"Remember, we wouldn't want my grandmother to have to call your superiors. Have a great day."

I close the door and run for the phone to call mother. Two rings seem too long to wait for Mother to pick up the phone. She does, "Hello my..."

I don't wait for her to complete her greeting, "Mother, where's daddy?"

She answers quickly; I'm sure she can hear the excitement in my voice. "He's at his office. Why? What's the matter Rietta? What's going on?"

I take a moment to catch my breath. "Mother, Detective Mayfield just left here!"

She pauses. Then very nonchalant, she responds, "Oh really, what did he want?"

"What did he want is not the response I was expecting to hear. I mean there actually are a few reasons why he would come by; funny how she seems so calm.

"He came to ask me about Robin."

"Really? Robin, huh?"

"Yes mother, Robin, you know the psycho Robin!"

Again, in a very settled tone and totally unconcerned demeanor, she says: "Yes, I know who you're speaking about. Are you okay, did he call before he came?"

Why isn't she asking me what he said about that woman? "No Mother, he didn't call first."

"Oh, he didn't huh; I'm going to call mother and tell her so she can deal with him on his manners. Well, what are you doing today?"

Okay, now I'm getting a little agitated by her disconnection to the subject of Robin. I'm missing something here.

"Mother!"

"Yes, and why are you sounding so upset? Did the detective upset you by coming by your house unannounced?"

"No, I know how to handle him..."

Cutting me off; she takes the conversation in another direction. "Well good, let's just forget he even came over. I know you have some last-minute things to do for the opening of the center; how about you and I go take care of those things."

I remove the phone from my ear for a moment. I need to think about her entire demeanor and why she hasn't she asked me what that man wanted. I take a deep breath and try to calm myself before I put the phone back to my ear.

I can hear mother calling my name, "Rae, are you there?"

"Yes ma, I'm here. I guess we are not going to talk about Mayfield's visit, are we?"

She pauses for a moment, then says: "I don't see any reason to take up our valuable time and energy on what's no longer a problem in our lives. Do you?"

Wait a minute, how does she know Robin is no longer a problem? Never mind, I will not ask, I don't think I want to know.

"No mother, you're right. However, just understand this one thing; what you are not telling me today, you will have to tell me one day and I mean soon. No more family or individual secrets, right?"

I can hear her chewing on something, and then I hear her snicker. "Rae, one day you will see, secrets are not such a bad thing when they are well placed and for unselfish reasons. Now, if you are ready to take advantage of this wonderful, gorgeous day. I will be headed that way."

I respond the only way I can for now. There is something in her tone that has me feeling quite uneasy inside. One part of me feels comforted and protected, the other part I feel like mother has taken a stand in her position, reminding me we are not on equal grounds.

Regardless of my impulsive and sometimes demanding personality, I heed her wishes and wait for her to arrive without saying another word. I have no intentions of mentioning this to her again. Now, talking to daddy is another story.

Mother and I spend the majority of the day together; however, in the back of my mind, I cannot help but wonder why she's not interested in knowing why that man came asking about Robin. Could she have done something to her, and that's why she hasn't asked any questions? Nah, not my mother!

Daddy, Lamont, and the children are at the house when we get back home. Ms. Elaine has the table set. We sit to have dinner together. Perhaps this is a good time to at least tell Lamont about Detective Mayfield's visit.

I wait until the children are finished eating and playing with daddy and Lamont. Mother and I retire into the family room waiting for the men to join us. I get glasses ready for after-dinner drinks.

Once I turn around, I see mother staring at me with this piercing glare. Before I can ask, she speaks. The look on her face is stern and serious.

"You listen to me Rietta Richardson-Mason-Thomas-Harper," She used every name she could think of! "I know you and I am warning you; just in case you missed something earlier when we talked about Robin."

Mother takes the glasses out my hand and points her finger in my face. "You are to say nothing; I do mean nothing to your father about the conversation with

Detective Mayfield. Do you understand me?" The seriousness in her tone makes me feel like a little child. I cannot believe how she's acting. Now I'm concerned about her involvement in Robin's death. Before I can speak, she continues, "Now, whatever happened to that woman; happened! It's over and done with, just let that sleeping dog lie."

I feel tears filling my eyes, I try to speak, "Ma..."

She cuts me off, using the same stern tone without acknowledging my fear or pain. Still pointing her finger in my face, "Don't you ma, mommy, mother or Irene me. I have spoken and that's it. Now go wipe your face and do as I say. If you want to talk to your husband, I strongly suggest you do it without accusations going in any direction. Do I make myself clear?"

I shake my head and attempt to wipe the falling tears from my face. Without softening her tone, "No, uh, uh, shaking your head is not going to do it. Do you understand me? Answer."

Still shaking my head, I answer, "Yes, ma`am I understand."

Now, with the loving tone I am accustomed to, she hugs me and kisses my cheek, "Good; your family loves you. That's all you need to know. We all love you and whatever we all have to do to protect our family, we will do. So please just leave it alone, please."

Still shaking my head, I hold my mom, I hold her tight. My heart suddenly feels such a flood of love and comfort. Imagine that; without the answers I thought I need, I am fine.

"I promise mother, I promise, I will leave this topic alone."

We hear Lamont and daddy coming down the stairs. I quickly get my composure together and put on a smile.

Daddy speaks first, "Hey what are the two most beautiful women in the world up to? I know that look."

Mother quickly wraps her arms around daddy's waist and lifts her head to kiss him. "See, that's why I stayed married to you for all these years, flattery. It will get you every time."

I follow suit and hold on to Lamont. We all take seats on the couch and talk about everything but the off-limits conversation. After about ten minutes, I totally forget about it all. Family is what's important and I may very well have the most precious family in the world.

We talk and laugh so long we pay no attention to the time. Ms. Elaine comes into the family room, "Is there anything I can get for you guys? Perhaps some cake or fruit?"

Lamont looks at me and asks: "Do you want something sweet?"

I think for a moment and shake my head yes, "Yeah, I think I'll have some fruit."

Lamont repeats the question to daddy and mother. They too will have fruit. Ms. Elaine returns with a tray filled with grapes and cheese. She is so perfect. While she is setting the tray on the table she says: "I know you all are grown, and you don't need me telling you what to do but do you know it is 11.pm? Work, school, business, and Kristie moving day is tomorrow. So, don't stay up too late. Ben and Irene, your room is always ready. You all have a good night. I'm going to bed if you do not need anything else."

We all laugh at Ms. Elaine. I declare she has been mother, grandmother, and protector for so many years. I don't know what we would do without her.

We talk for a while longer and then retire to our rooms. Daddy said he has a trial to prepare for. Daddy is an amazing man; I admire him so much more than I can say.

Once the doors close, I feel the off-limits question twirling in my mind. Mother did say I can talk to my husband. I wait until we are in bed.

"Babe," Lamont rises up on one arm, looking in my face, "Yes, my love, what's on that pretty mind of yours?"

"Detective Mayfield came by today."

With one eyebrow raised and his mouth in a position of so what, he hunched his shoulders then says, "Did he call you before he came over?"

Okay, he didn't ask me what the man wanted.

"No, no he didn't. He just showed up. But..."

Cutting me off, "Really, didn't grandmother tell him to call her first? Did you tell her?"

Wait a minute; this is not how this conversation is supposed to go. Lamont has not asked me what he wanted. So, I try to tell him.

"Babe, he came to talk about..."

Interrupting me again, "Sweetie, do we have to talk about this now? Big-Daddy is feeling real wanting right now. And I rather my body do some talking to yours. Wouldn't you rather do that?"

First Irene, now Lamont. What is going on? Okay, I will enjoy the wonderful love-making my husband gives so well and forget about this...for now. I'm calling Danna and Kristie tomorrow and see where their heads are at concerning this web of avoidance.

For tonight, I enjoy every touch, kiss, and nasty word from my hubby.

CHAPTER TWENTY-ONE

Sister's Love

Kristie takes a break, leaving Lamont, Curtis, and Nathan in charge of the movers. The children, Irene and Nathan Jr. are with Ms. Elaine; Ben and Charmin will be so happy to see them. Kristie and Danna are meeting me for lunch.

I arrive at the restaurant before they do and patiently wait with thoughts flooding my mind. Hopefully, my conversation with my sisters will go much better than it did with mother and Lamont.

Kristie is the first to arrive. We greet and hug; before she can take her seat, Danna is walking through the door. With extended arms, "Hi, my dear sisters, how's it going?"

She looks around and says, "You know, I almost forgot how beautiful this place is. I'm so glad to be back here with you guys."

Another hug and we all take our seats. The server comes to our table before we can start a conversation. This is one reason I love this place; besides the great food, the service is wonderful.

Danna turns her attention to Kristie, "How's the moving coming along?"

"Great, we are actually almost done. Lamont is at the house with Nathan and your hubby, getting the last of it done. Or should I say giving the last of the orders. Those three together are a mess. You should hear them, "No, put it over there, no not there, there." I would quit and I did."

Danna laughs and says: "They better stop with all the orders before the movers quit."

Kristie sips her water and looks up, "Movers, shoot, they were talking to me not the movers. They and the movers are fine. I think they just wanted to get rid of me."

We all laugh-out-loud.

The server brings our drinks and takes our order and I decide to take this wait-time to tell them about the detective.

"Yesterday I had a visit from Detective Mayfield."

Kristie almost chokes on her drink while staring at Danna, and Danna quickly sips on her drink. Neither, say a word…really?

I decide to continue my pursuit.

"He just showed up at the house yesterday to ask me some questions."

This time Danna responds, "Well, I hope you told him not to come back without speaking to grandmother first."

Kristie lifts her drink, "That's right. You know grandmother don't play that. I hope you told him to take a hike."

Okay, I must have fell through a vortex, left Kentucky, and took up residence in the twilight zone. I am definitely not imagining things. Neither of them asks why he came by.

After sipping my drink, "Look you two, I don't know what's going on, but something is, and I want to know what it is."

Kristie gulps her drink and says: "Look baby-sis, I just moved here, and I'm not too sure I know what you are talking about; however, I strongly suggest, you move past whatever it is and simply enjoy your wonderful life you have been fortunate enough to be living."

She gulps and raises her glass for a refill.

I peer at Danna. She turns up her glass as well and raises it for a refill. Following suit, I do the same. However, this is not over, not by a long shot.

"Don't patronize me, you two; don't you dare try to make me think I am imagining things. You both should know me better, now if you know something and are not going to tell me. I rather you say that, than pretend you don't know what's going on."

Danna thinks for a moment before responding.

"You know what, you're right..."

Before she can finish Kristy interrupts, "Danna, I think..."

Now Danna interrupts Kristy. Holding her hand up in a stop position, "Don't worry, I got this. Your right Rae, we should not pretend as if we don't know what you're talking about. So, yes, we know what you're speaking about and no, we are not at liberty to discuss it. Therefore, let's enjoy our sisterly lunch and forget about all that nonsense concerning Robin and Detective Mayfield. It is over and done with. There is no need to continue to talk about it and you don't need to know the details. You and the children are safe and that is what's important; nothing else. So please let it go, let it go. Do not ask us any more questions."

I cannot believe this. I want to scream but I can't, besides, I know my sisters, it will do no good. I sit in awe, with my mouth open, without a clue what to say.

Kristie breaks the silence. "Now, have you gotten everything ready for the opening? I know you are excited, I'm excited."

I nod my head yes. I am furious inside. How dare this family have a secret, a big secret and not tell me. How dare they? I'm going to the source, grandmother. As soon as I leave this luncheon, I am going straight to the mansion.

As we eat our food, I remain quiet. Kristie and Danna are acting completely normal. While inwardly, I strategize my approach to grandmother. This family has the uncanny ability of mind-reading. I'm almost sure it's a hereditary trait; one that seems to be used against me most of the time.

Kristie puts her fork down and pats my hand, "Rietta, listen to me sweetie, stop thinking about it. Do not ask grandmother or anyone else. I know it's all inside of you and you feel you must have the answers but understand this; some things are better off left alone. This is one of them. I will tell you this; you are not the first one in the family Detective Mayfield spoke to. So, leave it, please enjoy your peace and happiness."

Okay, that's how everyone knows, that smelly-turd-gruesome-side-wipe-used-up-toilet-tissue-miniature-detective, already spoke to the family. Inside my heart, I want to punch him in the face. However, she's right, but this is hard. I hug her and allow peace to flow.

"I know you're right, but I can't help it. Everyone knows something and you all are keeping it from me. Why?"

Danna joins in on the conversation, "Listen, I am going to say something and after I say this, please allow it to settle in your heart. Promise me if I tell you this one thing you will let it go."

"That's not a fair agreement. I don't know what you're going to say."

Danna gives me that big-sister look, "It does not matter what I say, if you don't give your word, you won't get this information. Now, swear and promise, it ends here, right here Rietta."

Reluctantly, I agree.

"Good, do you remember Solomon Pritchard?"

Chills are running through my body. I suddenly feel cold.

"Well, do you remember?"

I nod yes.

"Great, then this conversation is over for good. Now let's get another round of drinks and finish eating."

I do just that and I do all I can to reject the notion of talking to anyone else. Of course, I remember Solomon. I cannot forget what he did to my sister and I will never forget how he ended up. I guess I know no more details about Robin than I do him. Just that they are in a place where they can do no more harm to my family. Besides, I'm sure if I asked about Solomon; Uncle Douglas will either tell me a different story or pretend he knows nothing. So will grandmother and mother. Family is important and precious. I remember hearing someone say.

"You can pick and choose your friends, but you cannot pick and choose your family. Family, you're stuck with, so you may as well love each other, enjoy each other, and above all, find a way to live with each other in peace."

I believe we have learned to do just that. Our family is so much better. I will not mention this ever again. Shoot, it's not like anyone is going to have a conversation with me about it anyway.

CHAPTER TWENTY-TWO

Lies Have No Memory

*O*pening night is finally here. We have a ribbon-cutting ceremony this morning. One of the perspective mayoral candidates, my handsome daddy, cuts the ribbon. After, the doors remained open for the community to tour the facility. The band Lamont hired is a fantastic touch. They will be here throughout the day and night. Tonight, is a free-food and musical for the potential sponsors. The youth worked so hard for tonight's opening and their performance proves it.

We shake more hands and hug more people than I thought lived in all Kentucky. Grandmother is on her husband's arm all night. The stares are too funny to ignore. One of her old friends that grew up with her, Mrs. Amy Sant Clair, approaches grandmother and asks to speak to her in private.

As grandmother pats Mr. Charles' hand and asks to be excused for a moment she strolls just a few feet from her devoted beau. Now, you know I am going to eavesdrop; I move close enough to hear their conversation.

"Yes Amy, how can I help you? Are you enjoying the festivities?"

Mrs. Amy nods her head in approval, "How have you been Catherine? We haven't seen much of you lately. Is everything alright?"

Grandmother reaches out her hand and pats Mrs. Amy's shoulder, "Absolutely, Amy, all is forever well with us."

Mrs. Amy, then goes straight for the juggler, "Catherine, I cannot help but notice how your chauffeur is hanging on your arm. Are you not physically doing well, and need him to help you walk or something?"

Boy, oh boy, am I glad I saw this in the making. I can hardly wait to hear how grandmother is going to handle this question. Grinning grandmother even chuckles, "Amy, my dear, I am doing better than I have been almost in my entire life, physically, mentally and mostly emotionally. Charles has not been my chauffeur for years. He is actually my husband."

As Mrs. Amy's mouth opens wide enough for a swarm of flies, grandmother hugs her one-sided and walks away while reaching for her man. Priceless, that's all I can say ; priceless. Right after the eye-opening conversation with my wonderful, sweet, dear grandmother, I saw Mrs. Amy grab her husband and practically drag him to the door.

By the time the lights go out in the center, I have enough donated funds to offer college scholarships and pay my staff. All this, from the creativity of my own mind. Once all doors are double-checked, we head to the mansion to have a more adult party. In the limousine, we talk, laugh, and reminisce over the past couple of years; only touching on the positive and happy points. No, Mr. Charles is not driving. As a matter-of-fact, they hired a driver. He doesn't need to drive anymore unless he simply wants to.

After Uncle Douglas surprisingly hung up his bachelor's hat and married Nylah, and grandmother and Mr. Charles got married, we all have been tossing around what to call Mr. Charles. I wonder how that works. Granddaddy-Charles; yes, I said granddaddy-Charles, well technically, he is my grandfather.

The music is playing at a decent level; considering the older family members and of course grandmother's prestigious reputation. I look around Lamont's arm, which is wrapped around me while we sway. I see grandmother and my granddaddy, swaying to the beat of the music as well. So much love in this room.

Ms. Rochelle comes in and whispers something to grandmother. I see granddaddy-Charles pat grandmother on the arm and leave with Ms. Rochelle. The look on her face is puzzling. Everyone stops dancing and waits for Mr. Charles to return. When he does, he instructs Ms. Rochelle to assist the guests to the parlor. He then tells the family to follow him into the same room.

Unbelievable, as soon as we enter, I see Detective Mayfield. We all pair off with our mates and sit. I look around the room to see the expressions on my family's faces. I cannot read any of them. Each face is cool, calm, and collected.

I would think grandmother would be upset considering this man is unannounced, but she isn't and this I find strange.

Mr. Charles keeps in control of the situation, "We are all here as you requested Detective Mayfield. So how can we be of assistance?"

As the detective reaches into his pocket to pull out his pad; he does his usual assault on the gum in his mouth. It must be a fresh piece since he can hardly talk between his smacking and swallowing. I can hear him actually moaning while he chews.

I see the agitation in grandmother's face. No sooner than I think I cannot take any more of his smacking, grandmother speaks. In her dignified, very calm voice she says, "Excuse me, Detective Mayfield." She waits for his attention to be focused solely on her.

"Yes ma`am." He faces her.

"You have already interrupted our private party, which is not very courteous of you. My husband saw it fit to allow you entrance. I feel you can at least show him and his family a little civility and spit that gum out your mouth."

She points to a box of tissue for him to use to extract the gum. Oh, thank God, he is getting rid of the gum!

Showing no shame, no embarrassment, and not one bit of distraction from his task at hand; he simply begins his conversation as if grandmother did not shove a little tactful humiliation on that ass. Without addressing anyone in particular, Detective Mayfield fumbles through his little note pad and begins to tap his teeth with his pen...ugh!

"I need to speak to each of you again to get an understanding of what you've already told me."

Grandfather-Charles takes the lead. He is really good at this. I'm starting to wonder where all the spunk in this family really came from.

"Excuse me, Mr. Mayfield..."

The detective switches from tapping his teeth with that pen to tapping his pad; the scrawny-over-confident-getting-ready-to-be-totally-smashed-glutting-for-punishment-crazy-detective; interrupts to correct his title. Oh boy, this is going to be so good!

"Ah, that's Detective Mayfield, sir."

Grandfather-Charles looks directly into the eyes of the detective and takes a deep breath. He slowly walks within a foot of his face.

"As I was saying before you very rudely interrupted me. Mayfield is it? Well, Mayfield, you barge into my home without being announced or invited. Therefore, you don't give out any orders in here, much less your personal-preference for a title. Therefore, in your eagerness to have a title, I feel it is much easier to simply call you, Mayfield. Further, I believe you got statements from my entire family and there is nothing else to tell you except good-night."

Holding up his pen; Mayfield, attempts to speak; however, Grandfather-Charles is not finish. I glance around the room and there is not a straight face in this place. Oh, this is going to be good. Any minute now, someone is going to let out a snicker, laugh, or run out the room. There is one thing for certain, I'm not leaving; no way will I miss one second of this.

"Listen Mayfield, I will allow you exactly three minutes to ask, and, or say whatever it is you disturbed my family gathering for. So now, please tell me what it is?"

I guess his moment came too soon for him to respond. It almost looks as if Mayfield is somewhat muddled and lost his words. We all continue to stare at him, which I am sure is making him even more uncomfortable.

Finally, after using about two minutes of his limited three minutes, with totally uncomfortable air-space, the detective finds his voice. And apparently his confidence; he's back to tapping that annoying pen on his rotten-brownish-yellow-I'm-sure-smelly-and-gingivitis-filled-teeth.

"After going through my records, I find some discrepancies in each of your statements concerning each of your whereabouts when Ms. Robin Petrez was murdered. According to my records, some of you say you were with certain family members and others don't give that same information."

Grandfather is still the spokesperson. We all keep silent.

"What discrepancies are you referring to, Mayfield?"

Oh, I'm sure somewhere in this universe, the total joy I am experiencing because of this man's loss of any title whatsoever, is not right. However, it feels so good! The tapping stops for a moment as he reads over his little paper in his little pad. Now he is tapping on the pad while he speaks.

"Well, when I spoke to Ms. Mason, she stated she was with her daughter, Mrs. Irene Thomas. When I spoke to Mrs. Thomas, she stated she was with her husband, Mr. Thomas. When I spoke to Danna, she stated she was with both her sisters, Mrs. Harper, and Mrs. Miller. When I spoke to..."

Grandpapa again interrupts, "Mayfield, please get to your point. It's quite obvious you spoke to my entire family. Therefore, I have no clue why you are back asking questions again."

Tapping his pad for attention, "Well, it's right here. Each of you says you were with a family member and that family member states they were with another family member and all I want to do is get some clarity because I am somewhat confused."

We all look at our spokesperson as he continues to handle this matter quite well.

Chuckling, "Oh really, is that all? Then please allow me to help you out." Charles puts his hand on the detective's shoulder and turns him towards the door and slowly walks him towards it while he makes his final statement.

"See this is why I call you Mayfield; a good detective would have known we were all together. We have family business meetings, family and friends gatherings, and family dinner-parties; like this one you so rudely interrupted. Now a good detective can understand each of them told you the truth since we all were together at the same time. So please have a great night and please do not come again unannounced or it will mean you may have an employment problem."

Without another word the door closes behind Mayfield just as he places a piece of gum in his mouth. Once pappy-Charles re-enters the parlor we all burst out laughing. However, I know we were not all together at the time of Robin's demise. None of us were. I know for sure I was not with any of my wonderful family. Since lies have a way of catching up to the liars, and the fact that lies have no memory, it's a darn good thing this one lie has more influential participants who have no worries except a simple-old-dried-up-trying-to-hold-onto-his-last-piece-of-nasty-gum-detective.

Oh, I guess you want to know who actually killed that evil-child-abusing-mentally-deranged-so-glad-she-will-not-be-bothering-my-family-ever-again-tramp. Well, I would tell you; however, so many lies, so little memories.

ABOUT THE AUTHOR

Yvonne Dean Anderson is the fourth child in a family of five. Yvonne, interestingly, is the only name she knew until a fire caused her to request her birth certificate. That is when she discovered the name on her birth certificate was DEBRA. Yvonne wrote her first song at the age of eight and from that moment, she knew writing was one of greatest things she wanted to do.

Yvonne remembers not only writing sentences for her second-grade spelling words but pondering how she could write better sentences. She would challenge herself to use words that created pictures, and suddenly her imagination was awakened. She began to crave words that formed poems, songs, stage plays, movies and books.

At 16, Yvonne became a young wife and eight years later found herself a single mom. Unstoppable, she became the Founder and Coordinator of The Drug Free Youth Movement and received an Accommodation from Mayor Bill Campbell of Atlanta for the work the movement undertook with youth. Yvonne has been an educator of elementary through high school and an Administrator at The Metroplex Theatre in Atlanta. Her love for the art of creation is eminence. Writing, drawing and creating a space to perform, write books and stage plays is where her heart finds the most joy.

Having had the AWESOME experience of worshipping with diverse intelligence, Yvonne says her desire to know The Will of The Most High and do it is her goal. Now living in California, she has the opportunity to mentor sisters of all nationalities and spiritual beliefs. She is remarried to her bestie, the love of her life and her knock-around, Dion Anderson.